Endorsements

"In *Deliver Me from Evil* Kathi Macias brings readers a startling encounter with the real-world horrors of sexual trafficking. In an intricate story that could have come from the pages of any major newspaper, her fictional account makes readers confront the hard facts that slavery still exists and that everyday people may be only a brief encounter away from its victims. *Deliver Me from Evil* reminds us of our need to be alert to the signs of exploitation that surround us, and summons us to be bringers of Christ's light, hope, and healing to a dark and hurting world."
—**Lisa L. Thompson**, MA, Liaison for the Abolition of Sexual Trafficking, the Salvation Army National Headquarters

"*Deliver Me From Evil* is a book with many themes. One challenges Christians to see suffering and to put feet on faith. Jesus said, 'My yoke is easy, and my burden is light.' When we take up His yoke, are we not taking up the burden of love? A young man overcomes fear and follows the Lord's call, despite personal danger. Other characters endure the horrors of child sex-trafficking, but find Christ's love. work with Breaking Chains, an organization that has rescued over 500 child victims. Even before rescue, many have called out to the Lord, and have felt His presence. I have talked to young victims, hugged them, and prayed for them, and have seen many healed by God's love. Yet, so many more are waiting for help. I pray that this book will open the eyes of many. May our hearts be broken by what breaks God's heart and may we be moved to action. As the young man and his family discover, nothing but abolition will do."
—**Christine Nicolayeff** (Prayer Chain), Breaking Chains

"Macias tackles one of our world's most perplexing social issues with intense realism and hope. *Deliver Us from Evil* reveals depth, honesty, and grace to guide readers toward a deeper faith and a heart challenged to make a difference in our world."
—**Dillon Burroughs**, activist and coauthor of *Not in My Town*

"*Deliver Me from Evil* will grip your mind and heart from the opening chapter and refuse to let go till you reluctantly close the back cover. Kathi Macias tackles a dark and difficult issue with compelling, complex characters, and vivid prose. This novel will change you."
—**James L. Rubart**, best-selling author of *Rooms, Book of Days,* and *The Chair*

"Why are people so evil toward others? Over money? *Deliver Me from Evil* by Kathi Macias is more than a book, a story, or a message. It opens our eyes to the pain and suffering of human-trafficking victims in a very personal and touching journey through the lives of captives and 'normal' families. The very broken rawness of what these women and children experience is brought to light in the pages of *Deliver Me from Evil* while God's love is shown ever-present and moving in the lives of those He wants to act to end the degradation."
—**Angela Breidenbach**, speaker and author of *Gems of Wisdom: For a Treasure-Filled Life*

Deliver Me from Evil

Kathi Macias

New Hope Publishers
Birmingham, Alabama

New Hope® Publishers
P. O. Box 12065
Birmingham, AL 35202-2065
www.newhopedigital.com
New Hope Publishers is a division of WMU®.

Library of Congress Cataloging-in-Publication Data

Macias, Kathi, 1948-
Deliver me from evil / Kathi Macias.
p. cm.
ISBN-13: 978-1-59669-306-7 (sc)
ISBN-10: 1-59669-306-1 (sc)
1. Human trafficking victims--Fiction. 2. Human trafficking--Fiction. 3. Sex crimes--Fiction. I. Title.
PS3563.I42319D45 2011
813'.54--dc22
2011012686

ISBN-10: 1-59669-306-1
ISBN-13: 978-1-59669-306-7

N114140• 0911 • 5M1

Dedication

This book and series is humbly and heartbreakingly dedicated to all who are held in modern-day slavery. We stand together with you with the united cry of "Abolition!" And we look to the One who died to set us all free.

On a more personal level, I dedicate this book and series to my partner and best friend, Al, who daily supports and encourages me as God calls me to "write the vision . . . and make it plain" (Habakkuk 2:2).

Prologue

MARA FOUGHT TO BREATHE AGAINST THE THICK DARKNESS that pressed her down. The closet was so small…so dark and cramped. Impossible to stretch out, whether lying down or standing up. How long had it been now? Hours? Days? The blackness was too complete, the confines too cramped even to venture a guess.

She'd been in what they all termed "the hole" before, but not for a while now. In the beginning, before she'd learned to obey the rules without question or hesitation, she had often found herself confined in what felt like a tomb, wondering how long it would take before she crossed so far into insanity that there was no way back. And though the times in the hole were the worst, life outside the silent box wasn't much better. To survive, Mara had quickly learned to remove herself from the horrifying reality that had become her life, to travel far away in her mind where the torture was only a distant terror, one she could endure if she disciplined herself to think of something else. Eventually she had become one of the most compliant of the twenty or more wretched creatures that dwelled in this nameless location, which she had come to understand was somewhere in the San Diego area of Southern California, not far from the Mexican border. As a result, her trips to the hole became only a vague yet obedience-motivating memory.

But this time she had dared to break a rule, not openly but secretly, praying to a god she didn't really believe in to protect her. Unfortunately, the nonexistent god had apparently chosen not to answer her prayer, and she had been caught and severely punished—beaten mercilessly and thrown into the hole without food or water—because she had allowed the face of a young child to entice her to venture beyond the tentative bounds of safety.

And for what? Not only had she failed to help the girl escape, but she had probably caused her to be thrown into the hole as well, for there were several such confines within the compound. Nearly as bad as being in the claustrophobic enclosure herself was knowing that a captive no older than six or seven was being held in a similar prison nearby, terrified beyond imagining.

When would Mara learn? She herself hadn't been much older than the tiny child when she was spirited away from her previous life, never again to see her home or family or anything else familiar. Thrust into a world of violence and perversion, Mara had learned to endure the most nightmarish and degrading of conditions. Though at first she had cried and begged to go home to her parents, even though they too had beaten and abused her, she finally came to understand that it was her father who had sold her into this new life from which there was no escape—and her very own uncle, her "*tio*" who had arranged the sale and was now her owner. And that was the worst part of it all—realizing that no one would ever come to rescue her, for those who should care enough to try were the ones who put her there—all for the price of a few weeks worth of drugs or alcohol, possibly even some food.

With that realization, Mara had chosen to harden her heart and do whatever she must to get through, one day at a time—sometimes one moment at a time. That was how she had gained the tiniest amount of freedom and privileges, being fed more regularly and even allowed to walk relatively unhindered around the small compound that had become her world—so long as she continued to obey her tio and his two henchmen without question.

But then the little girl with the terrified eyes had arrived, bound and gagged, bloody and bruised... and everything had changed.

Chapter 1

JONATHAN HAD JUST TURNED EIGHTEEN AND WAS LESS than a couple of weeks away from his high school graduation, but his lifelong dream of becoming a major league pitcher was no closer to materializing now than when he first entertained the thought while he was still in grammar school. He'd worked hard to try to achieve his goal, but it seemed that good just wasn't good enough—not for turning pro, anyway. The best he could hope for was to enjoy the game as a leisurely pursuit and maybe coach his own children's teams one day.

Meanwhile, he had to get serious about what seemed his only viable alternative—heading off to Bible college in the fall, just as his parents had always prayed he would. It wasn't that Jonathan didn't believe in Jesus or want to serve Him, but he really had no clue what that looked like in reality. His parents had been missionaries for several years, and his dad now served as an associate pastor at a healthy, growing church, so Jonathan and his younger sister and only sibling, Leah, had plenty of experience as missionary and pastor's kids. But did Jonathan want to be a missionary or a pastor himself? Not really. He just wanted to throw a baseball faster and harder than anyone else in the history of the world.

Jonathan sighed. Just proved how totally unspiritual he really was. If he were a real on-fire Christian like his parents or even sixteen-year-old Leah, he'd be up already—even if it was Saturday—praying and reading his Bible. Instead, all he could think about was getting enough of the guys together to play a few innings before he had to head off to work this afternoon at his part-time pizza-delivery job.

He inhaled deeply and dragged himself from bed, standing to his full six-foot two-inch height. He might as well jump in the shower before Leah locked herself in the bathroom for the morning or he'd never make it to the field on time.

He smiled in spite of himself. Leah. He'd spent the better part of his life complaining about his "pain in the rear" little sister tagging along behind him and doing her best to ruin his life in every possible way imaginable, but he couldn't fathom not having her around. Sure, he'd miss his parents when he went off to school in a few months, but it was Leah he would miss the most—though he'd rather have his tongue cut out than admit it.

Wait a minute. The door to the hallway bathroom that he shared with his sister was closed. Surely she wasn't up already! He tried the handle. Locked. Jonathan shook his head. Maybe life without her would have its advantages after all.

Leah swallowed a giggle. She'd heard Jonathan jiggle the bathroom doorknob, but when he called to her and asked how long she'd be, she'd turned on the shower and pretended not to hear. On weekdays she always let him have first crack at the bathroom, while she snuggled under the covers for a few extra minutes. It was only fair. Jonathan could shower and be dressed and out the door in less time than it took her to figure out what to do with her thick, curly mane of long red hair. And since her parents had allowed her to start wearing a touch of makeup, her morning beauty regimen took even longer, driving her brother crazy if he was pacing outside the door. So she allowed him first dibs on school days or when he had to get to work early. But Saturdays? Nah. He'd just have to wait his turn. Besides, if he'd really wanted in there first, he could have gotten up earlier.

When you snooze, you lose, she thought, grinning as she climbed into the shower and adjusted the water, all the time considering how irritated Jonathan got when she threw that phrase at him.

"Will you quit saying that?" he'd demand. "I'm not the one who lies around in bed until the last minute and then hogs the bathroom!"

She'd shrug and raise her eyebrows nonchalantly. "I'm just saying..." Her voice would trail off then, and she'd scoot past him before he grabbed her and they ended up in a wrestling match. True, he always cooled down and let her win, but her mother had made quite a big deal lately about their being too old to roll around on the floor and holler at one another.

"You're going to break something one of these days," she'd warn. "Either one of my lamps or one of your bones. So could you please settle down and try acting your age for a change? Honestly!"

By that time the siblings would become conspirators, grinning at one another behind their mother's back. The thought that Jonathan would soon be gone away to college came like a streak of hot lightning to her heart, and her playful mood evaporated. She was glad her brother was going to attend Bible college, though she doubted it was for the right reasons, but she was going to miss him nonetheless. He'd been her protector and confidante her entire life, and things just wouldn't be the same without him. On the positive side, she could only hope and pray that Jonathan's stint at college would be the catalyst for launching him into the ministry she was sure God had for him. Selfishly, she hoped that ministry wouldn't take him far from their San Diego home, as she really couldn't imagine her life without Jonathan in it.

Mara's feet still felt numb, as if she couldn't get enough blood flowing through them to make them work right. And so she hobbled as best she could—and as quickly as possible—to do the bidding of her uncle or any of the others who claimed ownership over her. The time in the hole, which had so restricted her movement that her limbs no longer seemed to work right, had reminded her that even the confines of the compound and the humiliation that went with her position as slave were preferable to what could happen to her if she disobeyed again.

As she busied herself preparing a simple meal for her tio and the two other men who currently oversaw the twenty-plus young slaves in the compound, she wondered at the fate of the little girl who had precipitated her most recent punishment. Mara hadn't seen her since being released from the hole the previous day. She didn't even know the child's name—and little else about the others in the compound, for that matter—as the captives were forbidden from discussing personal information. The names assigned the overseers were quite obviously made up, since Mara's uncle's real name was Tomas but they were all instructed to call him "Jefe" or "Chief." The other two that assisted Jefe were known as "Destroyer" and "Enforcer," no doubt for intimidation purposes, Mara presumed. And the customers who "dated" the girls—or even one of the two young boys also being held there—seldom divulged their real names.

Don't ask names; don't look at faces. Mara had learned that rule long ago. Her own name had eventually been changed from Maria to Mara because her uncle-turned-owner said that Mara meant "bitter" and it fit her personality since coming to live at the compound. Looking back, it was probably one of the few true statements she could remember Jefe ever making.

Bitter. What else could she be, growing up in a place like this? She might as well have a name that fit her.

Don't ask names; don't look at faces. The warning still echoed in her mind. If only she'd remembered that when the little girl came in a few days earlier, maybe they both could have been spared some time in the hole.

So where is she now? Mara wondered again, using a large spoon to scoop the steaming canned stew into three bowls. Though it was her job to feed her captors, she had to wait to eat anything until they gave her permission. She hoped it wouldn't be too long, as she'd had very little since emerging from her punishment the previous evening.

The kid probably hasn't had anything at all yet, she thought, remembering how it was when she first arrived. Part of the painful process of breaking her down had been keeping her hungry, so much so that her stomach growled and burned almost constantly, and she was soon willing to do anything for a piece of stale bread. No doubt the new girl was receiving the same treatment.

It doesn't matter, she told herself, steeling her heart. *She's not my problem. If either one of us is going to survive, I've got to remember that. And if she doesn't survive... that's not my problem either. The only problem I've got right now is getting these men fed before they get mad and throw me back in the hole.*

Walking gingerly on feet that still felt like partially thawed blocks of ice, she concentrated on balancing the tray with the three bowls of food. More than once she'd paid the price for spilling even a drop, and she was not about to let that happen again. The memory of the beatings, plus two or three days with no food at all, were more than she could bear on top of what she'd already endured.

As she stood in her uncle's office in front of the three men, her eyes downcast and her back straight, hoping her arms wouldn't start shaking from the weight of the tray, she waited for them to acknowledge her, even as she sneaked peeks at them from under her lashes.

"How many healthy ones have we got right now?" Enforcer asked, his shaved head gleaming in the overhead light.

"Counting this one," Jefe answered, jerking his head in Mara's direction, "twelve or thirteen. But we'll need to clean them up first. Tonight's customers are particular. They want us to bring them clean and healthy." He smirked. "And young, of course. A few more years and this one won't be acceptable to them anymore."

Mara's heart constricted with fear. As much as she hated what she knew would be required of her this night, she had grown used to it. She knew how to escape in her mind and not even feel what was being done to her. She also knew the night's activities, as distasteful as they were, meant she would get a bath and clean clothes, as well as something to eat, before going to meet the man or men—or occasionally a woman—who would be her companion through the long, dark hours. But when she got to the point that she was considered too old—as had happened with several others since Mara joined the group nearly ten years earlier—her life would hold no more value. She would become a liability to the men, and she would quickly disappear, like the others, sold to anyone who would take her or turned out on the street to fend for herself, sleeping behind deserted buildings and scavenging for food. As bad as it was to be used by the highest bidder for whatever his pleasure might be, it was better than the alternative.

Or so she tried to convince herself. There were also times when the bidder's pleasure was such horrible torture for her that she wondered if death wouldn't be the best option after all.

"Don't just stand there," her uncle barked, nearly causing Mara to drop the tray in front of her. Only years of disciplined practice kept it steady in her hands. "Give us our food and get out of here. We'll get you ready for your night out later."

Doing her best to control her breathing, Mara placed the bowls on the round glass table in front of the men and then, still gazing at her feet, turned to leave.

"It's too bad about the new one," she heard Destroyer say. "She was young and small—and you could smell the fear on her. She would have brought a lot of money."

"Would have," Jefe growled, the familiar lust in his voice evident. "Too late now, though. Who would have thought two days in the hole would kill her? I just wanted to teach her who was boss, that's all." He laughed, and the sound of it sent a chill snaking up Mara's spine. If her stomach hadn't been so empty, she might have vomited. "I wanted her myself," her uncle continued. "Wanted to train her right before I turned her over to the customers." He laughed again, and Mara could picture his lecherous grin. "Guess we'll have to make a point of finding a nice young replacement for her real soon, now, won't we?"

The overweight middle-aged man and his two slightly younger companions laughed heartily, continuing with their lewd conversation about what they would like to have done to the little girl whose fear they could smell. Mara hurried as quickly as she was able into the cramped room that served as home to her and several others. Hot tears stung her eyes, and she rebelled at the emotions she had thought were dead, now rising up within her once again.

So, the little girl with the terrified eyes had escaped after all. Perhaps there really was no other way out of this horrible place.

Chapter 2

JONATHAN LOVED THE COOL EVENING BREEZE THAT BLEW IN from the Pacific, often bringing with it a thick marine layer that settled down over the city like a fluffy fleece blanket. It was typical for this time of year and probably would continue to be the norm for several more weeks, until the clear summer nights warmed enough to keep the fog away. As the last hint of daylight evaporated behind the oncoming darkness, Jonathan gunned his ancient, once-blue VW Bug, willing it to keep going until he could coast into the gas station on the other side of the intersection.

Why hadn't he remembered to stop and fill up before going to work? His dad was always on him about running the tank to empty, but he'd been caught up in the ballgame he'd managed to put together that afternoon, and by the time he realized he needed to get to work, he scarcely had time to shower and change. Now, with a pile of cooling-fast pizzas encased in a heavy plastic carrier in his back seat, he knew he didn't dare take too long at the pump or he'd lose out on the tips he counted on from satisfied customers.

Fortunately he didn't have to wait in line for an available spot, and he was soon on his way, weaving through traffic in the direction of the first address on his delivery list. When he pulled up in front of a motel, he groaned. He never liked delivering to places like this. Occasionally the people were very nice, respectful, and big tippers. More than once, however, Jonathan had found himself standing in front of a bunch of intoxicated partiers, each fumbling with their change and hoping someone else would pay for the food. Worse yet, Jonathan had heard of employees being robbed and beaten for a couple of twenties and some change. Fortunately, that hadn't yet happened to him.

Taking a deep breath and sending up a quick but silent "foxhole prayer," as his dad called the "help me" type of petitions, he retrieved the two pizzas marked for the motel address and made his way to the office to get directions to the correct room. He had just reached the top of the stairs on his way to the second floor when a door jerked open not twenty feet from him, and a nearly naked girl who couldn't have been more than twelve or thirteen bolted from the motel room, her long blonde hair streaming behind her. The look of terror on her face froze Jonathan in place, pizzas in hand, unable to speak as he watched the drama unfold in front of him.

The middle-aged man who dashed from the room after the girl was dressed in dark suit pants and a pale blue shirt, his tie loosened as if he'd been relaxing and watching TV. When the two spotted Jonathan, they halted, as if undecided as to what to do next. Then the girl ran to him and nearly knocked the pizzas out of his hands as she cried, "Help me! Please! I don't want to—"

Before she could say another word, the man from the room grabbed her from behind, pulling her gently but firmly against him as he smiled at Jonathan. "Forgive us," he said. "My daughter is...mentally unstable. She hasn't had her medication today, and I was just trying to give it to her. I'm afraid she always puts up a fight about it, but this is the first time she's actually tried to escape."

He lifted the girl's face until she was looking up at him, and then he spoke, firmly and, in Jonathan's opinion, a bit coldly. "This is why I told you to take your medicine, sweetheart. You can't be running around out here like this, upsetting people. Now come back inside with me, and—"

Her eyes wide with what Jonathan could only assume was fright, she opened her mouth, but no words came out. Instead she shook her head no, a low moan accompanying the action. Jonathan was beginning to collect his wits once again and thinking the man's story didn't add up when another girl, a few years older, appeared in the open motel room door.

"Jasmine, get back in here now," she said, leaning against the doorjamb, her voice as calm as her demeanor. "You know Daddy is trying to help you, just like the doctor said. Come on now. Come back inside, and everything will be all right."

Jonathan was struck by the older girl's beauty, though he imagined she was somewhere between his own age and Leah's. Her clothing, however, was much more provocative than anything Leah would ever wear, but he knew girls often dressed that way these days. When she smiled at him, he couldn't resist returning the gesture. Her hair was long and dark brown, her eyes hazel. She didn't really look like the younger girl's sister, but she had referred to the man as "Daddy," in a way that implied they were all family. Of course, that must be the case. What else could it be?

"Sorry if we alarmed you," the man was saying, pulling Jonathan's eyes and thoughts back from the girl in the doorway. "It's difficult being a single parent with two daughters, especially when one is mentally challenged."

The young girl turned her wide blue eyes toward Jonathan, and she opened her mouth again as if she were about to say something. Then she closed it and dropped her head, her shoulders slumping in apparent resignation.

When Jonathan looked back at the man who still held the girl around the waist, he saw that the older girl had come to stand by his side.

Jonathan nodded in response to the man's statement. "I can imagine," he said, still wondering why the whole scene just didn't feel right and trying to keep his gaze on the girls' father and not on the older daughter. "Well, if you'll excuse me, I really need to deliver these pizzas before they get cold."

The man's smile was immediate, though it appeared forced, as he backed up to let Jonathan pass. "Of course," he said. "Sorry to have interrupted you."

Another moan escaped the younger girl, so soft Jonathan wasn't sure he really heard it. But he pressed ahead, anxious to finish his delivery and move on. The entire encounter had unnerved him, and he wanted nothing more than to leave it behind and drive away as quickly as possible.

As he stopped in front of a door a few rooms down and raised his hand to knock, he dared a glance backward, only to see the father nearly shoving the young girl back into the room, with the other girl following close behind. Just before stepping inside, she raised her head and looked straight at him. When their eyes locked, Jonathan felt a chill pass over him. Was it just his imagination, or was the fear on the older girl's face even more pronounced than it had been on the younger one's?

Mara breathed a sigh of relief. Her practiced, cool-under-fire demeanor had helped avert what more than likely would have been a disaster. Various scenarios had flown through her mind in the few seconds that passed from the time she realized the girl known as Jasmine was trying to escape and the instant Mara laid eyes on the handsome stranger in the hallway, delivering pizzas. The various possibilities included the "elimination" of the delivery guy, severe punishment for Jasmine, and no doubt retribution against Mara for having been there and not preventing the situation.

But how could she have known? Jasmine was different than the other girls. She hadn't been brought across the border, but was in fact the only real blonde, white-skinned girl in Jefe's stable. It was unusual, though certainly not unheard of, for pimps to cross racial boundaries, and apparently Jasmine was Jefe's exception to the otherwise dark-haired, dark-eyed Hispanic girls in his brothel. Mara looked now at the younger girl, no doubt kidnapped and wondering why her family hadn't come to rescue her. Her parents, on the other hand, were probably frantic and frustrated, as the police labeled their missing child a runaway. It happened all the time, Mara knew—right here in the United States. And because Jasmine was so new to the "business," she still held out the slimmest of hopes that escape was a possibility, even though she'd been warned of the punishment that would follow such an attempt, not only to herself but to her family.

Mara had long since given up trying to escape. Her family was too far away and had sold her into this life in the first place. Still, she didn't blame Jasmine for taking advantage of the split second of opportunity that had presented itself when their "date" for the night had excused himself to go to the bathroom, but Mara should have been more vigilant and kept a closer watch on the younger girl. For that, though she had done her best to compensate, Mara would no doubt still suffer some sort of punishment once her dear uncle heard of the incident.

Tio, she thought. *To think I once called him by that name and thought he cared about me. When my own parents had no time for me, he always seemed to have a smile and a kind word. I remember when he used to bring me candy... before—*

She stopped, shaking her head to clear her thoughts. Dwelling on the past just made the present that much more difficult to bear. And though it was obvious that Jasmine was the main attraction for the night, Mara too would have her part to play in the evening's entertainment. And from the look on the man's face as he stood, belt in hand, glaring down at the whimpering girl on the bed, things were about to get underway.

It had been a busy night, but Jonathan's shift had finally come to an end. The last pizza was delivered, the last utensil washed and put away, and the building locked up for the night. Jonathan said goodbye to his two fellow employees and nearly sank into the front seat of his car. It wasn't so much that he was tired from working, but rather from holding in the emotional turmoil that had swirled within him throughout the evening.

No matter how hard he tried, he had not been able to shake the vision of the young, half-dressed girl, in the clutches of a man who claimed to be her father, while another girl—one whose sultry good looks had not escaped Jonathan's notice—made what appeared to be an attempt to diffuse the situation.

Why was he interpreting it that way? He started the car and backed out of the parking space, then pulled out onto the road, still asking himself that question. The older girl and the father had explained the circumstances—hadn't they? But if they had, why did the incident still nag at him? And why did the faint memory of the younger girl's moans and her wide eyes still haunt him?

He continued to wrestle with that question after he got home and climbed the stairs, heading to his room. When he noticed a light peeking through the crack beneath the door to Leah's room, he took a detour.

"Come in," she called in answer to his rap on the door.

"What's up?" he asked, walking in to find her sitting at her desk, books and papers spread out in front of her and her computer waiting patiently behind the screen saver of an empty cross standing against a muted sunrise. He winced to think that his screen saver was a baseball, swirling and bouncing like a pinball. How shallow was he?

Leah looked up and rolled her eyes. "I'm building a rocket for NASA. What does it look like, Mr. Genius?"

Jonathan grinned. "Okay. So you're doing your homework. I figured that. But on Saturday night? This late?"

She shrugged, her cascading red curls moving with her shoulders. "I've got a report due on Monday. What can I say?"

"That you should have started it sooner?"

Leah laughed. "Whatever."

Jonathan plunked down on the bed, and Leah scooted her chair around until she was facing him.

"So what's bugging you?" She grinned, her green eyes sparkling with what Jonathan knew was mischief. Teasing her older brother had long been one of her favorite pastimes. "Need some girl advice—again?"

He shook his head. "Nah. Not this time anyway."

Pausing, he wondered if he should just let it go. After all, he was probably blowing the whole thing way out of proportion. But it really bothered him, and he sure couldn't talk to his parents about it.

"I saw something tonight," he said after a moment, taking a deep breath before plunging ahead. "While I was delivering pizzas at a motel."

Leah's eyes widened. "You probably see all kinds of stuff at places like that."

Jonathan nodded. "More than I want to, sometimes. Most of the time, though, it's OK. But tonight..."

Eyebrows raised, Leah waited. When he didn't continue right away, she said, "So tell me. What happened? What did you see?"

"There was this girl—"

Her shoulders relaxed, and she rolled her eyes again. "See, I knew it was a girl! Why didn't you just say so? Was she hot? She was, wasn't she?"

Jonathan smiled. "Not really. I mean, well.... Actually, she was just a kid. Twelve or thirteen, I think. And she was... undressed. Sort of."

It was obvious he had her attention again. Leah frowned. "Sort of undressed? What does that mean? Was she naked?"

"Not...completely. She had...underwear and...a bra on. That's it. Nothing else. And she came running out of this room, looking wild and scared and—"

"Wild?" Leah's frown deepened. "What do you mean, wild? Jonathan, what are you talking about? You're not making any sense."

Jonathan shook his head. "I know. It doesn't make sense to me either. But...I'm just telling you what I saw. This young girl burst out of this room running straight toward me. She nearly knocked me over. And then this guy—her dad, I guess—came after her. She looked like she was scared of him or something. But he said he was her father and that she didn't want to take her medicine. And then this other girl came and stood in the door—"

"Another girl? Now there are two girls in this story?"

"It's not a story," Jonathan insisted. "It really happened. Just like I told you. And the older girl—the one in the doorway—she backed up what the guy was saying. About him being their dad and all. But—"

"Was the older girl half naked too?"

Jonathan shook his head again. "No. She was dressed, but...well, not in the kind of clothes you'd wear to school or church, if you know what I mean."

Leah watched him for a moment, as if trying to discern just what he did mean. When she finally spoke, her voice was hushed. "Do you think they were hookers?"

Jonathan's head snapped up. He hadn't allowed himself to consider it until then, but now that Leah had said it, he realized the thought had definitely been dancing around the fringes of his mind all evening. Hookers? The older one, maybe. But the younger one? How could that be?

His voice cracked when he spoke. "She was just a...a kid. Like I said, twelve or thirteen, maybe. How could she be a hooker?"

Leah's face softened. "I don't know. That does seem awfully young, but...I've heard of things like that happening. You have too."

Jonathan nodded. She was right, though he didn't want her to be. He didn't want to admit that he had heard of such things, and that now he might even have seen the reality of it. He knew there were a lot of evil and unfathomable things going on in the world, but they had never come close enough to him or to his family to become personal before. Now... He sighed and caught his sister's eyes, as the thought flashed through his mind that the second of the two girls he'd seen earlier that evening was probably only slightly older than Leah, and the other one, much younger. His heart constricted at the implications.

"What are you going to do about it?" Leah asked at last.

Jonathan felt his eyes widen. What did she mean? What could he possibly do? Even if he called the police, what would he tell them? That he saw a man with two girls at a motel, the older of whom claimed he was their father? Would the police even follow up on something so vague? And if they did, what would they find when they arrived? If what the so-called father and older sister had said were true, everything would check out just fine. And if it weren't true and something illegal or immoral had been going on, they had undoubtedly all moved on by now. So what was the point?

"What do you think I should do?" Jonathan asked, hoping Leah would tell him to pray about it and leave it alone.

"You know," she said. "You already know what you have to do."

After a moment, Jonathan nodded. She was right. He knew. And though he would never admit it—to Leah or anyone—the thought terrified him.

Chapter 3

LEAH LAY IN BED, STARING INTO THE DARKNESS AT A CEILING she couldn't see. Occasional lights from a passing car in the street below her second-story window briefly cast enough glow into the room to catch the familiar outline of her furniture and belongings, but her mind was too preoccupied to notice them.

Jonathan. What had her brother stumbled across during his otherwise uneventful evening of delivering pizzas? A middle-aged guy and two young girls—one nearly naked—in a motel could be exactly what the man claimed it was: a father and his two daughters, in the middle of a family dispute. But it was obvious that Jonathan suspected it was something much less innocent, and she had to admit that his suspicions seemed likely.

She shivered under her blanket. Hookers? Girls her age—younger even? Was it truly possible? It was one thing to hear about such a thing, but to actually stumble across it in your everyday activities... that was something else entirely.

Leah closed her eyes and pictured her brother's face as he told her of what he'd seen. His warm brown eyes had been intense, boring in on her from beneath his close-cropped auburn hair. She smiled and shook her head at the vivid memory. It just wasn't fair! Why did Jonathan get their mother's great coloring, while she inherited her dad's wilder, more traditional Irish looks? Many times she'd imagined how her long hair would look with an auburn tint instead of a fiery red glow! Why should such a lovely color be wasted on a guy who kept his hair cut short? And though her parents had insisted for years that her bright red hair perfectly complemented her deep green eyes, she would have traded it all for her older brother's more moderate coloring any day.

"Forgive me, Lord," she whispered into the empty room. "There I go, envying again! I know I should be grateful for the way You made me—and I am, truly, especially when I think of those girls Jonathan told me about."

Her voice trailed off, and her heart grew heavy as her thoughts circled back to where they'd been before she got sidetracked. It seemed envy was the least of her shortcomings. How could she be concerned about her looks when quite possibly Jonathan had discovered some sort of underage prostitution ring? The thought stabbed her conscience with the realization that she had just hit a whole new level of shallow.

Church tomorrow, she reminded herself. *And boy, will I be glad to be there! Now if I can just turn my mind off for a while and get some sleep before that alarm goes off.*

Mara had been up since before sunrise, helping one of the other girls prepare breakfast. As the gray light of the sun, muted by thick fog, slowly dispersed the lingering darkness, she caught herself daring to hope that she just might avoid punishment for Jasmine's attempted escape the night before. The man in the motel room had treated the two girls with contempt and even cruelty, but when it was over and Destroyer showed up to take them back to the compound, the man hadn't even mentioned the incident. He had, however, indicated that he'd had an especially good time and would put in a special request for Mara and Jasmine again soon. Though it was hardly something to look forward to, Mara had experienced worse and was relieved that so far Jefe and the others seemed unaware of the near crisis with Jasmine and the pizza man.

Mara stirred the huge pot of oatmeal, the sole nourishment she and the other slaves would receive that morning, while her companion, Goldie, fried bacon and scrambled eggs for their keepers. The smell made Mara's mouth water, but practice and experience had taught her to ignore the temptation and be glad for the oatmeal that would fill her stomach at least for a few hours.

The pizza man. His gentle brown eyes filled her memory, creating a stronger temptation than the aroma of sizzling bacon. She knew it was impossible. Regardless of the kindness she imagined she'd seen lurking behind his good looks, Mara knew there was no such thing as a kind man. Some weren't as mean or vicious as others, but all had only one purpose for someone like her—and it wasn't good. Given half the chance, she was certain the tall stranger would have thrown his pizzas over the railing to the ground below and gladly taken advantage of her and Jasmine for as long as he could get away with it.

She sighed. Gentle? Kind? What a joke! She'd once thought her beloved tio, who treated her with kindness and gentleness, cared for her; now she knew he'd sell her to the highest bidder, for whatever depraved purpose he or she wished. After all, Jefe had already sold her so many times she'd lost count. And when he could no longer use her to turn a profit, he would dispose of her like so much trash, the way he had with the others.

No, she thought, giving the mushy cereal one last stir and resisting the urge to sling the long-handled wooden spoon across the dingy kitchen. *I will not allow myself to think that the pizza man is any different than any other man. They're all scum—and I'm lower than that because I belong to them. And there's no way out.*

She gazed down into the large, dented pot that contained their morning food and realized this was just about as good as it was going to get. In the distance, a church bell rang, and Mara blinked away the hot tears that seemed to have surfaced from nowhere.

Michael Flannery stared in the mirror and fussed with his tie. Just once he'd like to get it right before Rosanna sashayed out of the bathroom, dressed and made-up and ready to go, and came to his rescue. Twenty years they'd been married, and twenty years his wife had been fixing his tie. What in the world did single men do anyway? No doubt attended a less formal church where ties were optional.

He chuckled and dropped his hands to his sides, leaving the tie to dangle at a crooked angle until the cavalry arrived. To be fair, ties were optional at their church too, but as associate pastor, he felt obligated to wear a suit for Sunday morning services. The evening and midweek services were much less formal, and for those occasions he seldom donned anything dressier than slacks and a nice shirt, but he simply couldn't get past his childhood training to do the same for the two main services. It was as if he could still hear his late mother's voice, scolding him for daring to enter "the Lord's house" in anything but his "Sunday best." She'd been gone for nearly ten years now, but "old habits die hard," as she was also known to say. And she'd been a stickler for establishing what she considered the right habits in her three sons from a very early age.

Is that why I became a missionary and then a pastor? Michael wondered. *No.* He shook his head. *Absolutely not! I've asked myself that question more times than I can count, and I always come up with the same answer: I became a missionary and a pastor because that's what God called me to be. Period. I love God and want to serve Him, and this is where that desire brought me.* He glared at himself in the mirror, disgusted. *But couldn't You at least have given me the ability to tie my own tie, Father? After all these years, you'd think I could have—*

His silent prayer was interrupted by Rosanna swinging open the bathroom door and stepping into their room. Just as Michael had expected, her pale green dress fit perfectly, complementing her shoulder-length auburn hair. Was it really possible his beloved wife was in her early forties? She looked better than most twenty-year-olds he'd ever met, and she was certainly more pleasant to be around. He was a blessed man indeed...even if God had never allowed him to learn how to fix his own tie.

Rosanna's brown eyes sparkled as she stepped up behind him and peered around his shoulder into the mirror. With a grin she placed her hands on her hips and sighed. "Michael Flannery, what am I going to do with you? Aren't you ever going to learn how to tie a tie properly? Here, turn around and I'll fix it."

Michael smiled and turned toward his wife, who was already latching onto the two ends of his unruly tie. And suddenly he had his answer. Why should God enable him to tie his own tie when He had given him a perfectly good wife who took great pleasure in doing it for him?

In less than a minute, his attire was acceptable and they were ready to go. Now to be sure, Jonathan and Leah were up and ready as well. If they hurried, there would be time for a light breakfast before they headed out the door into the gray Sunday morning light.

Chapter 4

JONATHAN FIDGETED HIS WAY THROUGH THE SERVICE, EVEN more than usual. Though his mind often drifted during the singing and sermon, today was worse. He hadn't slept well, so his preoccupation with the previous night's events had quickly partnered with his heavy eyelids, making paying attention to the senior pastor's teaching on the importance of relationships from the Book of Ephesians nearly impossible. Occasionally Leah, who sat at his right side, nudged him, bringing him back from the edge, but he was never able to regather his thoughts enough to focus on anything that was being proclaimed from the pulpit. He might as well have stayed home and slept through the morning.

And he would have, if he'd had anything to say about it. But of course, he didn't. He had learned early on that regardless of his age, if he lived under his parents' roof, he was expected to attend church regularly. Usually he didn't mind because there really were some attractive girls in the congregation, and he'd had his eye on a couple of them for a while now. He'd even considered making his move today and asking one of them—whichever he ran into first—out on a date. But the way he was feeling this morning, he opted to wait another week before reconsidering it.

He leaned to the left where his shoulder rested against the end of the wooden pew, right next to the center aisle. At least Leah sat as a buffer between him and his parents, so maybe they wouldn't notice his elevated level of inattention this morning. He really didn't want them pursuing what was on his mind, and possibly dragging the motel incident out into the open. Leah had told him he knew what he should do about it, but did he? The only thing he was sure of was that there probably wasn't anything he *could* do. If his worst suspicions were true and he had stumbled across an underage prostitution ring, then chances were there were kidnapping and human trafficking issues involved as well. What could one single eighteen-year-old, lukewarm Bible-college-bound guy do about something that evil?

Then again, how would he live with himself if he didn't at least try? What if those girls really were being held against their will? He nearly scoffed aloud at the thought. Of course they were being held against their will! Hadn't the younger girl tried to escape in her underwear? And though the other girl was obviously older, that didn't mean she was there by choice. From what little he'd heard about these situations, there wasn't much choice involved.

And so it came back to him—his choice. What would he do? What *could* he do? As selfish and slimy as it made him feel to think it, he wished he'd been anywhere else but at that motel last night when that terrified girl came running out the door. The honesty of his feelings made him ashamed, but his life would have remained so much simpler if he hadn't seen what he saw in those few minutes during an otherwise uneventful evening.

But he had. And now he was challenged at the very core of his being, and faced with the reality that he was a selfish coward at heart. He wished himself out of the situation so he could go on with his comfortable life. And yet, even if he hadn't been at that motel when the girl ran out into the corridor, it wouldn't change the truth that those two girls—and who knew how many others—were very likely a part of the sex slavery he'd heard about in the last few years. Whatever he decided to do about what he'd seen, he could never again deny that such a thing existed. There was simply no other logical explanation for it, no matter how desperately Jonathan tried to convince himself that the man had been telling the truth.

Mara had seen Jasmine a couple of times that day, but they always dropped their eyes and made no attempt to connect. Since it was forbidden for them to discuss anything personal and unwise to develop emotional attachments, Mara had long ago learned to avoid looking directly into someone's eyes unless commanded to do so.

The pizza man had been an exception. As hard as she'd tried to avoid looking directly at him, she'd told herself she had to in order to convince him of the truth of their customer's story. Had the tall, good-looking stranger believed it? Probably. People tended to believe what made them the most comfortable and prevented them from being nudged from their comfort zone. The young pizza deliverer no doubt lived in a comfort zone that included family and school and friends—something Mara knew little or nothing about—and he certainly wouldn't be anxious to step outside that familiar circle to examine the darker side of life where slaves were bought and sold, used and reused, until they no longer had any purpose. Mara supposed that was just the way life was—some landed on the side with opportunities and privileges; some did not. It was obvious where she belonged.

She leaned back on the rickety lawn chair in the overgrown courtyard of the compound. She determined to dismiss the image of the handsome stranger and to take advantage of a rare break in her daily duties to catch a few hours of sleep in the lazy afternoon sunshine before she once again began her nightly routine. The morning fog had burned off around noon, and Mara looked forward to absorbing some of the sun's warmth during the break they were usually afforded each afternoon. She'd already been informed that tonight she would be part of the entertainment for a group of businessman who were away from home for a few days and needed someone to help them forget their loneliness. Mara wouldn't even allow her mind to wander there; the evening's requirements could include any number of activities, none of which she would enjoy. But then, her existence wasn't about enjoyment; it was all about survival.

Jasmine strolled by, her eyes averted, and plopped down in a wicker chair several yards from Mara. She leaned her head back and closed her eyes, and Mara knew her younger counterpart was also trying to get some rest while she could. Darkness would arrive far too quickly for both of them, and it appeared that perhaps Jasmine had accepted her fate and abandoned her attempts to escape. Mara hoped that was true, as it would simplify both their lives.

The last of the food was back in the refrigerator and the dishwasher was loaded. Rosanna punched the start button and wiped her hands on the dishtowel as the washer started its familiar hum. Flipping out the kitchen light, she headed for the family room where Michael had settled in to watch a basketball playoff game. It was nearly impossible to tear him away from the television this time of year, particularly if his beloved Los Angeles Lakers were still in the running—which they often were. Personally, Rosanna didn't care who won; she just counted the days until the season was over. Of course, football season would start soon, and baseball overlapped the two. Was there no break in all this sports mania?

Michael was leaned back in the brown leather recliner, his shoes kicked off and his feet up. Rosanna knew before she looked that his eyes were closed, though if she woke him he'd swear he wasn't asleep and had been listening to the game all along.

She smiled and sat down at the end of the couch adjacent to the recliner. Michael didn't move, confirming her suspicions that he was indeed asleep. And why shouldn't he be? He kept a crazy schedule at the church all week and was ready for a little relaxation by the time the weekend rolled around—although Sunday was a work day for him too. But at least in the afternoon, between services, he could relax and enjoy himself.

To be truthful, she wouldn't mind a little quiet time herself. Leah had gone home from church with a friend, and Jonathan had gone straight to his room after lunch, saying he had some last-minute homework to finish up, so it appeared that quiet time was definitely on the agenda.

Deciding to give her husband the acid test as to whether or not he was sleeping, she gently retrieved the remote from the end table that sat between them. Slowly, carefully, she pushed the channel button to see if Michael would react to the change. Nothing. She knew she was home free!

Before she could punch the menu button to find an old movie or "golden oldies" sitcom rerun, the image of a sad-eyed little girl filled the screen, and she froze. "Slavery is alive," the caption read, and she thought her heart would break. It wasn't that she was unaware of human trafficking, but for the most part she was able to keep its horror at bay. After all, she and Michael regularly gave to their denomination's missions fund, and one of the outreaches that fund supported was the rescue of human trafficking victims. But this was so...personal. This face, with its hopelessness and despair, nearly knocked her from her chair. Though she resisted the urge to fall on her face and pray for this child, she was unable to stop the hot tears that popped into her eyes and threatened to overflow onto her cheeks.

"Oh, Father," she whispered. "Father!" It was all she could say, though her heart cried out as she continued to watch the documentary unfold. Was this hideous crime really as widespread as the narrator made it sound? Did it really take place right here in their own country, possibly even in their own neighborhoods?

"Are you all right?"

The question jarred her, and she snapped her head around to face her husband. Apparently he hadn't been sleeping quite as soundly as she'd thought.

She cleared her throat and immediately began to swipe at her eyes, wiping the tears from her face onto her pant legs. "I'm fine," she said. "It was just—"

"I know," Michael said, interrupting her as he reached across the expanse between them and took her hand. "I was watching too."

Rosanna dropped her head, glad for the reassurance of Michael's hand around hers. "It's awful," she said. "I know it goes on—all over the world. But here? In our own country? Surely it's not as prevalent as it seems in this documentary!"

"I want to believe that too," Michael said. "To accept the figures I've seen, some estimating there are at least 27 million people enslaved around the world, is almost more than I can fathom. And then you see a face—just one face, tortured, miserable, helpless—and it becomes personal."

She heard him sigh, and she raised her head. The encroaching gray scarcely showed in his bright red hair, but his green eyes shone with tears. Already a few had escaped to trickle down his cheeks, but he made no effort to hide them or wipe them away. She loved him for that. Michael's heart was tender, which was why she trusted him implicitly. He would always do the right thing, and if he wasn't sure what that might be, he'd err on the side of compassion.

Rosanna's heart constricted. What a blessed life she had, while others suffered unimaginably. Surely there was something they could do to help, though she couldn't imagine what it would be, beyond the small amount they already gave at church. It was just that seeing the little girl's face, having the issue become personal, made her want to respond in a personal way as well. But how was she to do that?

A sound caught her attention, and both she and Michael turned toward the doorway to see Jonathan standing there, his eyes moving from the television to his parents and back again. Had he too been troubled by what he saw? The shadows that played across his face told her that he had.

Chapter 5

Chanthra had somehow managed to survive in the Golden Triangle region of Thailand for several years—exactly how many she wasn't sure. Her memories of her life before coming to this infamous corner of the world where Thailand, Burma, and Laos meet grew dimmer with the passing of time. She had been a small child then, the beloved and only daughter of peasant farmers who treated her well and cared for her as best they could, naming her Chanthra because of the full moon that shone the night she was born. The only thing she knew for certain was that her father had worked long and hard to try to provide sufficient food for them to eat and a small hut in which to sleep. The rest was too hazy to identify—except for her parents' strong faith in *phra yaeh suu*, the Lord Jesus Christ, and the sound of her mother's singing. Now, as a teenager, when she lay down at night in the filth-ridden brothel she called home, ready to entertain yet another string of customers in order to keep her owners happy and to ensure that she would be fed at morning light, she escaped her circumstances by wrapping herself in the memory of her mother's voice. It was all she had left of the life she had known before her parents agreed to let her be adopted by a wealthy family who promised to care for her and give her a chance for a good life and a promising future. But when she'd been torn from her mother's arms, screaming and kicking while her parents watched with tears streaming down their faces, she had not gone to live with a rich family. She had instead been brought to this place where her life had become a living hell and where she had begged and pleaded with God to let her die. But she was still here, and she had never seen her beloved parents again. At least they were at peace, she told herself, believing their daughter now lived a prosperous life. Thank God they didn't know the truth!

Tonight was no different from all the others. With her eyes closed in the dimly lit room, which served as her living quarters as well as her working space, Chanthra had no idea what the man looked like who now abused her for his own pleasure. And it didn't matter. They were all faceless—and nameless. None cared for her, nor did she care for them. Even her hatred of them was generic. She tolerated them in order to earn two meals a day and, if all went well, to avoid any serious beatings or mistreatment.

Chanthra supposed it could be worse. After all, hadn't she heard that some slaves didn't even have beds but had to sleep outside? Yes, her owners had told her many times that she was a lucky girl to have such nice accommodations and such a steady job. She supposed it was true, but even after all these years, she would rather be back with her parents, listening to her mother sing her to sleep—even if they didn't have enough to eat.

Jonathan was more disturbed than ever. When he had walked to the door of the family room and found his parents watching a program about human trafficking, while tears stained their cheeks, it was nearly more than he could bear. He almost burst into tears himself, as the desire to tell them of his bizarre encounter at the motel the previous night burned within him. But at the last moment he had swallowed his pain and walked away, returning to his room where he flopped down on his bed and stared at the ceiling, wondering why—if there really was a God up there somewhere—He didn't come down and do something! What kind of omnipotent Deity ignored such evil and suffering? The only thing worse than believing that no God existed was to think that He was there but simply didn't care.

Jonathan knew better, of course. After all, he'd been raised in the church and had heard Bible stories from the time he was old enough to understand words. God was good and merciful and wanted to have a relationship with us—but He also allowed us to make our own choices, including to reject Him and go our own way if we so desired. Jonathan imagined that the vast majority of people must have chosen the latter for the world to end up in such a terrible mess.

Bible college. Who was he kidding? What did he hope to accomplish by going there in the fall? Everyone would know he was a fraud. He'd probably be expelled before the end of the first semester. Why couldn't his parents understand that he'd be better off going to some secular school and studying business or something? At least it would be an honest pursuit, one that he could get involved in without feeling like the biggest hypocrite on the planet.

The young girl's face swam before his eyes again, and he nearly hollered at the vision to go away. It had plagued him throughout the night, even in his dreams, and had continued to haunt him during the daylight hours. Leah's words hadn't helped any either.

"You already know what you have to do," she had told him. And at the moment, he had thought she was right. But was she? No. All he knew was that he had to do something—but what? What could anyone do? If those two girls were some sort of sex slaves, how could he help them? What was he supposed to do, ride in on a big white horse and rescue them? He didn't even know where they were—or if they even wanted to be rescued!

The terrified girl's face pricked his conscience. Who was he kidding? Of course they wanted to be rescued—at least the younger one did, or she wouldn't have been trying to escape. What kind of slime ball was that guy who claimed to be their dad anyway? Jonathan smirked. *Their dad. Sure! Like I'm gonna buy that story!*

What bothered him most was what he did after he completed his pizza delivery and left the motel—or, to be more accurate, what he didn't do. He didn't call for help. He didn't report what he'd seen. He didn't do anything except tell Leah. How many other people had seen things just like that and done nothing to help? The thought chilled him. That was the reason this sort of thing existed—because others felt as inadequate as he to stop it... or simply chose to ignore it.

What do You want me to do, God? he cried silently. *Show me what to do!*

When he realized he had just prayed his first heartfelt prayer in a very long time, he released the tears that had lurked behind his eyelids for nearly twenty-four hours now. As they dripped down his face and into his ears and hair, he waited, not sure which was worse—the thought that God wouldn't answer... or that He would.

Mara bolted from her sleep, nearly choking on the stench. Had it been only a dream? Her racing heart cried out for it to be so. Yet she could almost taste the dry, dead smell of the huge reeds that surrounded her like a cave, intermingled with the putrid odor of sweat, lust, and unwashed bodies. And oh, the heat! It was nearly as oppressive in her dream as it had been when she was actually there.

She shuddered at the thought, and then shook her head and tried to focus. Of course! She remembered now. She had leaned back in the webbed lounge chair, hoping to get some rest before starting her nightly duties. Instead she had fallen asleep and dreamed of The Reeds, that horrible place where her very own tio had taken her as a child to "break her in," as he called it—to teach her "the trade," as well as her place in it. And she had learned quickly.

"Are you all right?"

The words were almost inaudible. Mara wondered if she had dreamed that too, though the voice sounded vaguely familiar. Turning in the direction where it seemed the question had originated, she spotted Jasmine, still sitting in her own lawn chair and watching her intently. Mara realized how different the girl looked with concern defining her features, rather than terror.

Mara nodded. "I'm fine," she said. "Nothing to worry about. Just a dream."

"Must have been a real nightmare," Jasmine said, lifting an eyebrow. "You were boxing the air, like you were fighting for your life."

Fighting for my life, Mara thought, *even in my sleep!* She shook her head. "Yeah, so what else is new?" She forced a smile and shrugged. "Fighting for our lives. It's what we do, right?"

The concern melted from Jasmine's face, as the familiar look of fear returned. Leaning her head back, she closed her eyes. The conversation was over.

Chapter 6

Jonathan knew his parents preferred that he not work on Sunday, and he never did in the morning, but afternoons and evenings were different—especially during any sort of sports playoff season. When it came to big tips, Sunday was the absolute best money-maker, and he always volunteered for that day. Of course, his parents didn't know that. He had them convinced that he tried to get out of it, but his boss just wouldn't give him any special consideration. And to be truthful, Jonathan knew he'd sign up for Sunday deliveries even if it weren't the biggest tipping day. Going in to work on Sunday afternoon was the perfect out for not attending church again in the evening.

A stab of guilt nudged him as he loaded the stack of pizzas into the back seat of his VW, ready to begin his deliveries. But he dismissed it as quickly as it came. After all, he went to church that morning, didn't he? Wasn't once enough? He really didn't see any need to overdo it, though he imagined he'd be spending a lot more time in church once he got to Bible college. He'd heard it was nearly mandatory several times a week. And he'd be studying books of the Bible all day, every day—in class, doing homework, taking tests. Would it help? Would it finally light a fire in him like the one he saw blazing in Leah and his parents? What was wrong with him that he didn't share their passion for church or their depth of faith? Sure, he believed in God and Jesus and...well, most of what was in the Bible. He'd heard it all his life, so why wouldn't he believe it? But somehow it just hadn't soaked in the way it did with Leah. And it sure wasn't the greatest passion of his life.

He shook his head and climbed into the front seat. OK, so what was the greatest passion? Baseball. Hands down. But reality had already convinced him that there wasn't any future in it for him, so he was doing the next best thing—going off to a school that would make his parents happy and that just might give him enough time to figure out what he *really* wanted to do when he graduated.

He tapped the gas a couple of times and then gunned it, the way he'd become accustomed to doing in order to keep his rattle-trap car running, and headed down the street. The first delivery was an easy one, practically a regular. A nice house in a nice neighborhood with a nice family who always gave him a nice tip. Jonathan hoped they'd never get tired of pizza.

By the time he'd delivered the large, piping hot pepperoni and extra cheese pizza and pocketed his expected tip, he'd nearly forgotten his self-absorbed musings and was beginning to enjoy the warm San Diego weather. The mornings might be gray and foggy this time of year, but the afternoons were great. He loved early summer because he could drive with the windows down and feel the wind on his left arm, which he always rested on the window. Since his heater didn't work and he didn't even have an air conditioner, this was the perfect weather for driving around in his old faithful Beetle.

Wait a minute. How had he ended up over here? He pressed on the brake and slowed to a stop in front of the motel where he'd seen the girls with their so-called father the night before. He hadn't meant to come here... had he?

Pulling his eyes from the second story corridor where the terrified girl had almost knocked him down as she came running from her room, he looked down at his delivery list. No, he definitely did not have any deliveries in this area. So what was he doing here? Was it some sort of subconscious pull that had dragged him to the front of the motel, hoping to see the girls again? Possibly. He didn't really have any other answers. And he didn't have any business here either. What he did have was a backseat full of pizzas that were going to get cold and rob him of his tips if he didn't put yesterday's events out of his mind and get back to work.

Taking his foot off the brake, he tapped the gas and gunned it once again, determined to focus on his job and complete his deliveries on time.

Leah loved Sunday evenings. For her it was the best of both worlds—being at church with people who shared her love for Jesus and getting to work in the nursery with the babies and toddlers, and even a few preschoolers. Jonathan teased her that she should quit babysitting for free and get a "real" job, but she always countered with the fact that this was her ministry. More than once he had admitted that she was good at it, and she knew he was right. The kids loved her, and so did their parents. On the Sunday evenings when Leah was on duty in the nursery, parents didn't have to peel their little ones off their legs to get them to stay; the children who had been there before and knew Leah were eager to spend some time with her.

Tonight was no exception. As one of four nursery workers, Leah and her companions oversaw nearly twenty children under the age of four—a few still in cribs, but most either crawling, toddling, or racing around. The biggest challenge was to keep the younger ones from finding things on the floor and sticking them in their mouths. Leah accomplished that task best by keeping those who were old enough to pay attention entertained with her singing and hand motions. It wasn't long before the mobile ones were following her around, singing along and doing their best to copy her actions, while the other workers took turns feeding and changing the infants and hovering over the crawlers. To an untrained eye, it might look like chaos, but to Leah, it was more fun than she'd had all week.

As she and the children who had been following her collapsed on the floor in fits of giggles at the end of a song, one child in particular caught Leah's attention. Anna, her wide, dark eyes looking far too big for her tiny face, smiled shyly at her from the edge of the circle of little ones that surrounded Leah. Returning the smile, Leah held out her hand, and Anna hurried into her arms. Leah pulled her close and kissed the top of her head, as the smell of baby shampoo filled her nostrils. Anna was one of Leah's favorites, as well as one of her regular babysitting assignments. Smiling, Leah took Anna's arms in her hands and held her away so she could look into her face.

"How are you today, Anna?" she asked, watching the child closely while she waited for an answer. She had known the almost three-year-old since she'd first arrived from her home country of Thailand, adopted by Kyle and Nyesha Johnson, an interracial couple who had long attended the church and nearly as long prayed for a child. When they'd flown across the seas to retrieve their new daughter, the church had thrown a huge welcome party when they returned, nearly frightening little eighteen-month-old Anna—whose name was then as new to her as her surroundings—into a nonstop crying fest. But at last she had fallen asleep and rested peacefully in her adoptive mother's arms, as the congregation *oohed* and *aahed* over her short, silky black hair and soft, creamy skin. Leah remembered wondering what could have happened to the little girl's mother that would make her willing to part with such a perfect child. As she gazed into the child's eyes even now, the same question crossed her mind.

"I fine," Anna mumbled, pulling one arm loose from Leah's grasp so she could shove a couple of fingers in her mouth, a nervous habit that she had clung to since arriving in her new home.

"I can see that," Leah agreed, smiling. "You have a beautiful pink dress on tonight."

Anna's eyes dropped to examine her clothes before she looked up and removed her fingers from her mouth to offer a hesitant smile. "My daddy buyed it for me," she said.

Leah laughed. "Bought it," she corrected. "Your daddy *bought* it for you."

Anna nodded in agreement, her eyes sparkling as if she were very proud of Leah for understanding the situation.

Before Leah could say another word, she was attacked from behind by two rowdy boys who wanted to play trucks. Pretending to yield under protest, she shot an apologetic look at Anna, wondering if the girl might want to join in. But Anna was already turning away and moving toward the corner where two other girls about her size played with dolls.

Leah smiled and watched her go, pleased that Anna was beginning to gain enough confidence to attempt playing with the other children. She'd come a long way from the terrified state she'd arrived in more than a year ago.

A small dump truck *vroomed* past her, powered by one of her two former assailants, who looked up at her and laughed. "Don't you want to play?" he asked. "I have a truck, and Tony has a truck. But you don't."

Leah laughed aloud. "You're right, buddy. I'm the only one without a truck. Guess I'd better get one, huh?"

The towheaded boy grinned and nodded. "Yep," he said. "You can't play without a truck."

With one last glance at Anna, who now clutched a doll of her own as she sat between the two other little girls, Leah moved on to playing trucks with the boys.

Mara could scarcely stand, let alone walk, in the ridiculously high heels they'd given her, but apparently a couple of the businessmen who had requested her and two of the other girls for the evening had also specified stiletto heels. As long as Mara had been wearing them now, she wondered why she hadn't gotten used to them. Jasmine and an even younger girl named Reina walked in front of Mara, looking like awkward storks as they followed Enforcer up the stairs to the room or rooms where she and the others would spend the next several hours. The motel, the same one they'd been at the night before, wasn't as nice as some Mara had been to, but definitely better than most. And it seemed Jefe had recently made some sort of deal with the owners, as Mara had overheard him mentioning it to Enforcer and Destroyer and telling them to plan on using it more often in the future.

When they reached the second floor, Mara hesitated, glancing to the left even as the others turned right. Just a few feet away is where the handsome stranger had stood the previous evening, holding his pizza and watching the drama unfold before his wide brown eyes. Mara wished she could forget those eyes. It seemed he'd looked right through her—and she'd almost liked it. It wasn't anything like it was with other men, whom she didn't even look at unless ordered to do so. The pizza guy had caught her attention in a way that disturbed her, and she couldn't figure out why.

"Get moving!" came a command from behind, just as she felt a jab to her back. Destroyer. Who else? Enforcer always led the way, and sometimes Destroyer would come too, staying behind to make sure there were no stragglers. Mara quickly moved to get back in line.

"You've got work to do," Destroyer growled. "The clients are waiting."

Mara nodded and picked up her pace. What good would it do to dawdle? Like Destroyer said, she had a job to do, and she would do it, whether she liked it or not. But she knew before they even stepped inside the room that she wouldn't like it.

Chapter 7

CHANTHRA WOKE TO THE SOUND OF HOWLING WINDS AND a heavy downpour—again. It was monsoon season, so she wasn't surprised, but she hated the heavy, wet heat and the added business that invariably came her way when one of these seasonal storms hit. She found herself wondering why men didn't stay home with their families in this kind of weather; instead they seemed to become more restless than ever because they couldn't work or carry on their normal activities. And so their thoughts turned to female companionship.

It wouldn't be so bad, Chanthra reasoned, if it meant more money for her and a better chance to one day save up enough to break free from her horrible life. But the added customers just meant more money for her owners and more work for her. Who was she kidding? She'd never get out of this nightmare—at least not alive. Her dream to one day see her family again had nearly disappeared into the hopelessness that surrounded her.

She rolled to one side and saw the pipe that had become her constant companion sitting on the floor beside her thin mattress. Her heart skipped a beat at the sight of the fresh supply of drugs her boss man had left her while she slept. It was one of the few bonuses that accompanied being a sex slave, and she had long since learned to take advantage of it. Its effects dulled her senses as she went through the motions of her job each night, and it highly increased the likelihood that she wouldn't have to endure it much longer. For that she was grateful, though she knew it was no great sacrifice on her boss man's part to get it to her. They were, after all, living and working in the Golden Triangle, where poppy fields were plentiful, nearly funding the entire region financially. If it weren't for the workers who grew and harvested the profitable plants, there would be little need for girls like Chanthra.

Reaching out with trembling hands, she took the pipe and began to prepare for the day. She couldn't do anything to change what she must do, but she could at least change the way she experienced it.

Rosanna lay in bed beside Michael, listening to the sounds of the early night. Leah was in her room, no doubt finishing up some last-minute school assignment, her worship music playing softly in the background. Michael had fallen asleep the moment his head hit the pillow, the way he usually did at the end of another busy Sunday, but a day off on Monday would enable him to rest and recover.

She wished she could fall asleep as easily, but since Jonathan and Leah were born, her sleeping habits had changed. Even at her points of deepest sleep, she was always on the ready to awake and bounce out of bed at the first hint of a sound from either child. It didn't matter that they were no longer babies or toddlers who needed her to do everything for them. They were still her offspring, and she would no doubt always live up to the name "helicopter mom," which Jonathan had teasingly bestowed on her because of her constant hovering.

It's my job, she thought, smiling into the darkness. *Well, OK, maybe it isn't—not really, anyway. Maybe my job is just to pray for my kids and trust God to take care of them. But how do I stop feeling what I feel? When do I discover the off switch for worrying mode?*

She glanced at the illuminated dial of the clock radio on the bed stand. Almost eleven. Jonathan wouldn't be home for at least another hour. She hated the thought that her son was driving around in all sorts of neighborhoods in an unreliable car, carrying nothing but pizzas and just enough cash to get him robbed at gunpoint. And all for minimum wage and a few paltry tips! Still, she knew he needed to learn the responsibility of working, and in today's economy a not-quite-yet high school grad couldn't be too picky.

A dog barked in the distance, as her mind drifted from her children to the children she'd seen on the documentary earlier that day. Human trafficking! How was it possible that it went on right here in their own country—according to the program, even in their own San Diego area? And it wasn't just women who were forced into such degrading and illegal work, but children as well. *Children! Oh, Father,* she thought, *how can people be so cruel? How can these little ones suffer so?*

Fighting tears, she found herself wondering if there was something tangible she could do to help. The problem was so widespread, and she was just one person. But wasn't there some sort of saying that one person plus God equals a majority? Besides, surely there were others who were equally touched by this tragedy and wanted to help. If they banded together...

Tomorrow, she thought. *Tomorrow I'm going to go online and find ministries that are involved in rescuing these people—or see if I can find out something at church. There have to be some somewhere!*

And I have to get involved, Lord. Help me, Father. Guide me into what You want me to do about this.

With that prayer on her heart, Rosanna finally drifted off to sleep.

The last pizza was delivered and, as expected, Jonathan's tips had been generous. He was feeling fairly flush with cash when he backed out of his last customer's driveway and headed back to the restaurant. It was times like this, when his deliveries were made and the streets were fairly quiet, that he really missed having a radio in his car. He'd learned to live without heat and air conditioning—after all, this was Southern California, and the weather was never all that extreme—but no music? Man, he was going to have to use some of this extra tip money to get that radio fund built up. As bad as he needed to save up to have extra cash when he started school this fall, he really needed to remedy this quiet before much longer.

Humming to himself and hammering the beat on the steering wheel with his right hand, he rounded the corner and realized he was only a couple of blocks from the motel. What could it hurt to drive by there on the way back to work? It wasn't really all that far out of his way—wouldn't take more than an extra five minutes or so. But even as he made the decision and veered to the right at the next cross street, he asked himself why.

What do you expect to find there? It's not like those girls are going to pop back out of that room again. And even if they did, what would you do? When you saw them yesterday, you didn't do a thing. What makes you think it would be any different now?

He shook his head at his own foolishness as the pushing-toward-seedy motel came into view. Several cars in the parking lot, but not a soul in sight. *Just keep driving, big man,* he told himself. *You've got no business here. None.*

He slowed to a stop directly across the street from the motel, where he could see the room from last night. *Why? What am I doing here?* But this time he sensed he wasn't talking to himself. Somehow he had switched into prayer mode, and he was talking to someone a lot bigger than himself. *What do You want me to do, God? Do You even want me to do anything—or am I just imagining all this? Why can't I just forget about it and get on with my life?*

A siren in the distance was the only sound that floated to him on the night breeze, as he sat and stared at the closed door on the second floor. *Where are they, God? Where are those girls? Why did You let me see them? There's nothing I can do to help them. Nothing!*

In an instant his eye were filled with hot tears. "I don't know where they are, God," he whispered, "but You do. I also don't know if You're listening to me because I really haven't been very faithful lately—at least not compared to Leah and my parents. But...for their sake, for those two girls, please...will You help them? Somehow? Do something for them, God. Please."

With a silent amen he tapped the gas and then gunned it, resuming his trip to the restaurant. It was getting late, and he had to get back and help clean up so they could close the place.

Chapter 8

ROSANNA JERKED HERSELF AWAKE AND SAT UP IN BED. She'd heard something. The front door? Yes, of course. It had to be. Jonathan was home from work.

She glanced over at Michael, though it wasn't necessary to determine if he was still sleeping. His soft but steady snores assured her of that. Moving carefully, she sat up on the side of the bed and slid her feet into the waiting slippers, then donned the light robe that lay across the foot of the bed. Stepping to the window, she moved the curtain to one side and peered downward, confirming that the porch light was indeed turned off. Jonathan was home.

Avoiding the two spots in the floor that always creaked and that she'd memorized to keep from waking her husband, she padded softly to the door and let herself out into the hallway, hoping to intercept Jonathan before he reached his room. That usually wasn't difficult because he almost always stopped in the kitchen for a snack, even if he'd been munching on leftover pizza all the way home. At the head of the stairway, she saw the light from the open kitchen door shining into the entryway, and she smiled. She still knew her children well, despite the fact that they were nearly adults.

When she reached the kitchen, she stood in the doorway and watched her son spreading peanut butter on a couple slices of bread. He was so intent he didn't realized he had company, and she took advantage of that to drink in her tall, handsome man-child. Peanut butter had been his favorite snack since he got his first set of teeth and was able to eat solid foods. Some things never changed, and she was glad. It gave her a sense of security.

"Hungry?" she asked, grinning as he swung around to gaze at her, his eyes wide.

"Mom," he said. "I didn't know you were there. I thought you were sleeping."

Rosanna's smile widened. "I was," she admitted. "But you know I don't sleep soundly until I know you're home." She stepped toward him. "Did you have a good shift at work?"

Jonathan nodded and turned back to his task. "I did," he said, putting the two slices of peanut butter-covered bread face-to-face and smashing them together as he always did. He picked it up and looked back at her. "I was busy, so it went fast. Made lots of tips." He smiled and bit into his sandwich.

Rosanna couldn't imagine how he could chew a sandwich so absolutely overflowing with sticky filling, but instead of saying anything she simply went to the refrigerator and got out the carton of milk. She poured a glass and handed it to him, watching as he nearly inhaled it. Why didn't he ever pour himself a glass when he made those horrible sandwiches? She might know her children's habits, but she certainly didn't understand their quirks.

"Want to sit down?" she asked, nodding toward the small but comfortable maple dinette set in the corner breakfast nook that had seen more family meals and discussions than she could count.

Jonathan didn't answer—he probably couldn't since his mouth was filled once again with peanut butter—but went straight to a chair and sat down. Rosanna joined him.

"Anything unusual happen today?" she asked, hoping to draw him into a conversation, something she knew she would miss when he went away to college in a few weeks.

Jonathan's eyebrows shot up, and for a moment she wondered why her question had elicited such a strong reaction. But then, Jonathan had a tendency to be dramatic at times. She waited for him to swallow.

When he did, she was sure she saw a look of guilt cross his face before he answered. "No, nothing," he said. "Why?"

She shrugged. "No reason. Just wanted to know about your day."

He nodded slowly and shoved the remainder of the sandwich into his mouth. It was obvious he wouldn't be able to say anything further for a while. And something told her that by the time he could, he would have found a way to change the subject.

Mara was relieved. All five businessmen had been drinking so heavily by the time she and the others arrived that the girls' involvement in their evening was limited. The men were all sleeping soundly now, spread across the two double beds and the sofa. The floor was littered with cast-off clothes, empty bottles, and glasses. The youngest girl, Reina, who couldn't have been more then nine or ten, had cried herself to sleep on the floor after covering herself with a towel from the bathroom. Jasmine sat quietly in a corner, watching Mara, who gazed back at her wordlessly. If all went well, the men would stay asleep until Enforcer or Destroyer returned for them.

Mara frowned as Jasmine moved from her sitting position to all fours and stealthily crawled toward her. What was she doing? The last thing Mara wanted was to risk waking their customers.

Jasmine stopped in front of Mara and resumed a sitting position, cross-legged in front of her. Leaning toward her and whispering so softly Mara had to strain to hear her, the younger girl whispered, "Tell me about The Reeds."

Mara's heart nearly stopped. The Reeds? Why would anyone want to know about that horrible place? And besides, didn't Jasmine realize they were forbidden from talking of such things?

Jasmine's blue eyes spoke only of innocent curiosity, as her long blonde hair fell forward over her shoulders. Mara knew the girl must be at least eleven or twelve, but at the moment she looked so much younger. Though she knew it was a foolish decision, Mara realized she was going to tell Jasmine what she wanted to know. Mara could only wonder what it would feel like to finally give voice to the horrors she experienced in that place when she was no more than six or seven years old.

"The Reeds," she whispered, leaning forward as Jasmine did the same, "is the worst place in the world. Never, ever let them take you there."

Jasmine frowned. "But... how can I stop them? If they want me to go..."

Mara shook her head. "No. Never. Never let them take you there. Tell them you'll do anything else, but don't go there." She paused for effect, and waited until Jasmine nodded. Then she went on. "I haven't heard of anyone going there for a while, so I don't know what happened. I only know that I had to go there every Sunday afternoon to entertain the workers. Jefe said it was to break me in and teach me the ropes." She shuddered. "If I had been old enough to find a way, I would have killed myself after the first day."

Jasmine gasped, and her eyes widened in horror. "It's worse than..." Her voice trailed off and she glanced around at the sleeping men. "Than all of this?"

Mara fixed her eyes on Jasmine's, willing her to understand. "A hundred times worse," she hissed. "A thousand. Never go there."

Fear and understanding mingled in Jasmine's eyes, and she nodded. Satisfied that she had made her point, Mara continued.

"It is a huge field—maybe many fields, I'm not sure—filled with tall, thick reeds. Jefe and the others go in and hollow out little caves in the reeds, and then spread old blankets on the ground inside them. That's where we—where we lay and wait for the customers. They come and line up to wait their turn, and Jefe and the others set timers—ten minutes, fifteen, I'm not sure—and they come in and do whatever they want to us. When the timer rings, they leave and the next one comes. All day long they do this. Only once every hour we get a drink of water and then we must start all over again. I tried to count how many customers I had one day, but I couldn't count that high." Mara ducked her head. "I never really got to go to school."

Jasmine reached out and laid her hand on Mara's, and the older girl jumped as if she'd been burned. Gasping, she looked up, horrified to see tears in Jasmine's eyes. "I'm so sorry," Jasmine whispered. "I shouldn't have made you talk about it."

Their eyes locked for several seconds. At last Mara said, "It's all right. You needed to know so you would never go there."

Jasmine nodded. "Thank you for telling me. And I will never go there. I promise." She hung her head. "But... what about...?"

Mara frowned. "What about what?"

Jasmine raised her head, and her blue eyes glistened.

"There's something else I've been worried about."

Something else? Only one other thing? Mara marveled that the girl had only one concern when they lived in a world where their very lives could be ended at any moment by the whim of one angry or vengeful man. "What is it?" she asked.

Jasmine swallowed, hesitating before continuing. "Babies," she said at last. "I... I know where babies come from, how they're... created. What if...?"

Mara sighed. This was a common concern among all the girls, at least once they were old enough to conceive. She herself had been forced to deal with the issue more than once.

"It happens," she said, her voice softer than she'd expected it to be. "We try to take precautions so it won't, but... it does. And then we deal with it."

Jasmine frowned. "Deal with it? What does that mean?"

"We have an abortion, of course. What else can we do? The customers don't want pregnant girls. They want us slim and trim, so we have the abortions as soon as we know so our stomachs don't stretch out."

The tears that had glistened in Jasmine's eyes now spilled over onto her cheeks. "You mean... you kill them? The babies?"

Mara shrugged. "We have no choice. Just like we have no choice in anything we do here. Jefe makes the arrangements, Enforcer or Destroyer drives us to the clinic, and we're back in a couple of hours. The only good part is that we get a couple days off work so we can heal."

"Have you...?"

"Sure," Mara answered. "The first time was the hardest. I was only twelve—about your age, right?"

Jasmine nodded, as tears continued to drip down her face. "How many times...?" She stopped and held up her hand before Mara could answer. "Don't tell me," she said. "Please. I don't want to know."

Good, Mara thought. It was better that way.

Rosanna watched her only son, her firstborn, walk away from the kitchen table, having kissed her on the cheek and announced that he was tired and was going to bed. He had to be at school at eight the next day, so she couldn't really argue, but she sensed that his hasty departure was about a lot more than his concern for getting enough sleep.

What was going on with him? Rosanna had always felt so close to her children, had prided herself on the fact that they didn't keep things from her as so many of her friends complained that their kids did. Suddenly she wasn't so sure.

Wearily she rose from the table and spotted the peanut butter jar and bread still sitting on the counter—very out of character for Jonathan. Lazy just wasn't in the boy's vocabulary. If he got something out, he put it back. If he opened something, he closed it. What was going on with him?

She raised her eyebrows as a thought popped into her head. Returning the peanut butter and bread to their rightful spots, she wondered if Jonathan had met someone. Was it possible that he had a girlfriend and hadn't told them? As handsome as he was, he certainly didn't lack for interested young ladies, but he never seemed to get serious about any of them. He might take them out a time or two, but after that...

No. She was nearly certain that Jonathan's odd behavior wasn't about a new love interest. Was it possible that his hesitancy about going to Bible college was resurfacing? They'd had that conversation several times throughout his senior year, and she thought it was settled. Maybe she'd look for a chance to bring it up with him in the next day or two and see how he reacted. Meanwhile, she'd better head up to bed and get some sleep herself. Tomorrow was Michael's day off, and he just might want to spend it doing something special—like taking her to the beach or out to lunch.

She smiled. Maybe, if he didn't already have plans, she could drop a couple of hints and get him moving in the right direction. A day at the beach sounded very tempting at the moment.

Chapter 9

MARA WAS NERVOUS. THOUGH SHE AND JASMINE HAD discontinued their discussion about The Reeds long before Enforcer showed up to escort them back to the compound and their customers hadn't shown any signs of waking or overhearing them while they talked, it almost seemed too good to be true. The exchange with Jasmine a few hours earlier was the closest thing she'd experienced to a personal conversation since she was a little child, still living at home. Even then the extended conversations hadn't been with her parents; amazingly enough they had been with her tio.

Daring to spend a few extra minutes in bed before getting up to tend to breakfast, Mara closed her eyes against the early morning light that tried to penetrate the one tiny window in the room she shared with several others. Though it seemed another lifetime ago, she could still recall the sunny neighborhood in Mexico where she'd lived with her parents and three brothers, all of whom had called her Maria. She'd known from the time she was old enough to understand anything that her parents preferred their sons to her, but it was all she'd ever known so she didn't expect anything else. She was just content to live in the run-down shack they called their *casa*, where she slept on a tiny mat in a corner and rejoiced in the days when there was enough food to eat and she wasn't beaten by one of her parents.

Her visits from her tio were the highlight of her life. How she looked forward to seeing his smiling face appear in the doorway! He was the only one who seemed to seek her out above the others. Though he stopped to tousle his nephews' hair and to greet his brother and sister-in-law, he always made a point to pick her up and carry her outside where they could be alone and talk. He would arrive in his fancy car and tell her of his grand life on the other side of the border, less than two hours away, and how someday he would take her there to see the beautiful ocean and the big homes, and to meet the people who would welcome her with open arms. But the best part of his visits was when he began to teach her to speak English. He even brought her simple books and taught her to read a few words. Oh, how grand that made her feel! Even her parents and brothers couldn't read anything in English—and very little in Spanish, for that matter.

In between the visits, she practiced reading and rereading her books, and dreamed of the day when her tio would finally take her with him to the city of San Diego. She trembled with excitement and a bit of fear as well at the thought of going so far away, but she always reassured herself that she would be with her tio, so she would have nothing to fear.

At last the day had come. The first she realized that something was different about that visit was when she saw her tio handing money to her father. Then she'd been told to kiss her mama and papa *adios* because she was going on a trip with her tio. She was overjoyed and didn't even stop to wonder why she was saying what seemed like final farewells to her family when she would surely be back in a matter of days.

But of course, that hadn't been the case. From the moment she climbed into the front seat of her tio's shiny red car, she had sensed something was different. Her tio no longer smiled at her or kissed the top of her head. Instead, his voice became very gruff and he ordered her to be quiet and to say nothing as they crossed the border. If anyone asked if she were his daughter, she should nod—nothing more. Mara had done as she was told, hoping the tio she knew and loved would resurface once they were on the other side of the border. The memory of what happened next sent a chill snaking up her spine, even as she lay under the covers in her familiar room at the compound.

At first she had been encouraged, for truly it seemed that her familiar, loving tio had returned. He smiled down at her and spoke to her in a gentle voice, stroking her cheek and pulling her hand into his lap, where he held it tightly against his leg. When he turned into a motel parking lot and took her up to a room, she marveled at the television set and clean towels that awaited them.

And then it had changed—everything. After locking the door he ordered her to disrobe. "Everything," he'd said. "Take it all off." Why would he ask her to do such a thing? She couldn't imagine, but she knew it didn't feel right. She shook her head no, and averted her eyes so she wouldn't have to look at him.

When he grabbed her arm and yanked her toward him, picking her up and holding her face only inches from his, her eyes opened wide in alarm. What was her tio doing?

She began to cry. "You're hurting me, Tio," she whimpered, as she felt the tears pooling in her eyes and spilling over onto her cheeks.

"And I will hurt you a lot more than this if you don't obey me," he growled. "The first thing you must learn is that you are no longer to call me Tio. My name is Jefe, and yours is Mara, not Maria. Do you understand?"

When she didn't answer immediately, he shook her and raised his voice. "I said, do you understand?"

Trembling, she whispered, "Sí, Tio. I understand."

Jefe threw her on the bed and slapped her. "It seems you don't understand at all," he said, leaning down until she could feel his hot breath on her face. "What is my name?"

She swallowed, blinking to try to rid herself of the stars that seemed to dance in front of her eyes. Her cheek burned where he'd hit her, and her head pounded. What did he want from her? What had she done to make him so mad? What could she say or do to make him be nice to her again?

Jefe. That was it. He wanted her to call him Jefe, not Tio. She took a deep breath and opened her mouth. "Jefe," she croaked. "Your name is Jefe. And I'm... Mara."

Her vision was clearing enough by then that she could make out the smile that crossed his face. She had answered right! What a relief. Maybe now things would return to the way they'd been before.

But again she was wrong. As he lowered himself onto the bed beside her, she was about to learn how very wrong she had been—about everything. Nothing would ever be the same again, most of all the little girl from Mexico whose name had just become Mara.

Rosanna was thrilled. Not only had she not had to mention or even hint to Michael about taking her to the beach because he had come up with it all on his own, but he had even gone out of the way to take her to her very favorite beach town—San

Juan Capistrano—even though it was much more of a drive than hitting one of the local beaches in San Diego.

They sat under the early afternoon sun now, relaxing after a long walk on the beach, where they'd dipped their toes into the cold water as it foamed up onto the sand and listened to the sounds of the seagulls swooping and diving overhead. Michael had wakened early that morning and encouraged her to do the same, telling her he had a surprise for her. Though she longed to luxuriate under the covers a bit longer, she knew that Jonathan and Leah were already up and getting ready for school, and she really wanted to see them off. So she'd pulled herself from the comfort and warmth of her bed, her curiosity mounting as she wondered just what Michael's surprise might be.

That it was a drive north along the coast to Capistrano hadn't even crossed her mind, but once she realized that's where they were headed, she couldn't have been happier. Strolling barefoot on the damp sand and dodging the waves that rolled up around their ankles had been a delight, and she felt more relaxed than she had been in weeks. The shrimp enchiladas had been the perfect transition from morning to afternoon on what was turning out to be an absolutely delicious day.

"What next?" she asked, watching Michael as he sat across the table, sipping his iced tea and alternating between gazing out at the sun sparkling on the ocean and staring into her eyes. What had she ever done to deserve such a remarkable husband? She knew that not all women—not even those in the church—were as happy and fulfilled in their marriages as she. Some had confided in her about how they felt unloved by their husbands and unappreciated by their children. Rosanna had listened attentively and prayed faithfully, but all along she'd thought about how blessed she was. Michael loved her passionately and unconditionally. What more could a wife want from her husband?

He turned his face from watching the waves and grinned at her. "So, a walk on the beach and lunch in the sun isn't enough for you, eh?" He shook his head. "Boy, there's just no pleasing you, is there?"

She returned his smile and reached her hand across the table to lay it on top of his. "I couldn't be happier or more content," she said. "I just don't want it to end—not yet."

He nodded. "Neither do I. Have any suggestions?"

Did she have any suggestions? She nearly bit her tongue to keep from blurting out the first though that popped into her mind. San Juan Capistrano was not only famous for its historic mission—which they'd toured countless times—but its antique shops were some of the best anywhere. Rosanna could spend hours browsing just one of the town's charming stores, but she knew Michael would probably prefer getting a root canal—sans anesthetic!

He squeezed her hand, his eyes sparkling. "Don't tell me. I already know." He held up his hand to stop her protest. "Really, I thought about it before we even got in the car this morning. A perfect day for you would be a walk on the beach, lunch outside, and then an afternoon looking at old stuff in dark, musty shops. I may not understand or appreciate your passion for that sort of thing, but I'm with you all the way. An afternoon of antiquing, and then a nice ride down the coast as the sun sets. The kids will be fine. I already told them what I was planning, so they're covered for dinner. We'll find a nice spot to eat on the way home and extend our day as long as we can. What do you say?"

Rosanna could scarcely say anything. "I'm overwhelmed," she managed at last. "Have I told you lately that you're the best husband in the entire world?"

Michael frowned and tilted his eyes heavenward, as if trying to remember something. "I think maybe you did," he said, "but I wouldn't mind hearing it again."

She laughed. "Then listen up," she said. "You, Michael Flannery, are the very best husband in the entire world—bar none! And don't you forget it. In fact, I'll make a habit of telling you more often so you can't."

He smiled and lifted her hand to his lips. "Sounds like a great plan to me, Mrs. Flannery. Now let's see if we can get someone to bring us our bill so we can get started on this shopping. I can see an entire row of antique shops from here, just waiting for you to invade them."

Rosanna laughed again. "For us, you mean. They're waiting for *us*!"

He rolled his eyes and sighed. "For us, yes. That's what I meant, of course. I can hardly wait."

The evening fog hung like a gray blanket on the horizon, framing the darkening ocean and hiding the setting sun. But Michael didn't mind. He'd had a great day with Rosanna, even if his feet were killing him after several hours of shifting from one to the other while his wife compared Betty Boop memorabilia to that of *I Love Lucy*. She ended up buying neither, as she said they just wouldn't go with anything they had at home. Michael wanted to ask her why she spent so much time considering them if she already knew that, but he decided against it. It had been a nearly perfect day; why ruin it?

He glanced at her before refocusing on the road ahead, three lanes on either side of the dividing line, filled with cars zipping along in opposite directions as if someone were giving away six-foot candy bars at the end of the highway.

Rosanna's eyes were closed, but Michael knew she wasn't sleeping. She never slept in the car. He teased her that it was because she didn't trust him and wanted to be alert to his driving—just in case. She countered that if that were the case, she'd rather die in her sleep than see the accident coming.

He smiled. Antiquing aside, she was the best life partner anyone could ever hope to find. What she saw in him he would never know, but he was glad she did. Oh, they'd had their ups and downs through the years like any other couple, but for the most part, their nearly twenty-year marriage had been the closest thing to heaven on earth that he could imagine.

What he really liked was that they seemed to think alike. How many times had he been thinking about something, only to find out that Rosanna's mind was running along the same track? He couldn't help but wonder if that was the case now, ever since they'd watched that documentary on TV the day before. The images, the faces, had haunted him so much more than the statistics, though they too had been horrifying. He'd been aware for some years now that such a thing as modern-day slavery still existed in some parts of the world, but that it was actually worldwide—even here, in his own country—and in such appalling numbers, was almost more than he could process.

And somehow he knew they hadn't seen that program just to be shocked by the staggering statistics or the emotional appeal of the haunted eyes of the victims of human trafficking. He sensed that God was calling him to get involved somehow, but where did he start? Quite obviously right where he was—with his wife at his side. If God truly was tapping him on the shoulder and telling him to make this issue personal, then He was undoubtedly tapping Rosanna on the shoulder as well. As soon as he found a good place to pull off the road so they could get some dinner, Michael determined to broach the subject and see what sort of reaction he got.

It's in Your hands, Lord, he prayed silently. *If this is something You want us involved in, please give me the right words to speak to her, and give Rosanna a willing heart so we can go into this together. And then show us where to start because I don't have a clue. Thank You, Father.*

Chapter 10

LEAH WAS SURPRISED TO SEE JONATHAN'S BEDRAGGLED Beetle in the driveway when she arrived. She glanced at her watch as she headed for her room to drop her books on her bed.

Almost four. Why wasn't he at work? He usually went there straight from school.

She knocked on his door.

"Enter at your own risk," he called.

She pushed the door open, laughing. "Yeah, like your room would ever be messy," she teased as she entered.

He looked up from his chair in front of his desk and grinned. "I might just surprise you one of these days and throw some stuff around in here."

Leah's laughter went into overdrive. "Oh, please, you wouldn't last five minutes before you'd be disinfecting the place."

He shrugged. "Nothing wrong with being neat."

"True," she conceded, plopping down on his bed. "So why aren't you at work? Get fired or something?"

"Not even close. They love me over there. Some people say I'm the best pizza delivery guy who ever lived."

She rolled her eyes. "Whatever. So why aren't you working?"

His tone was a cross between teasing and sarcastic. "I do get an occasional day off, you know. Especially since I worked till closing last night."

"Oh, yeah, I forgot about that. So what are you doing then?"

He glanced at the pile of books on the desk and then back at Leah. "Care to guess?"

"Homework." She sighed. "I need to go get that done myself, especially since I'm babysitting later."

"For the Johnsons?"

She nodded. "Yep. They're my best customers. And I love Anna."

"You love kids, period. But at least you get paid for this—not like the free babysitting you do every Sunday at church."

Leah bristled. "That's not just babysitting! We're teaching them something."

Jonathan laughed. "Yeah. How not to eat dirt or sit on their little sister's head."

"Very funny."

Jonathan's smile softened. "Hey, you know I'm just kidding, right?"

"I guess."

"So when are you going over to the Johnsons? Do you need a ride since Mom and Dad aren't back from Capistrano yet?"

"Actually, the Johnsons are coming over here any minute now. They have some sort of meeting to go to, so they're just going to drop Anna off for a little while."

"Cool. Well, just remember, I'm doing homework so don't expect me to help."

"I can handle Anna by myself."

"Who couldn't? She seems like a really quiet kid."

"She's adorable. Smart too. She's learned a lot since she came to live with the Johnsons."

Jonathan tilted his head. "Did they ever tell you why they decided to adopt a kid from another country?"

"Actually, yes, they did. They picked a child from Thailand because they wanted to rescue a potential human trafficking victim. That goes on a lot there, you know."

At the mention of human trafficking, Jonathan's head jerked upward and his jaw twitched. "From what I hear it goes on all over," he said.

Leah nodded. It was obvious she'd hit a nerve. "Still thinking about those girls you ran into at that motel the other night?"

Jonathan's gaze dropped for an instant. When he looked back up, she was certain she saw a hint of tears glistening in his eyes. "I try not to," he admitted, his voice low, "but I can't. I even drove by the motel again last night. I have no idea why, but... I just did. I even stopped the car and prayed."

Leah's eyes opened wide. It had been a long time since she'd heard Jonathan talk about prayer. She smiled. "Maybe that's why God let you see them in the first place... so you'd pray."

"Maybe," he said. "But I can't help thinking I should be doing more."

Leah nodded. She imagined he was right, but what could he do? What could anyone do? The problem was overwhelming.

Before either of them could say another word, the doorbell rang. The Johnsons had arrived, and the question of what to do about the girls at the motel would have to wait until another time.

Rosanna couldn't sleep. The day had been so amazingly full, leaving her with far too much information to process and ideas to formulate. She smiled. The new memories to add to her favorite files didn't hurt either. What a fantastic husband she had! First he surprised her with a trip to San Juan Capistrano, including several hours of browsing antique shops—though she ended up buying nothing—and then he treated her to a delicious seafood dinner while they watched the sun set on the Pacific. Could it get any better than that?

Actually, it had. Not only did they share a delicious meal at the end of a nearly perfect day, but the man who knew her better than she sometimes knew herself had brought up the exact issue that had been dancing around the edges of her thoughts.

Human trafficking, she thought, listening to her husband's peaceful breathing and the sounds of a modest but comfortable home settling in for the night. *Here I am, living a life that is so completely blessed, and people all over the world—*She interrupted her own thoughts with a shudder. *Not just adults, but children, are being bought and sold for profit. How is that possible? So many used for cheap or free labor, while others become sex slaves.* Tears stung her eyes. *Millions, all over the world, even right here in our own San Diego neighborhoods. Oh, Father!*

She brushed away a tear as the memory of little Anna swam before her eyes. The Johnsons were in the process of retrieving Anna from Leah's care when Rosanna and Michael had returned home, and the little girl's large eyes and shy smile had captivated Rosanna as they often did. She remembered the Johnsons explaining to their adult Sunday school class a couple of years earlier why they were going to try to adopt a child from Thailand, but somehow the reality of it hadn't impacted her until she watched the TV special on Sunday. Apparently the program had affected Michael in much the same way, because he now felt that they should seriously consider getting involved in some sort of ministry to trafficking victims.

She closed her eyes and remembered the corner table by the window where the two of them had enjoyed their dinner. When he'd brought up the topic of the TV special, it was as if God Himself were confirming what she was already feeling. Her acceptance of Michael's premise—that they would pray about a way to get involved in this outreach together—resonated with her immediately. It had been the perfect ending to their day.

The only difference between her reaction to this new calling from God and Michael's was that she couldn't stop thinking about it, while her husband seemed to have had no problem at all turning off his thoughts and going straight to sleep. But they'd always been pretty much that way, even from the beginning of their marriage, so there was no reason it should surprise her now.

She leaned over and kissed his bare shoulder. When he didn't move she got out of bed and decided to go to the kitchen for a cup of tea.

Jonathan had wandered downstairs for a snack and then into the family room, where he sat in the dark, munching on chips and sipping on a soda. He sure would like to be able to put this thing about the girls and the motel into perspective. He was past the point of just wishing it away because, quite obviously, it wasn't going anywhere. But the helplessness of knowing he should do something but not having a clue what that something might be was beginning to wear on him.

A noise from the stairway caught his attention, and he turned his eyes toward the dim light that shone in the entryway. He could see that small area surrounding the foot of the stairs that led to the front door straight ahead, to the kitchen on the right, or to the family room, where he sat, on the left.

When his mom's robe came into view, he was glad he had opted not to turn on the light when he wandered in and sat down to have his snack and think. He just wasn't in the mood to chat, and he was certain she'd head straight for the kitchen, which she did. If he sat quietly and waited, no doubt she'd find what she was looking for and, sooner or later, climb the stairs and go back to bed.

He stopped crunching chips. *Ridiculous*, he told himself. *Mom can't hear you from the kitchen*. But there was no sense taking chances.

After a few moments of listening to cupboards opening and closing and water running, Jonathan heard the teakettle whistle briefly before being turned off. Good. That meant she'd settle onto a stool or in a chair at the table and sip her tea for a while, giving him time to slip out of the family room and up the stairs unnoticed. She'd never even know he hadn't been in his room.

Slowly he made his way toward the bottom of the stairway, carrying his half-finished soda and nearly empty chip bag with him. He hadn't climbed more than half a dozen stairs when he heard her voice behind him.

"Jonathan? What are you doing up? I didn't see you when I came down."

He turned sheepishly, not sure why he felt guilty but feeling it nonetheless. He smiled. "I was in the family room—having a snack."

She raised her eyebrows. "In the dark?"

He felt his face flush, and he shrugged. "Just didn't feel like turning on the lights."

She studied him with the look he remembered so well from when he was young, the look that said, "I know you're up to something, and you're not getting out of here until you tell me about it."

He sighed. It was hopeless. She was going to get it out of him sooner or later, so it may as well be sooner or neither one of them would get any sleep that night.

Chapter 11

THE MAN WHO HAD CLAIMED TO BE THEIR FATHER WHEN Jasmine tried to escape and nearly ran into the pizza guy had requested them again. This time, however, he specified a different location, and Jefe wanted to know why.

"What happened that night that made the customer not want to return to that motel?" he growled, glaring at Enforcer.

The younger man, who stood at least six inches taller than Jefe and was more muscular, seemed to shrink at the implied accusation. "I don't know, Jefe," he mumbled. "He didn't say anything when I picked up the girls, and he seemed happy." He shrugged his broad shoulders. "He must have been if he asked for them again."

Jefe stepped closer to the man who had sworn his allegiance to him. "He asked for the same girls but a different motel. Doesn't that tell you something?"

Enforcer frowned. "He didn't like the place?"

Jefe took a deep breath and forced himself to keep his voice calm, though he wanted to grab the ignorant fool's throat and squeeze until his eyes popped.

"Do you really think our customers take time to notice what the rooms look like or what channels they can get on TV?" He shook his head. "No, they do not. If he requested a different motel, then something happened at that one that made him not want to return. Maybe it was something personal—somebody he knew who worked there or something. But I doubt it. He would have said something before you left the girls there—asked to go somewhere else maybe. No. I think something happened after you left the girls with him, and I want you to find out what it was—preferably not from him. Ask the girls. Mara knows enough not to keep things from me, but I still don't trust her. She's my own flesh and blood and should be loyal to me, but even after all I've done for her, I don't think she is—not really. She'd turn on me if she had a chance."

He turned away and banished the thought from his mind of what he would do to Mara if she ever tried such a thing. Now was not the time. "Talk to the young one—Jasmine, is it? She's been here just long enough to understand who's in charge but maybe not long enough to give up any ideas of outsmarting us." He turned back to Enforcer and allowed his eyes to emphasize his words. "Get her to tell you what happened—but not until after she and Mara take care of the customer tonight. He's not going to want her if she's too beat up." He glanced at his watch. "It's midnight. Don't say anything when you pick them up tonight. I've got them set up to meet their repeat customer late tomorrow afternoon. After they do whatever he requires to keep him a satisfied customer, take Jasmine aside and get the truth out of her. If she doesn't tell you, I'll get it out of Mara myself—but you'll pay the price right along with her. Understand?"

Enforcer's dark eyes widened, and he nodded. "I understand, Jefe. Completely."

Jefe nodded. "Good. Now get back to work. We have a business to run here."

Mara could hardly believe her good luck. She'd been personally requested by a lonely middle-aged man who only wanted to talk with her and hold her hand. Occasionally he caressed her cheek or hair, but said he just wanted her to keep him company. She could get used to assignments like this!

Now Enforcer had picked her up, along with a couple of the other girls who had been in other rooms with different customers, and he was taking them all back to the compound. It was one of the easiest evenings she'd had since—since she couldn't remember when. She could probably count on one hand the number of times she'd been with customers who treated her without at least some roughness, and when one touched her with gentleness and something bordering on respect or even awe, as tonight's date had done, it was a night worth remembering.

From the looks of the other girls in the van, she doubted any of them had experienced such an easy few hours. Jasmine looked especially exhausted, and the red mark on her cheek told Mara the girl had been slapped at least once. For disobeying or refusing to perform a requested act? Possibly. It could also be because her companion for the evening just enjoyed inflicting pain. It went with the territory.

As they rode through the night, Mara wondered at the sights outside the darkened windows of the van. But even if they managed to peer through the dark tint and make out lights or shapes, they'd been warned not to even try looking outside, so of course they didn't.

Mara found herself nodding off just as the van drew to a stop. The back doors opened only from the outside, so the girls waited to be let out. Mara let the others go ahead of her, and when she stepped onto the familiar ground of the compound, Enforcer grabbed her arm and pulled her ear next to his lips. "You and Jasmine have been requested for tomorrow night—the man from Saturday night. You must have made a good impression."

Mara suppressed a shudder at the memory of the motel and the handsome pizza man with the wide brown eyes that spoke of shock—and yet kindness as well. It was the kindness that alarmed her and that she struggled to forget. She reminded herself to be grateful that Jasmine's attempted escape had never come to Jefe's attention.

She nodded her answer to Enforcer and hurried away the moment he released her. She wasn't crazy about seeing the guy from Saturday night again, as he'd been rough and even mean to both her and Jasmine. But then, that was more the norm than the gentle treatment she'd received from the guy tonight. Besides, Mara had endured a lot worse, as had all the slaves in the compound—mostly from the hands of her own tio. She'd deal with tomorrow when it got here. For now, she just wanted to get some sleep.

The storms had finally stopped raging, and the morning had dawned clear and slightly less humid than usual. But the chaos of living in close proximity with so many other people in such a small corner of the world didn't allow for quiet or peaceful sunrises.

Nor did Chanthra's living conditions. She'd worked most of the late afternoon and night, taking care of nearly a dozen customers before falling into an exhausted sleep. She was nowhere ready to begin another day when the loud commotion invaded her room and jarred her awake.

The crying sounds that flowed like an undercurrent to the familiar growls and yells of Chanthra's owner sounded more like the mewing of an injured kitten than the protests of a frightened human being. Though Chanthra knew better than to interfere, she peeked through half-opened eyes at the arrival of the one who would no doubt be her new companion and co-worker, though the poor girl had undoubtedly not accepted that yet.

Chanthra's boss threw the child, who looked to be no more than eight or nine years old and was already thin as a rail, onto a dirty mattress in the far corner. It had been vacated a couple of months earlier when its owner died of some sort of untreated venereal disease. Chanthra had wondered when her deceased roommate would be replaced, since few of the girls had the luxury of a room to herself.

The child who now lay shivering on the mattress looked too terrified to fight or run or even scream. She simply lay there, wide-eyed, staring at the man who tied her hands and feet together and then looped the rope around her wrists to the one securing her ankles so she was trussed in a fetal position on her side, her face turned directly toward Chanthra. Through it all the little girl continued to whimper and cry until the man was satisfied that the ropes would hold and she couldn't run away. Then he slapped her face and yelled at her to shut up, causing the decibel level of her crying to rise slightly. With that he stormed from the room, looking back only long enough to leave orders with Chanthra. "Take care of her. Shut her up and teach her what she needs to know to stay alive here. We can't afford to lose any more of you. We have customers to take care of."

He slammed the door and left them, and Chanthra knew it was up to her to obey her boss man's orders and to deal with her new charge. She told herself it wasn't that she cared, but if she didn't do as she had been instructed, they would both suffer.

Chanthra crept to the girl's bed and sat down beside the mattress where the new arrival lay, staring up at her and sobbing. "I want my mama," she gulped. "I want to go home."

"We all want to go home," Chanthra answered, keeping her voice level so the compassion that threatened to show itself would not win out. "But this is our home now. It is the only home you will ever have again. You must think of your mama as dead, whether she is or not. No more mama. Understand?"

The child looked on the verge of crying even harder, and Chanthra placed her hand over the girl's mouth. "Don't," she said. "Don't cry or scream or make any noise. The boss man means what he says. He will punish you—and me too—if you don't obey him. He will kill you if necessary. But first he will hurt you very, very bad. Worse than you can imagine. So much that you will beg him to kill you." She leaned down, her face only inches from the girl's. "Now do you understand?"

The child's eyes widened. After a moment she nodded, struggling visibly to control her crying.

Good. Better a terrified but quiet child than the punishment that would be meted out to them if she didn't obey. Now, to explain what would be required of her in order to survive...

Chapter 12

JONATHAN WAS RELIEVED, BUT IT WAS MORE THAN THAT. Encouraged? Possibly. Yet still more. He couldn't quite identify the feeling, but there was little doubt in his mind that it had to do with the flickering flame of his faith, which slowly but surely seemed to be gaining strength.

Was it because of his talk with his mom? Certainly that had a lot to do with it. What a relief to realize that not only did she not think he was crazy for what he believed was going on with that motel situation, but she was actually quite supportive of his need to do something about it.

"Not directly, of course," she'd cautioned. "You can't just go barging into some motel, looking for a couple of under-aged prostitutes. Even if they returned to the same place, you'd probably just end up getting yourself *and* them hurt—or worse. And where else would you look for them? In a city the size of San Diego, with all its suburbs that nearly blend together, you'd never find them." She'd leaned close to him then, as they sat side by side on the couch in the family room that was by then well lit. "And you're not meant to find them, Jonathan. God just allowed you to see them to open your eyes to the problem. Now you pray for them, and you find a way to get involved in one of the many outreaches already established to help rescue and rehabilitate these poor victims of human trafficking—which is exactly what your father and I decided today that we wanted to do."

She had laid her hand on his arm and waited until he raised his eyes to hers. "Do you understand what I'm saying, Jonathan? God orchestrated all this so that we could get involved as a family, together, in this worldwide rescue effort to free the slaves. And don't kid yourself, son. That's exactly what they are. As Christians, we need to lead the charge to free them."

He'd nodded his head, knowing she was right about everything she said—that he couldn't find and rescue the two girls he'd seen but he could pray for them and find some way to help rescue others, most likely indirectly through already established ministries and outreaches. Most of all he'd known she was right about God's involvement in the way things had come together to bring the entire family to a realization of the scope of this problem and the need for people to help. And yet...

His mom had long since gone to bed, and he lay silently in his own, trying in vain to fall asleep. He'd be worthless at school the next day, but his mind was racing with possibilities and challenges. He knew with every ounce of good sense in him that he needed to limit his involvement with the two girls from the motel to praying for them. That, quite obviously, required a more committed effort on his part to communicate regularly with God. But he still couldn't shake the feeling that at some point he would see those girls again. And then...

"No." The sound of his voice surprised him. He hadn't meant to speak out loud, but he had to convince himself to let this go. High school graduation was right around the corner, and he had one last summer to enjoy himself playing baseball with his friends and heading to the beach in between his shifts delivering pizza. Then it was off to Bible college, where he'd be so busy he'd be doing good to remember to pray for the girls even occasionally. What happened to them was out of his hands—and that's as it should be. Wasn't it?

He groaned and rolled over, glancing at the clock as he did so. It was nearly three. He had school tomorrow and then a four-hour shift at work. It was definitely going to be a major caffeine-induced kind of day.

The newcomer had finally cried herself to sleep, though at least she'd done so silently. Chanthra was relieved. She had learned not to grow attached to anyone, and she certainly didn't plan to make an exception for the girl that she had discovered was called Lawan.

Beautiful, Chanthra thought, glancing down at the sleeping child. *I'm sure her parents thought she was so when she was born, but if they saw her now they would be forced to rename her.*

She sighed and turned away. What did it matter what the girl's parents would think? They would never see her again; it was just that simple. The child's life was no more. Lawan would become a woman before the night was over. That the boss man had allowed her to sleep as long as he had only proved that he wanted her rested for her first customers, who would probably arrive shortly, as the stringy shadows of early evening were beginning to invade the room's sole window. Chanthra had already bathed and dressed for work; the little one would surely be next.

Commotion in the street below and voices as the outside door was opened told Chanthra the first customers of the night were beginning to arrive. The girls in the home's "day" rooms were nearly finished with their shift, and the boss man would begin to direct his clientele to Chanthra and the other handful of slaves who worked the night shift. That could mean only one thing.

Exactly as she'd imagined, the door to the room burst open and the brothel's owner stormed in, followed by a stocky middle-aged woman named Adung who often helped with new arrivals. Together they snatched young Lawan from her sleep, precipitating howls of fear that were silenced when the woman clamped her hand over the child's mouth and threatened her with a beating. She untied the terrified girl and then watched as the boss threw her over his shoulder and hauled her out of the room. The last thing Chanthra saw before the door shut behind the three of them was Lawan's huge round eyes, as she lifted her head and pleaded silently for help. The kindest thing Chanthra could do was let the girl learn quickly that help would never come. All they could hope for was survival—and that, she knew only too well, came at a terrible price.

Leah poured milk on her cereal and then watched Jonathan take the carton and do the same. They sat across from one another at the table in the kitchen, hoping to gulp down some breakfast before heading off to another day at school. With only two years of high school left, Leah looked forward to being away from it for a couple of months during the summer, though she'd stay plenty busy with babysitting. She could only imagine how Jonathan anticipated it, knowing it was his last summer before starting college. It must be like leaving your childhood behind, she imagined—exciting but a bit unnerving, to say the least.

"Just a few more days until graduation," she commented, watching her brother as they each scooped a spoonful of cereal into their mouths. His only answer was a grunt and an almost indiscernible nod.

She changed her tactic. "So what's on the agenda for grad night? You and the guys going to do anything?"

He raised his head and his eyebrows simultaneously and spoke around his half-chewed breakfast. "Seriously? I'm going to Bible college in the fall, remember?" He swallowed and leaned forward. "And by the way, have you met our parents?"

Leah grinned. "I wasn't asking if you were going to a bar or a strip club or something. I just thought you might be planning something special."

He shook his head and snagged another spoonful of cereal. "Nah. Mom and Dad asked me what I wanted to do, and I told them a family dinner out somewhere was fine. I'm working the next day anyway."

"You don't mess around, do you, brother?" Leah shrugged. "Suit yourself. I just thought you'd want to take a trip to Catalina or at least Disneyland or something."

Jonathan was chewing again. "Gotta save my money," he said. "College is expensive, you know. And that heap I call a car needs some major attention."

Leah smiled. "You're way too serious sometimes. You know that, right?"

"Maybe."

"No maybe about it. I mean, it's not like you have to do something illegal or immoral or anything. You can still have fun, you know."

He didn't answer.

She chewed a bite of her own cereal while she watched him do the same. "Still thinking about those girls at the motel?" she asked, not surprised when his eyes widened.

"Not really," he said. "Well, yeah. Sometimes. But I'm feeling a little better about it since Mom and I talked last night."

This time it was Leah's turn to be surprised. "You and Mom talked last night? I thought you both went to bed early, like I did."

"We did," Jonathan said. "But neither one of us could sleep, so we ended up downstairs looking for a snack. Somehow we got talking about human trafficking, and Mom said that she and Dad are thinking about getting involved in a ministry or outreach to help the victims." He paused a moment, dropped his spoon into the now-empty bowl, and stood to his feet. No matter how many times he did that, Leah marveled at how tall her brother was—especially when she was still sitting.

"I'm thinking about doing the same thing. Not sure how, but... I really want to do something."

He walked to the sink and rinsed out his bowl before leaving it there.

Leah spoke softly, but she could tell by the way he tensed his shoulders that he heard her. "That encounter with those girls at the motel really affected you, didn't it?" she asked.

Jonathan turned back to face her. "More than I ever thought it would. I guess I can't really help those girls directly, but maybe I can help some other way. Mom and Dad are going to check into some ministries to trafficking victims and let me know what they find out." Leah hesitated. "Good," she said after a moment. "When they do, fill me in. I want to help too."

Her brother's jaws twitched and he nodded before exiting the room and leaving her to wonder what sort of help they might offer to people in such horrible circumstances.

Chapter 13

TUESDAY HAD BEEN AN ESPECIALLY NICE DAY, WITH nearly perfect weather and not too much for Mara to do but rest up for the night's work that still lay ahead. It was obvious that Jasmine was aware of what they faced, as she'd seemed nervous and distracted all day. And no wonder. Jasmine had taken the worst of the man's treatment the last time the three of them were together. Mara wondered if it was simply because he was mad at the younger girl for trying to escape or whether he was one of those men who took pleasure in making others suffer. If he was like most men with that behavior, he would mete it out most harshly to the weakest among them—in this case, Jasmine.

Mara steeled herself against the compassion she felt for the girl. The last time she'd tried to run interference for someone she'd ended up being locked in the hole, and the little girl she'd tried to defend had died anyway. No. It did no good to sacrifice herself for someone else. Better to let others fend for themselves, as she'd done now for nearly all her life.

A light breeze rustled her hair as she lay dozing in the lawn chair, trying to keep her mind off the approaching hour when Enforcer or Destroyer would drive her and Jasmine to the motel. The fact that the man had requested that she and Jasmine dress like little girls did nothing to bolster her confidence. The humiliation that was sure to come was something she'd learn to expect and accept, but if they got away tonight without any serious pain or suffering, it would be a miracle.

She'd almost slipped away into a deep sleep when the vision of the handsome stranger delivering pizzas popped into her mind. She shook her head and sat up, trying to dismiss the memory. The thought that he might actually have some kindness in him was almost more frightening to her than what she imagined she faced in the night hours that were quickly drawing near.

Jasmine's anxiety seemed to increase as the night approached. By the time they were in the van heading for their rendezvous, she was noticeably trembling.

"Are you all right?" Mara whispered, as she hunched down in the back, next to the younger girl, hoping Enforcer wouldn't hear her over the sound of the engine.

Jasmine raised her bowed head, and even in the semi-darkness Mara could tell there were tears in the girl's eyes. "No," she whispered in response. "I'm not. But I don't have a choice, do I?"

Mara shook her head. Choices had long since ceased to exist in their lives. Jefe made their choices for them—and they obeyed. That's the way their life was. Trying to change that was far too dangerous. Mara had paid the price more than once, and she wasn't willing even to consider it again.

"We'll be OK," she whispered, hoping she was right and wondering why she bothered to try and reassure her companion. It wasn't her job, after all. As a matter of fact, Jasmine's disobedience the last time they met with this man nearly cost them both some serious punishment. If Jefe ever found out—

No. She wasn't going to let herself even think of what could happen. The best way to survive in their situation was to focus on getting through one day at a time. What might happen tomorrow was too overwhelming even to consider.

The van drew to a stop, and Mara watched Jasmine's eyes widen and the tears spill over onto her cheeks. She put her finger to her lips in a wordless warning, and then turned to wait for Enforcer to open the door.

When he did, she stepped out and glanced up at what she thought would be the familiar hotel from a couple of days earlier. Instead an entirely different building stood before her—a dirtier, seedier place. Why would Enforcer bring them here, rather than the other place? Hadn't she overheard Jefe saying that he had made a special deal with the owners of the other hotel and that he planned to use it more often? Why, then—?

Enforcer grabbed her arm and shoved her ahead, nearly knocking her to the ground. "Quit gawking!" he ordered. "Just get moving—up the stairs and to the right. Room 212. Your friend is waiting for you." He turned and leered at Jasmine. "Both of you."

The younger girl seemed to shrink under his gaze, but he pushed her forward along with Mara, and together the girls climbed the stairs to face the predator who had requested their company.

Jonathan was never so glad to finish a shift. The four hours had dragged, and then his boss had asked him to stay over for a couple more. He could barely keep his eyes open, but he had made it and was now heading home. Twice during his delivery times he had passed within a couple blocks of where he'd seen the girls, and twice he'd had to resist the pull to go back there and—and what? Always he came back to that question. What would he do once he got there, especially if by some weird coincidence the girls were there? Because he had no answer for that question and because he really needed to complete his deliveries on time, he had kept right on going.

But now he was off and heading home at last. His bed called to him, but not as strongly as the motel. With little resistance he yielded to the call and soon found himself parked where, if he lifted his head, he could see the very spot where the fleeing girl had nearly knocked him down.

The memory tore at his heart. The girl had been younger than Leah, and if he knew someone were abusing his sister in some way, forcing her to participate in prostitution just to stay alive—and he was thoroughly convinced that was what was going on with the trio he had seen here on Sunday—he would be hard-pressed not to want to kill them himself. That the two girls who'd stood on that second-story walkway hadn't been his sisters didn't change the fact that they were certainly someone's daughters. But whose? Who allowed their little girls to be caught up in such horror? Did the parents even know where their babies were? Worse yet, had they played a part in their ending up in such a place?

When he allowed his thoughts to run wild, it nearly overwhelmed him. He forced himself to stop thinking such things and to concentrate on prayer. He'd heard a lot of sermons on the importance of communing with God, but none had impacted him and convinced him to begin doing so like seeing those two girls with a man who claimed to be their father.

"He's not their father," Jonathan nearly spit out with contempt. "He's some sleazy pervert who uses girls like toys and then throws them away. But You're their real Father, God. Help them, please! Somehow, get them out of that horrible situation—and show me what You want me to do to help. There must be so many like them. So many..."

Glad no one could see him, he wiped away a tear and tapped his gas pedal before gunning it and heading down the street. He had to get away. He'd seen enough, and he'd prayed. For now, it was all he could do.

Chapter 14

When Chanthra finally forced her eyes open the next day, something seemed off. She listened. Nothing unusual. Just the midmorning street sounds outside in contrast to the silence of her room.

Her eyes snapped open all the way. Of course. The new girl. Lawan!

Chanthra turned toward the girl's mattress where just last night she had experienced her first night of work in a brothel. Her muffled screams and sobs had continued throughout most of the night but had finally deteriorated into barely audible whimpers. Was she asleep at last? Is that why she made no noise?

The girl lay on her back, naked and motionless, her face straight forward toward the ceiling. Chanthra crawled across the few feet that separated their beds and was stunned to see the girl's eyes open. Was she dead? The thought forced the oxygen from Chanthra's lungs, as she slowly reached her hand to the girl's mouth. Air! She was breathing. Relieved, Chanthra felt her body relax, even as she wondered why it mattered to her that the child was still alive.

"Lawan," she whispered. "Lawan, look at me."

The girl didn't move. Even her eyes didn't blink.

Chanthra touched the girl's shoulder and shook her gently. Her skin was like ice. Chanthra reached for the dirty blanket at the foot of Lawan's bed and pulled it over her. Then she shook her again, harder this time.

"Listen to me, Lawan," she ordered, keeping her voice down so as not to be heard outside their room. "You must listen!"

Slowly, agonizingly so, the little girl whose name meant beautiful turned her head ever so slightly toward Chanthra. The bruises on her face tore at Chanthra's heart, but she couldn't let it weaken her resolve. After all, she'd had such bruises herself, and worse—many times. The child would have to learn to live with such treatment, as they all did. Hadn't she herself been even younger than Lawan when she spent her first night working in a brothel? And she had survived, hadn't she? Lawan would too—if she paid attention.

"Last night was terrible," Chanthra said. "I know. I have been here for many years. And I can tell you that it will not get better. I know what you're thinking, but no one will come to rescue you. Your family is dead to you now. We—this—is your family." She swept her arm around in a circle, indicating the room, the brothel, and all that went with it. "This is all we have, and we must work together to stay alive. We each do our job, understand?"

She waited, but when the girl didn't respond she continued anyway. "Now you know what your job is. It's anything the boss man wants you to do. If you don't do it, you will be punished—and so will I. So do what you're told. It doesn't matter how awful it is or how much it hurts. Just do it. If you don't, the pain will be much, much worse."

This time as she waited, she knew the girl heard her, because her puffy, swollen eyes widened at the thought of a pain worse than she'd already experienced. At last she nodded, and Chanthra sighed with relief. Perhaps little Lawan would make it after all—at least for now. None of them lived to a ripe old age, but if they could just hold on for a while, it was the best they could hope for.

It had been a long night; in a couple of hours the dawn would begin to dispel the darkness, though Mara was certain there wasn't enough light anywhere to rid her of the darkness that seemed to smother her much of the time.

She watched Jasmine, sleeping from exhaustion in the corner of the room, where she had crawled after the man who had once portrayed himself to the handsome stranger as being their father had finished with her. Naked and thin, the girl lay curled in a fetal position, trying to cover herself with a towel from the bathroom even as the early signs of bruises and welts were already beginning to show in the muted light of the room.

Mara turned away. She would have markings of her own as a result of the last few hours, but nothing as severe as Jasmine's. For whatever reason, this particular customer had chosen to vent most of his perverted anger on the young blonde. Mara hated him for that, though she couldn't imagine why she hated him worse than any of the others who had abused her and her fellow captives all these years.

I don't hate him as much as I hate Jefe, she thought, squeezing her eyes shut in an effort to block out the memory of that first time in the motel when her very own tio had stolen her innocence so many years earlier. She had trusted him, believed in him, hoped in him when he taught her to read and promised her a better life. And he had betrayed her beyond anything she could ever forgive or understand. If she had her way, she would kill him—slowly and painfully—and not shed one tear of remorse. It was men like her tio who enabled others like the one who now snored on the room's only bed to fulfill his lusts by torturing others.

The noise of a key in the door interrupted her thoughts, and she realized Enforcer had returned for her and Jasmine. She was relieved to think they would be gone from the room before their customer awoke and decided to hurt them again. As awful as it was at the compound, at least she and Jasmine would get some food and a few hours sleep before they had to entertain anyone else.

Something was wrong. Mara knew it the moment Enforcer snatched Jasmine from her sleep and threw her clothes at her, demanding that she get dressed and get in the van immediately. He urged Mara to do the same, but with less urgency. Now they were almost back at the compound, and she could sense the tension in the vehicle was growing, even as Jasmine's fear seemed to escalate as well. What was going on?

Enforcer jerked the steering wheel and turned into the alley behind the compound, and then slammed on the brake, nearly throwing the girls into the seat in front of them. What was he so mad about? It wasn't as if Jefe or any of his sidekicks were ever nice to them, but they seldom showed so much anger unless something was very wrong. Mara's skin crawled to think what that something might be.

"Get out," he growled, throwing the door open and yanking on Jasmine's arm, nearly tumbling her to the ground. Mara hurried out as quickly as possible right behind her. Any hope she'd had that she might just be imagining something was wrong vanished in the wake of Enforcer's exaggerated stomp to the locked gate of the compound. It was obvious to her now that he wanted them to realize he was angry and that one or both of them was in trouble. Why?

What had happened? What had they done... or not done? She ran through the recent events of the past few days and could think of nothing except—

She nearly froze as she stepped through the gate. Of course. It had to do with the man they'd just been with—the one who had requested them again after the episode with the pizza delivery guy. Somehow Jefe and the others had found out. Had the man told them? Is that why he met them at a different location? Had he complained about their behavior? If so, why would he ask to have them back? Why didn't he just request someone else?

Unless he wanted to punish us, Mara realized. *Jasmine most of all. Of course, that's why he treated her so badly. He's mad that she tried to escape. But that doesn't explain why Enforcer's mad too—unless they know. They must know. They have to know! It's the only thing that makes any sense. But... if they do, Jasmine won't be the only one punished.*

Memories of her last stint in the tiny dark closet danced through her mind, and she nearly cried out with horror. Jefe had told her that if he ever had to put her in there again, he'd leave her there to die. Is that what was going on? Was she truly about to go to her death in that horrible place? And Jasmine... would they kill her too?

She glanced at the girl who cowered in front of Enforcer, waiting for his instructions. No. She couldn't allow herself to become concerned for the other girl. It was about survival now—her own, and no one else's. She had taught herself that early on, and this was no time to forget it. Jasmine was on her own. Mara couldn't help her anyway. For now all she could do was hope the focus would be on the younger girl. If Jasmine had to be sacrificed for Mara to live, then it would just have to be so. And from the look on Enforcer's face as he grabbed the girl by her arm and dragged her across the yard and into one of the empty rooms, that just might be what was about to happen.

Chapter 15

ROSANNA WAS ENCOURAGED. BETWEEN HER ONLINE research and Michael's asking around at church the day before, they'd found many more ministries and outreaches to human trafficking victims than they'd anticipated. The senior pastor had recommended a couple to Michael, and they were praying about where to go next.

"I'm thrilled that both the kids want to be involved with us," Rosanna commented as the two of them sat at the table on Wednesday morning, relishing their last few moments alone together before Michael had to hurry off to work. "I think that episode Jonathan had with running into those people at the motel on Sunday really affected him."

Her husband nodded, a few gray hairs scattered among his red curls showing up clearly under the kitchen light. "More than I would have imagined," he commented, taking another sip from his favorite mug and fixing his green eyes on hers. "I think maybe it's a good thing, don't you? Maybe it's what God is going to use to light the fire of his faith once and for all."

Rosanna smiled. "I've been wondering the same thing. We both know Jonathan has a call on his life, and I'm so grateful he's going to Bible college in the fall. But I must admit, it would nice if he made a serious commitment to Christ before he left."

"Exactly. He believes with his head; it's his heart that's missing." Michael's smile was warm and lit up his eyes. "All in God's time."

"True." Rosanna dropped her eyes and picked at her toast, though she didn't eat any. She wasn't sure why she'd even fixed it. She almost never ate anything this early in the morning. She raised her eyes to find her husband was still watching her. "What do you think about those girls Jonathan saw at the hotel? Do you really think it was some sort of illegal prostitution situation?"

Michael's smile faded, replaced by his serious "pastor" look that Rosanna loved so much. "What else could it be?" he asked. "We know it goes on, but we never really expect for it to intersect our lives, and certainly not our children's lives. Ever since you told me about it, I haven't been able to stop thinking about those girls. I pray for them, of course, and I pray for those who use them too, though it's tough at times." His jaw twitched before he continued. "I confess that I have to resist a feeling of hatred toward them. I know Christ died for them too, but that they could do such horrible things to people against their will, children especially..."

His voice trailed off, and Rosanna reached across the table to lay her hand on his. "I fight the same feelings," she said. "Who wouldn't? I have to remind myself that the Bible says that vengeance belongs to God, but that doesn't mean these people shouldn't be punished."

Michael nodded. "That's true. They should be prosecuted to the full extent of the law. This sort of thing has to be stopped." A sudden onslaught of tears filled his eyes. "Thank you for wanting to get involved in this with me—whatever our involvement may mean. Do you want to pray about that now before I leave for work?"

Rosanna nodded. "Yes. Please." She bowed her head as Michael began speaking to the Father about their desire to help and asking Him for clear direction. Though she had no idea how God's answer to their prayer would play out in their lives, she trusted that it would be for the best for all concerned.

The day passed with agonizing slowness, as Mara tried to sleep but was unable to drown out the occasional noises she heard coming from the room where Enforcer had taken Jasmine. What was he doing to her in there? Would she survive? Though Mara repeatedly told herself that it wasn't her concern, she struggled with imagining what tortures Jasmine might be enduring. And if all this was because of what had happened at the motel, then it was just a matter of time until the whole story came out and Jefe or one of the others would come for her. It wouldn't matter that she hadn't been a part of Jasmine's failed escape attempt and that she had in fact diffused the situation with the pizza guy; it would matter only that she was there and hadn't stopped it from happening in the first place.

Her heart raced at the thought. She had survived for years by doing what she was told and never questioning authority. The few punishments she'd endured had been because she let down her guard momentarily and dared to cross even the smallest line. After her last stay in the hole, she'd promised herself she would never again take such a risk, but some things—like being in the wrong place at the wrong time with the wrong person—just couldn't be avoided. If only Jasmine hadn't been so foolish and tried to escape, then she wouldn't be going through what she was experiencing now. The stupid girl had only herself to blame. And now Mara might very well have to pay the price as well.

Life was anything but fair—but then, she'd come to accept that years ago. All she hoped for now was to get through one day at a time with as little pain as possible. Jasmine's actions had diminished her chances for such an outcome.

Chanthra and little Lawan had made it through another night's work. Apparently the tiny girl had taken Chanthra's warnings to heart, for no matter what happened to her during those long hours after the first customer of the night made his way to their room, the little girl had endured it silently and without protest.

Chanthra was relieved. She had been living in this tiny, semi-dark room long enough to know the rules and to understand that the best way to make it from one day to the next was to remain silent and subservient. If Lawan learned that hard lesson quickly, she too might be around for several years.

Reaching for her remaining drugs to get her through a few hours of sleep, Chanthra saw that Lawan was awake, staring at the ceiling. Just as the night before, she hadn't even bothered to cover herself. Tears trickled from her eyes and down her cheeks, but she didn't make a sound.

For a reason Chanthra couldn't explain, even to herself, she ignored the drugs and crawled across the floor to Lawan's bedside. The child did not acknowledge her.

"Are you all right?" Chanthra asked.

Still the girl did not answer.

Chanthra's heart squeezed at the memory of what it had been like for her when she first came to this terrible place, and she knew what the one called Lawan was feeling. Pushing the child's hair from her face, Chanthra leaned down and began to sing softly into her ear. The words and melody were some of the only things she remembered clearly from the life she lived when she was a very little girl.

Almost immediately Lawan's head turned toward Chanthra, her eyes wide. "*Maae*?"

Chanthra stopped singing. "No," she whispered, shaking her head. "I'm not your mother. I'm just singing a song my own mother used to sing to me when I was even younger than you."

Lawan's eyes opened wider and the tears increased as they poured down her face. Without warning she lurched forward and buried her head in Chanthra's chest, weeping and trembling as Chanthra did her best to calm her.

What was wrong with the girl? What had happened? Whatever it was, Chanthra determined never to sing to her again. It had been a foolish thing to do anyway, something she never did aloud—only in her mind. It was all she had left of her mother, and she should have kept it to herself. When would she ever learn?

Chapter 16

Jefe brooded over the loss. He hadn't meant for Jasmine to die. What was wrong with Enforcer that he hadn't realized that? Didn't he know the difference between persuasive tactics and murder? Apparently not. But then, neither he nor Destroyer had been hired for their brains. Next time Jefe would deal with something like this himself. After all, he enjoyed the interrogation process, so long as he was the interrogator and not the one being interrogated. But he should be able to trust his employees with such simple tasks.

He cursed as he stubbed out a cigarette in the overloaded ashtray that sat on his cluttered desk. Ever since Enforcer had brought him the news about Jasmine—shaking and nearly crying as he did, which told Jefe that Enforcer knew he should have stopped before the girl expired—Jefe had been trying to determine the man's punishment. Jasmine was young and good-looking, innocent and fearful, blonde and fair-skinned, the type customers fought over. She had several good years ahead of her and could have brought in a lot of money. Now she'd have to be replaced. For that, Enforcer must pay.

Jefe had considered killing him outright, but it was more difficult to find someone to take his place than Jasmine's. No, he wouldn't kill him, and he wouldn't fire him. But he would do something that would ensure the stupid buffoon never forgot what he'd done and never, ever would do it again.

He smiled then, knowing that the man was a basket case, waiting and wondering what would happen to him. Jefe had locked him in the same room where, over several hours, he'd murdered Jasmine, leaving the terrified man to stew while his boss decided his fate. As a result, Destroyer had been pulling double-duty all evening, chauffeuring the workers back and forth to meet their clients. Jefe knew Destroyer was nearly as nervous as Enforcer over what had happened, but what pleased Jefe most in the midst of this financial setback was what he knew Mara must be feeling.

She has no idea how much Jasmine told us before she died, he mused. *But there's no doubt she's been thinking about it all day. Good. It'll keep her on edge, and the customers like that. Makes her look nervous and vulnerable—almost innocent. The older she gets, the more she's going to need a little pressure and incentive to keep that kind of look. When she loses it, she'll lose her value to me.*

He sighed. Mara was family, after all, and it would be harder to get rid of her than it was with the others—especially since he'd actually spent some rather enjoyable hours with her over the years. Still, business was business, and he couldn't make exceptions. For now he'd let Mara worry a while, though her punishment for not keeping Jasmine in line would have to be meted out at some point. Meanwhile, he wanted to get as much mileage out of her as he could before he had to make the painful decision to get rid of her.

He flipped off his desk lamp and rose from his squeaky swivel chair. He was feeling hungry and wasn't up to any of the slop the girls served around here. A nice drive to the beach and some lobster out on the pier would help him get his mind off all the responsibilities of running a business. People had no idea how stressful it was to be the boss.

Mara had been fighting tears all night. Her client no doubt thought it was because of him, and he seemed to like the feeling of power it gave him. Fine. Let him think that if it made him happy. She'd been through a lot worse than he could ever mete out, and if it hadn't been for what she'd seen just before leaving the compound she could easily have shut the customer out completely.

It had happened just as Destroyer was taking her and a couple of the other girls to the van. Each of the three had a different "date" for the night, but all at the same motel. Mara couldn't help but think of the previous night when Enforcer had taken her and Jasmine to meet with the man who had requested them both. Jasmine had been more frightened than usual, but Mara could only imagine how terrified Jasmine would have been if she'd known what was going to happen to her when they returned a few hours later.

Mara had spent the better part of the day trying to convince herself that she didn't care what happened to Jasmine, so long as it didn't extend to her. Yet she found herself peering toward the room where she knew Jasmine was being interrogated by Enforcer, listening for screams and hoping the door would open at last and Jasmine would emerge alive.

It wasn't to be. As Mara and her companions followed Destroyer to the van just before sunset, she'd heard the door to the interrogation room screech open. Gasping at the sound, she'd dared to turn back for a quick peek, only to see Enforcer emerge with blood all over his clothes. When no sound followed him through the open door and he didn't bother to turn back to lock it, Mara knew. Whether Jasmine had told Enforcer all the details of what happened Sunday night at the motel or not, it was certain that the girl would never tell anyone anything again.

Jonathan had made it through another day of school and work. He would be off the next day, and it was a good thing because he had one last final to study for—and then he was pretty much home free. He had a couple more days to show up at school, but he'd basically be taking up space, marking time until the ceremony the following week. He couldn't help but wonder why he wasn't more excited about it.

He resisted the temptation to kick off his shoes and leave them wherever they landed, instead untying and removing them and placing them in the closet. If they gave out awards for neat cowards, there was no doubt in his mind that he'd be at the front of the line.

You've got to stop that, he told himself. *You're not a coward because you didn't help those girls when you saw them at the motel that night. There was nothing you could have done, and besides, you weren't even sure what was going on.*

Yeah, right.

He flopped down on his bed, not even bothering to turn off the light. Everybody else was already asleep, so what did it matter? And who did he think he was kidding about not knowing what was going on? From the split second he saw that half-dressed girl with the terrified eyes racing toward him, he'd known something was wrong. He might not have known all the details—and he still didn't, really—but no way was that some innocent family situation. That poor kid was scared to death! She'd wanted his help, and he just let that pervert take her back to the room.

The older girl's face invaded his memory. What had he seen in her hazel eyes? Fear, sure, but what else? Acceptance. Yes, that was it. That was what was present in her eyes that was missing in the other girl's wide gaze. The younger one must still have held out the hope that she could escape. Why else would she have tried? The older one knew better and had long since given up that slim hope. How awful must life be when there was no hope left?

Jonathan shuddered at the thought. He suspected this would be another long, restless night. It was tough enough to pass finals, but tackling them on little or no sleep made it nearly impossible.

He sure would be glad when his parents made a decision about how they were going to get involved in helping these people who were being held against their will and treated like slaves. Who would have thought that slavery still existed in twenty-first-century America? Maybe that very fact was the reason he just couldn't get as excited as the rest of the seniors about graduating from high school. The importance of the event paled drastically in comparison.

Chapter 17

MARA WAS TOO NERVOUS TO BE TIRED WHEN THE VAN finally pulled into the alley beside the gate to the back entrance to the compound. She was the only girl not sleeping by then, but she just hadn't been able to block out the sight of Enforcer emerging from the doorway, covered in blood. That it was Jasmine's blood there was no question. By now her body had probably been removed—disposed of where it would never be found. As Destroyer pulled the van door open to let them out, she shivered. The cool night air didn't help, but it was the thought of how truly disposable they all were that chilled her to the bone.

Did no one care that Jasmine had lived or died? No doubt she had parents somewhere who would—if they knew. But they didn't and probably never would. They'd keep posting "missing" signs on telephone poles and holding candlelight vigils, hoping and praying that their daughter would one day return to them.

Mara nearly stumbled at the thought, her spike heels wobbling on the uneven ground. Her early life in Mexico with her family had been hard, but she'd had the hope that her beloved tio would one day rescue her and take her to a better life. He'd promised just that—and delivered the exact opposite. She wondered if it was possible to hate anyone more than she hated Jefe.

No sooner had that thought crossed her mind than he was standing in front of her, smelling of sweat and seafood and cheap cologne. She'd smelled worse, but still she nearly gagged. She hated it when he stood so close to her that she could feel his hot breath. The possibility that he might want her to come to his room for what was left of the night caused her heart to skip a beat or two. Would he force her into his bed, or beat her as Enforcer had beaten Jasmine—until she died? But then she realized he was smiling. Neither of the two possibilities she had considered would be preceded by his smile. In fact, his smiles were so scarce that she could come up with no plausible explanation for it.

She stopped in front of him and hung her head, gazing at her feet as she'd been taught. She waited for instructions.

Jefe reached out and lifted her chin with his finger. Still smiling, he spoke gently to her. "How are you doing, *mijita*? You are still my little one, you know."

Mara didn't answer, scarcely breathing as she wondered what would happen next.

"Of course you know that," Jefe continued. "Haven't I always treated you special? That's because you are. You are very special, sweet Mara. From the time you were a little girl, I promised you I would take care of you and give you a better life than you had in Mexico, and I have kept my promise, have I not?"

A vision of her last stay in the box flashed into her mind, but she blinked it away. "Sí, Jefe. You have kept your promise and given me a better life."

Jefe laughed, seemingly delighted at her response. "Good! I'm glad to hear you say that, for I wouldn't want to think I had let your parents down. I promised them to take care of you, and I have kept my promise. Even you have confirmed it! What a good and faithful man I am, sí?"

Mara swallowed the bile that rose to her throat. "Sí," she said at last. "You are the best, Jefe. So much better than I deserve."

Jefe blinked in what appeared to be surprise, and then laughed again, clapping her on the back and motioning her to continue on to her sleeping quarters. "Yes, Mara, you are right. I am so much better than you deserve!"

He was still laughing when Mara stepped inside her shared room and fell down onto her mattress, praying she would fall asleep without weeping or being sick. Jasmine was dead, and she had just complimented her tio for the deed. Could it get any worse than that?

Yes, it could. And no doubt it would. Jefe had been playing with her, and she knew it. Jasmine had no doubt told Enforcer what happened, and now Jefe knew about it. He would punish her in his own time and in his own way, but first he would let her imagine the worst. The only question was for how long.

Michael had been up since before dawn and left for work early. He loved the quiet of the church hallways, classrooms, and offices before anyone else arrived. Thinking he would spend some peaceful time in his office, preparing for the men's group he was leading on Saturday morning, he instead found himself sitting on a back pew in the main sanctuary, staring at the large cross that served as the sole adornment on the front wall behind the pulpit. One simple piece, and yet it said so much. Many had died to defend it through the centuries, while others had used it as an object of terror to threaten and bully people. Michael supposed it all depended on whether or not you stood before the cross—or knelt there in humility, recognizing your abject helplessness and need of a Savior.

That's where he was right now. Though he had long ago knelt in submission and received God's forgiveness, pledging himself to follow the One whose unfathomable sacrifice was symbolized by that cross, he sensed the need to yield his will once again.

"Am I resisting somehow, Lord?" he whispered. "Is that why Rosanna and I haven't received a clear answer or direction on our desire to get involved in some sort of ministry to victims of human trafficking? Or am I just being impatient? I know we haven't been praying and waiting very long, but I sense such an urgency in this call. And that part is sure to me—Your call to me and my family to be involved. Father, that TV program the other day showed me the ugly reality that slavery still exists in our world—and on such a huge scale! Abolition. That's the word I heard, over and over again. Abolition. The word takes me back to pre-Civil War days, and yet..."

He hung his head. Was he resisting the term abolitionist? Was that it? Was it a label he didn't want to wear?

The faces of modern-day slavery, so vividly and poignantly portrayed on the documentary, argued with his reason. When a tear plopped onto his hands, which lay folded in his lap, he realized he was crying.

"Forgive me, Father," he whispered, letting the tears flow. "Forgive me if I'm stumbling over terms or dangers or stigmas—or anything else. Just please, give me a Moses heart to stand in the gap and cry, 'Let My people go.' I know that's Your desire, Lord, and I pledge myself and my family to do whatever You call us to do to help make that happen."

As his heart lightened, Michael sensed God's smile upon him, and he knew the answer would come clearly when God was ready.

Chanthra and Lawan had not spoken beyond the tearful, nearly wordless exchange of the previous morning, and now night was upon them once again. The younger girl had remained silent during her working hours, enduring whatever came her way and even sleeping a little during the day. Her tears had lessened as well, though Chanthra still saw them glistening in her eyes more often than not. Chanthra's primary concern, however, was to convince the girl to eat. She'd scarcely consumed enough to stay alive since arriving in this horrible place, and though the food wasn't anything special, it was enough to sustain them.

And that was the problem. Chanthra had no doubt that the little girl had simply decided to starve herself to death. Perhaps it was the best thing for her, the kindest in the long run. But Chanthra felt she had to try to convince Lawan otherwise.

"Please," she coaxed, sidling up next to Lawan's mattress and sitting cross-legged on the floor beside her as she used chopsticks to shovel noodles into her mouth. "You need to eat something. The customers will be coming soon, and you must keep up your strength."

Lawan turned her sad eyes toward Chanthra and shook her head.

Chanthra sighed. Why not just leave the girl alone and let her die if that's what she wanted? Because she knew the boss man would punish her for not at least trying to keep her alive.

"Please," she said, holding the bowl close to Lawan's face and preparing to scoop some noodles into her mouth. "For me?"

Lawan hesitated. "You sang to me."

Chanthra nodded, remembering the girl's emotional reaction.

"Do it again."

Chanthra blinked. Sing to her? She'd thought the girl had hated her singing. Why would she want her to sing again if that were the case?

"Please?"

The girl's tiny voice moved Chanthra's heart, and she set her bowl down on the floor beside the mattress. She cleared her throat and began to sing one of the songs her mother used to sing to her so many years ago.

This time Lawan didn't cry. She watched Chanthra intently, and when the song ended, Lawan nodded and then picked up Chanthra's bowl of noodles and began to eat.

Chapter 18

LEAH LOOKED FORWARD TO A COUPLE HOURS OF babysitting at the Johnson home on Thursday evening. They always paid well and treated her kindly, but Leah would probably have done the job for free simply because she so enjoyed being with little Anna.

When Leah's father had driven her to the Johnsons' place, she thought he would drop her off and drive away. Instead he had come in for a few moments and visited with Anna's parents before leaving. Though Leah had gone into the other room with Anna, she had heard snatches of the adults' conversation coming from the entryway where they stood chatting. Leah was only mildly surprised that the topic of their discussion had been the adoption of little Anna and the human trafficking that was so prevalent in her homeland but was also present in their own.

Blocking out such depressing thoughts, Leah smiled as she watched her little charge stack wooden blocks, one on top of the other, until the crooked pile fell. Then both Anna and Leah clapped and cheered before Anna began the process all over again.

How is it possible, Leah asked herself, her heart squeezing at the thought, *that anyone would want to hurt a little child like this?* The memory of Jesus' words in Matthew 18 echoed in her mind: *"And whoever receives one little child like this in My name receives Me. But whoever causes one of these little ones who believe in Me to sin, it would be better for him if a millstone were hung around his neck, and he were drowned in the depth of the sea."* That people could be so depraved as to purposely buy and sell others, particularly helpless children, and then use them for their own pleasure was almost more than the sixteen-year-old could fathom.

Anna's tower of blocks took another nosedive, and Leah's depressing thoughts were interrupted by the little girl's cries of delight. Leah joined in, determined to put the tragedy of human trafficking from her mind—at least for now.

Michael parked his five-year-old red Toyota Camry in the garage and hit the button to close the door behind him. Then he turned the handle on the door that led into the kitchen and stepped inside.

Their modest three-bedroom house in a slightly older section of the San Diego suburb of Chula Vista struck him as both peaceful and secure. The Johnsons' home was slightly larger and newer, but it had a similar welcoming ambiance that was so common in many homes in America. At that particular moment, Michael couldn't help but wonder how much of that peaceful and secure ambiance was a façade. Just how peaceful and secure were they—really? For all they knew, similarly appearing homes in their very own neighborhoods were even now harboring ongoing crimes beyond their imaginings. That truth had danced on the edges of his conscious thoughts for years but only recently had penetrated those edges and taken up residence in his daily musings.

"Is that you, Michael?"

Rosanna's voice called to him from the family room, where Michael pictured her sitting in her favorite corner of the couch, reading or praying or possibly even watching TV. He knew his wife seldom turned the set on when he and the kids were gone, but occasionally she opted to watch the news or an old movie. He heard no voices coming from the room, however, so he immediately envisioned her with a book in her lap as she waited for him to come in.

He was right, of course. He dropped the car keys on the kitchen table and walked from the kitchen through the entryway and into the family room. The lamp on the end table next to the couch illuminated Rosanna's shoulder-length auburn hair, making her appear as if she had a halo.

And why not? Michael asked himself. *She's the closest thing I've seen to an angel in the flesh.*

He smiled as he stood in the doorway, watching her. "What are you reading?"

She appeared surprised at the question and raised her eyebrows in a shrug before lifting the book to hold up the cover. "My daily devotional," she said, laying the book back in her lap.

"Don't let me interrupt you, sweetheart."

She shook her head. "No, I'm done. Come and sit by me." She patted the cushion beside her.

Pleased at the invitation, Michael accepted and settled in next to her, putting his arm around her shoulders and nudging her closer. "Does this mean we have the house to ourselves?" he asked.

She looked up at him and smiled before shaking her head. "No. Jonathan's upstairs studying for his 'final final,' as he calls it. He'll be back at work tomorrow evening."

Michael nodded. "Hard to believe he's graduating next week."

He felt as much as heard Rosanna sigh.

"It sure is," she said. "How did that happen, Michael? How did our children grow up so quickly and our lives fly by with the speed of light? Weren't they just babies in diapers, toddling around and getting into everything that wasn't tied down?"

He chuckled. "Absolutely. Which means they're far too young to even think about going out on their own. Whoever heard of a toddler going off to college or an infant babysitting someone else's child?"

Rosanna laughed too, and then turned a bit more serious. "Leah loves babysitting for the Johnsons, doesn't she?"

"Absolutely. And why not? They're great people, they pay her well, and that little Anna is a really well-behaved child."

"Which is nothing short of a miracle," Rosanna observed. "I mean, when you think about all she's been through. We don't even know about her life before she came here, but even if it wasn't terrible, the complete uprooting of everything familiar must have been terrifying for her."

"True. I remember how she seemed to cry all the time when the Johnsons first got her. She doesn't do that anymore, but she's sure quiet until she gets to know you."

"Lots of kids are like that, though... shy around strangers. That's normal, don't you think? But you can only wonder what memories, if any, she has from her earliest months on this earth."

Michael took her hand and rubbed his thumb across her knuckles as he spoke. "I talked to Kyle about that one time, and he said they prayed that they'd gotten her while she was still young enough to start building her conscious memories here. Still, he said there are times when he sees her staring off into space and he wonders if she's remembering something... her mother or—"

Rosanna lifted his hand to her lips and kissed it. "You're a good man, Michael Flannery."

Michael raised his eyebrows. "Thanks. But what brought that on?"

She smiled. "You. You're just a good man, that's all. And I appreciate you. I don't need a reason." She stood to her feet and offered him her hand. "Now come on. Let's go into the kitchen and raid the pantry. I just happen to know where the secret stash of chocolate chip cookies are hidden."

Morning was upon them once again, and Chanthra knew as soon as she awoke that it would be their "dancing" day. Lawan would have to learn yet one more demeaning task as she served her owners.

Chanthra considered waking the girl and explaining it to her before they came for them, but the sight of little Lawan sleeping so soundly convinced her not to awaken her any sooner than necessary.

Taking advantage of the pipe and drugs beside her mattress, Chanthra prepared herself for what lay ahead. They would get little rest today before being required to start working again when the sun set. She may as well dull her senses as much as possible.

As she lay there, her mind beginning to drift as the edges of reality dimmed, Chanthra remembered the first time she'd been dragged down to the windows to dance for the passersby in hopes of enticing them to come inside. She'd already been through the initial pain and humiliation of nearly a week of servicing customers, and she thought it couldn't get any worse. Then they'd stripped her nearly naked and stood her in the window between two older girls, also scantily clothed, and told her to dance. Chanthra had no idea what that meant, as she'd never danced in her life; all she knew was that she was standing nearly naked on display for all the world to see, and for the first time she no longer wanted to survive her horrible ordeal. She wanted to die, and the sooner the better.

But she hadn't died. When she refused to wiggle and gyrate as the two older girls did to the beat of sensual music, she was taken from the window and "convinced" to try again. This time when she rejoined the others in the window, Chanthra bore fresh bruises and even a burn on the inside of her hand. She'd been told that if she didn't cooperate, her other hand would be burned as well—and then the bottom of her feet. With tears streaming down her cheeks, Chanthra had spent several hours in the window, moving along with the music as best she could, while the palm of her hand screamed in pain and her frail body shivered from a cold that came from deep within her bones.

Even now she still bore the scars of that unimaginable day. She lifted her hand and gazed at the palm that had never healed quite right. The little finger and ring finger had even attached themselves at the bottom with scar tissue. But at least it didn't hurt anymore. And she had learned to dance like she did everything else—with her mind carrying her somewhere far, far away, where her mother sang to her and *phra yaeh suu* declared her clean and forgiven.

The door to the room burst open then and Adung entered, heading straight for Lawan's mattress. Before the girl had even opened her eyes, the stout woman had grabbed her and pulled her to her feet, slapping her when the terrified child howled in alarm. Then she dragged Lawan out the door, slamming it behind her.

Chanthra knew the drill. Lawan would have a bath and have makeup applied to her eyes before being placed in the window. Chanthra might as well get up and get ready too, as she would no doubt be ordered to join her young roommate.

Chapter 19

IT HAD BEEN A LONG TIME SINCE MARA HAD ALLOWED herself to feel sad, but tonight it washed over her in waves. She did her best to harden her heart as she'd learned to do over the years, but the sense of loss continued to plague her.

Why did I allow myself to get close to Jasmine? I knew better than to talk to her. But when she asked me about The Reeds, I had to tell her. Even though they haven't taken me there in years, I had to warn her about it just in case.

The van jostled over pot holes and dips as it made its way down as many back alleys and backstreets as possible, avoiding main drags at all costs. Mara couldn't help but wonder how they hadn't been stopped more often. One peek in the back should have told any cop what was going on, but the couple times the police had pulled them over when Mara was in the vehicle, either Enforcer or Destroyer had somehow talked their way out of it and convinced the officer to allow them to continue on.

Were the police being bought off? Mara had heard of such things and imagined it was true, at least to some extent and with certain individuals. But all of them? Impossible. Still, she'd long ago given up hoping that an honest policeman would pull them over and rescue her. Rescue for Mara was just not going to happen—not tonight, not ever. Besides, even if the cops did stop them and arrest Destroyer, who had been driving the girls since Enforcer killed Jasmine, Mara would be deported to Mexico, and then what would she do? She wasn't sure if she was eighteen yet or not, so the government might want to return her to her parents. Were they still in the small town where they'd been when they sold her to her tio? And would they welcome her home or punish her and send her back to Jefe?

No, the cops were not going to rescue her, and she may as well accept it. She had lived in various compounds with her tio and some of the others for many years, and she would die here, one way or the other. Maybe Jasmine was the lucky one after all.

She shook her head as the sadness returned. Why had the stupid girl tried to escape? And why hadn't Mara seen it in her eyes and stopped her before it happened? If she had, Jasmine might still be alive today. Instead she had to go running out the door of the motel almost directly into the arms of the handsome pizza guy, the one whose deep brown eyes still tugged at her heart.

This had to stop, both the sadness at the loss of Jasmine and the attraction to the pizza delivery person whose name Mara didn't even know. These emotions were weaknesses, and Jefe would use them against her any way he could. If she was to survive a little longer and not end up like Jasmine, she would have to become as hard as steel. She'd thought she already was, but apparently she was wrong. How could she kill the emotions that endangered her?

As the van pulled up in front of the motel to unload the girls for another night's work, Mara decided she would have to stoke her hatred for her tio. And what better way than to imagine what it would be like to kill him? It was only fair. He had stolen her life; why not take his?

With that thought fueling her, she closed her mind to the loss she felt over Jasmine's death and the attraction she felt to the nameless pizza man, and focused instead on how much she despised her tio. What better way to get through the night, whatever pain or humiliation it might hold, than to imagine his painful if only imaginary end?

"So," Jefe said, blowing out a puff of smoke with his words while he played with the lit cigarette in his hand, "have you been thinking about what you did, how you robbed me of my income?"

Enforcer sat in a chair that was much too small for his bulky frame, fidgeting with every breath. Sweat beaded on his forehead, shining on his shaved skull, and Jefe loved every drop of it.

The big man swallowed and ducked his head, staring at his feet. He nodded. "Sí, Jefe. I have thought about it, and I know I was wrong. I shouldn't have killed her."

Jefe seethed. The fool was so ignorant he had no idea how much future income he had cost them. Jasmine was young and pretty, a *gringa* with several good years ahead of her. Blonde-haired *Americanas* were not easy to come by, especially for one who specialized in a Latina harem, but they were in high demand. The one Enforcer so carelessly beat to death could have brought in a lot of money. Jefe would have to take into account the financial loss when he meted out Enforcer's punishment, but he would have to exercise restraint as well—until or unless he found someone to replace the overgrown idiot.

He took a long drag from his cigarette and leaned forward, his elbows on his desk as he glared at the man who cowered before him—a man who could crush Jefe like he'd crushed Jasmine but who didn't seem to realize that.

"Perhaps I wasn't clear when I told you I wanted you to get the information from her. Is it possible that's the problem?"

Enforcer raised his head, a hopeful look daring to cross his ugly face. "Sí, Jefe, perhaps that is the problem."

Jefe frowned. "Yet haven't I made it very clear that you are never to kill anyone who works for me unless I specifically order it?"

The man's hopeful look faded, and he nodded as his gaze returned to the floor.

"Am I to believe, then, that even though I gave such an order, you may not have been listening?"

Enforcer didn't respond.

"Answer me!" Jefe ordered.

The man jerked his head up, and Jefe was disgusted to see that there were tears in his close-set eyes. "No, Jefe. I mean, yes," he stammered. "I... I don't know, Jefe."

"You don't know?"

The man shook his head. "I don't know, Jefe. I don't know why I did it. I didn't mean to kill her, but she—"

"She was a child," Jefe hissed, his voice low but his eyes holding the other man's in their grasp. "A child! You should have known how weak she was, that it wouldn't take much to kill her. And even if you didn't know that, you should have listened and paid attention to what I said. Am I right?"

Jefe saw the man's Adam's apple bob up and then down again in his thick neck. "Sí, Jefe," he nearly whispered. "You are right. I should have listened to you."

"Should have but didn't." An idea was forming in Jefe's mind, and he smiled, evoking a brief look of surprise from his prey. "So, it is obvious then that your problem is not listening. Therefore we must remedy that problem." He stubbed out the still smoldering cigarette and folded his now empty hands together, almost as if in prayer. "You are too valuable to me to kill," he said, watching Enforcer's face for a sign of relief. It came quickly, and Jefe continued. "Unlike Jasmine, I will allow you to live because I am basically a very kind and generous man, am I not?"

Enforcer nodded eagerly. "Sí, Jefe, very much so."

"Still," Jefe continued, rubbing his chin with one hand as if deep in thought, "such an act of disobedience cannot go unpunished. And if the act was caused by the fact that you weren't listening, I believe I have just the cure."

He glanced down and opened the middle drawer of his desk. The highly sharpened six-inch blade glinted back at him. He pulled it up and held it under the light, turning it back and forth slowly as Enforcer watched, his eyes growing wider with each turn of the knife.

"This punishment will not only remind you to listen and obey when I give you a command," he said, sliding his eyes from the weapon to his victim, "but it will also remind you of what a merciful boss you have."

He smiled. "Now, let's get this over with, shall we? It's long past time for my dinner, and I'm starved."

It had been a long and especially trying night for Mara and the two other girls who had accompanied her on their group date, but keeping her mind focused on her tio's demise had helped her get through it. Now all she wanted was to get back to the compound and get a few hours of sleep before the sun came up.

Tomorrow's Friday, she thought. *That means we'll be even busier for the next couple of days. The weekend warriors will be out in force. I wonder if anyone will request Jasmine.*

She thought of the man who more than once had requested that she and Jasmine come together, the man whose initial meeting with them had started the episode with Jasmine's failed escape and, eventually, her death. Did he know what had happened? Would he even care if he did?

The van turned into the alley and stopped near the gate. The two other girls pushed ahead of Mara to be near the exit the moment Destroyer opened the door. As they spilled out and Mara followed, she yawned as she dragged herself through the now open gate and into the familiar grounds. A noise caught her attention just as she was about to step into her room, and she turned to see Enforcer walking slowly across the yard toward his sleeping quarters. Was she imagining things, or was it possible the sound she'd heard was the giant of a man moaning?

And then he turned toward her, the side of his head illuminated by the full moon overhead. A large white bandage was taped to the side of his head, covering the spot where his ear should have been. But the bandage lay flat against his face, almost caving inward rather than bulging out as she would have expected, and the realization that Jefe had at last meted out his punishment for Jasmine's death nearly knocked her to her knees.

Her tio had cut off Enforcer's ear! She didn't have to see the wound to be sure. She just knew. And the battle between terror and her desire to see Jefe dead exploded inside her.

Chapter 20

Michael was excited. He couldn't wait to get home for lunch and tell Rosanna about the meeting on Sunday afternoon. He also enjoyed lunch so much more when he could share it with his wife.

She was in the kitchen when he arrived, preparing a chicken salad that made his mouth water. He'd eaten very little breakfast that morning, and his stomach was rumbling.

Rosanna turned her head when he walked in, greeting him with a smile as she continued her work. "What a nice surprise," she said, offering her cheek for a quick kiss and then turning back to her chopping and shredding. "I was so glad when you called and said you were coming, but how did you manage to get away long enough to come home and have lunch with me?"

He slid his arms around her waist and rested his chin on top of her hair, enjoying the familiar fragrance of rose petals. Did they make a rose shampoo? He had no idea, but if they did, Rosanna must use it.

"I took some extra time because I wanted to tell you about a meeting on Sunday. But let's wait until you're done and we can sit down and talk about it together."

She looked up with a cocked eyebrow, but when he smiled in return, she shrugged and returned to her task. "Well, whatever the reason, I couldn't be more pleased. I was going to work out in the garden this afternoon, but I can start that later. A lunch date with my husband always takes priority over weeds and seeds."

Michael laughed and turned toward the refrigerator. "How can I help? I see you already have the table set. How about dressing? I'll get that. Anything else?"

"There's a plate of sliced date nut bread in there. Why don't you get that too? And some butter."

He busied himself with the remaining details to complete their lunch, and then joined Rosanna as she placed the salad bowl in the middle of the table. By that time Michael had already poured two glasses of iced tea and was ready to dive in.

Joining hands as they sat side by side, Michael offered a brief prayer of thanks and then spooned out a small plate of chicken salad for each of them.

"Looks delicious," he said. "I don't know how you manage to come up with something so good on such short notice."

She smiled up at him. "Like I said, lunch with my husband always takes priority, expected or otherwise."

He shook his head. "How did I end up with someone like you?"

"Clean living," she said, and they burst into laughter.

"That must be it," he agreed, stabbing a large portion of chicken and lettuce and popping it into his mouth.

"So," she said, holding her fork over her salad, "what's this meeting about on Sunday? How big a deal is it that you took off long enough to come home and have lunch with your wife? Must be huge."

He smiled and swallowed. "It is. I've been talking to the rest of the staff about our concern about human trafficking—the scope of it and our desire to get involved in some sort of ministry or outreach to the victims—and we've decided we need to make it a church endeavor. We're going to put it in the bulletin and announce from the pulpit Sunday morning that we're having our first ever human trafficking outreach meeting right after the second service. We'll just use one of the classrooms, but I'm praying we'll pack the place out and people will respond to this massive problem."

Rosanna's dark eyes widened as he spoke, and he knew she was as excited at the prospect as he was. "Can Jonathan and Leah come too?" she asked.

Michael hesitated. "We talked about that. Some felt it wasn't an appropriate ministry for teens, while others thought they had a right to be involved at some level if they want to. We finally decided they could come, at least to the initial meetings, and if they want to become a part of the outreach, we'll find a spot for them, though obviously within limits."

Rosanna nodded. "Serious limits, I hope." She frowned. "There will probably be limits for all of us, don't you think? I mean, this is not the sort of thing you run into headlong without a plan and guidelines."

He laid his hand on hers and folded his fingers around her palm. "Strict guidelines," he said. "We'll get legal advice from a couple of the guys in the church who know about this sort of thing. And we've got one lady in our congregation—Barbara Whiting—who already works with an international group on this very subject, so she's going to come too." He smiled. "You know who she is, don't you? I didn't even know about her involvement in any of this until we started talking in the last staff meeting about a possible outreach from the church. That's when her name came up."

"I know Barbara, but I didn't realize she was involved in that sort of ministry." Rosanna squeezed his hand. "Things are falling into place for this, aren't they?"

Michael nodded. "They always do when we let God take the lead." He leaned toward her and kissed her forehead. "Now, let's eat. This salad is delicious, and I'm starved!"

Mara couldn't help thinking of Jasmine as she sat on the floor, leaning against the wall and waiting for Destroyer to pick them up. It would probably be a couple of hours yet, but she wasn't about to instigate a conversation with the other girls, nor enter into one if they started something. She'd learned her lesson with Jasmine: Don't ask names and don't look at faces when it came to their customers, and no unnecessary talk with the other slaves. It was the safest way to stay alive, and she knew better than to cross the lines. She should have learned with the little girl who died after being locked up, but she didn't. Now, with Jasmine dead, too, Mara would not make the same mistake again.

Bored, she dared to move the curtain a few inches to one side and peer out into the street. They were only a couple of rooms down from where she'd been with Jasmine when the foolish girl had tried to escape. Right out there, just beyond her line of vision, was where the pizza man had been standing. She could still see his eyes, surprised and confused, but kind too.

No. She dropped the curtain back into place. She had imagined the kindness, but it wasn't there. He was a man, and men were not kind. They used people like her, and then threw them away when they were done. Only a fool would trust a man—any man. And though Mara knew she might be many things, none of which were good, she refused to think of herself as a fool.

Jonathan couldn't believe his finals were over at last. From here on out it was just a matter of showing up at class and taking up space until the dismissal bell rang and he could go to work. And he'd be glad to get there. His VW bomb had been acting up and he knew it was overdue for a tune-up and oil change. Even though he could do that himself, he needed a little extra tip money to get the parts, and Friday night was usually a good night to pocket some serious change.

As he headed across the campus toward the parking lot, he appreciated the breeze blowing in off the Pacific, keeping him fairly cool on an otherwise warm day. That breeze was the only air conditioning he had while he delivered pizzas this evening, and he'd have his front windows rolled down the entire night. The back windows didn't even open, but that was just as well, since he didn't want the pizzas to get cold.

Once inside his car, he coaxed it to a start, tapped the gas a couple of times, and gunned it out of his parking space and into the line of other cars headed for the exit and freedom. There was something about this kind of an afternoon that made him want to turn right instead of left and keep right on driving up the coast instead of pounding the same old beat, delivering pizzas and pocketing tips before heading home. But the reality was that he had parents who believed their kids should work and pay their own way, and that required a left turn toward his place of employment.

Once there he loaded up with his first list of deliveries, which was fairly light. It would get busier as the evening progressed, but for now he had only three stops to make before returning for more.

Chugging down the familiar streets, he realized as he did each time he passed that he was only a couple of blocks from the motel where he'd seen the two girls nearly a week before. What had happened to them since then? Would he ever see them again? Was there any way out for them from such a nightmarish existence? There had to be. If not, what was the point of trying to get involved in an outreach to help the many victims of such a human tragedy? Someone had to rescue them before they could begin to be healed.

"Those girls are not your problem," he told himself out loud. "You can get involved in some organized ministry, and that's all that's required of you. It's more than most people do! And it makes a lot more sense than beating yourself up over not trying to help two girls you don't even know and will never see again."

But something about his words just didn't ring true. Something in his heart beat out the message he'd been hearing for days now: he would somehow cross paths with those girls again. And when he did, this time he would not be able to walk away without at least trying to help.

The music continued to pound out its repetitious beat, but not loudly enough to raise complaints from adjacent rooms. The two men who had paid for the company of Mara and the two other girls now slept soundly, passed out from a combination of alcohol and physical exertion. At least they hadn't been violent, and for that Mara and her companions were grateful.

Chapter 21

IT HAD BEEN ONE OF THE BUSIEST SHIFTS JONATHAN HAD pulled in a long time. Seemed like everyone was in the mood for pizza. He'd put a lot of miles on his already fragile VW Bug, and he just hoped it would hold out long enough to get him home tonight. He was tired and needed a good night's sleep. He'd be glad to spend his Saturday morning getting the car tuned up before returning to work in the afternoon.

He glanced at his watch as he passed under a street light. Nearly two in the morning. He'd get back to the restaurant just as the doors closed. At least he didn't have to stay and clean up tonight. When he delivered this late, someone else took care of that.

Once again he found himself chugging along just a couple of blocks from the motel where he'd seen the girls. He wished his deliveries didn't take him to this neighborhood so often. It made it that much more difficult to forget what he'd seen—and to convince himself it was OK that he hadn't done anything.

The pull was just too great. Meeting with only halfhearted resistance, he turned the steering wheel in the direction of the motel and soon found himself parked in front of the second story room where the terrified young girl had escaped and run toward him. The full moon was just bright enough to enable him to check his watch again as he reminded himself he couldn't stay more than a minute or two. They'd be waiting for him to return from his last delivery so they could lock up.

His stomach rumbled and he glanced at the one small cheese pizza that had somehow been slipped into his deliveries by mistake. He'd called work on his cell phone earlier to ask about it, and they told him to have it for dinner. Though he much preferred a pizza smothered in everything, even the plain cheese sounded good about now.

He flipped open the box and pulled out a slice, folding it nearly in half before shoving it into his mouth and chomping down. It was barely warm, but it would fill up the hole in his stomach that was screaming to be fed. One piece of pizza...and then he'd leave.

Where are they? His mind explored the possibilities as he chewed and swallowed. *Are they with that guy again—or somebody else? Do they ever come back to this place? Does that poor kid still think about trying to escape?*

But it was the large, hazel eyes of the older girl that danced in his memory this night. She was young, and yet she seemed...old. No, that wasn't right. Not old, but...experienced? Yes, that was it. And no doubt she was. Jonathan shuddered at the implications.

A slight movement in the window a couple of doors down from the room where the girls had been caught his eye. Was that someone's face, pressed up against the window while a hand held the curtain back? He was fairly certain it was, though he couldn't make out the person's features.

Enough, he told himself. *Close the box and get back to work. You can take the rest of the pizza home and eat it later.*

He tapped the accelerator and then gunned it, but nothing happened. Now what?

Disgusted, he climbed out of the car and went around back to open the engine cover and peer inside. His dad always said only the Germans would put an engine in the back of a car and expect it to push the vehicle instead of mounting it in front like everyone else.

Jonathan wished he'd brought a flashlight. He kept telling himself he needed to carry one with him, especially with a car that was older than he was and more than slightly temperamental. The moonlight just wasn't enough to enable him to see clearly.

He gave up and got back inside, opting to try to start the beast one more time before using his cell to call someone for a ride. Sure enough, this time it fired up without a hitch, and in seconds he was rolling down the street, headed for the restaurant and then home. It was a good thing he had raked in such good tips tonight, because this car was in need of some serious attention.

Mara's heart raced as she peered out the motel room window once again, this time spotting an old VW parked in front of the building with someone sitting inside. She remembered seeing a similar car the night she and Jasmine ran into the good-looking pizza guy. She had wondered if it might be his, and she now found herself hoping it was, though she couldn't imagine why. She strained her eyes to make out the person in the front seat, but the best she could tell was that he was a tall male. Was it possible . . . ?

Her heart nearly stopped as the driver's side door opened and the vehicle's sole occupant stepped out, unfolding himself to his full height, far above the top of the little car. Mara's eyes widened and she pressed in closer against the glass, watching the man as he stepped to the back of the car and raised what looked to her like the trunk lid and then leaned inside for a closer look. What was he doing?

After less than a minute he stood up and slammed the lid shut before getting back inside the car. Before she could decide if the man she'd seen at that distance was the same one she'd seen up close less than a week earlier, the old car had roared down the street, leaving her to watch the tiny taillights disappear into the distance.

The tears she'd been holding in since Jasmine's death suddenly flooded her eyes, and she jerked herself from the window and leaned back against the wall once again. Where was Destroyer? She sure wished he'd get here and take them back to the compound so she could get some sleep. She needed to forget the reckless thoughts going through her mind. They were dangerous, and she knew it. Even if the man in the VW was the same guy she saw on Sunday, that didn't mean he was there looking for her. He might have stayed on her mind, but that didn't mean he'd thought of her even once since their brief run-in nearly a week earlier. She was a prostitute, after all. If he'd figured that out by now—and surely he was smart enough to have done so—then his only interest in her would be to use her the way other men did. No one came looking for someone like her for anything else. Her tio had explained that to her long ago, and her years of experience had convinced her he was right.

Even with the moonlight shining in the room's one dirty window, the darkness seemed heavy and thick. Enforcer lay on his bed, confused; he was also very angry. It was one thing to pledge loyalty to his *jefe,* but something else altogether to allow the man to mutilate him. Sure, he'd made a mistake—a bad one—by beating the girl until she died. But she was trash, just like all the slaves who served them in the compound. Why should she be any different just because she was kidnapped from a nice neighborhood in the States instead of being sold into this disgusting life by some family member in another country who needed money to survive? It didn't matter where these lowlifes came from and whether they wanted to be here or not; they were worthless except to bring in a steady stream of income for their owners.

And that's where Enforcer knew he had messed up. He'd been thinking about it for nearly twenty-four hours now, ever since the man he had once trusted had done this terrible thing to him. He grudgingly concluded that he understood Jefe's reasons, even if he didn't agree with his punishment. If the girl had been older and less attractive, with few good years left in her, Jefe would probably have congratulated him on getting rid of her. But the girl had just begun to turn a profit and had plenty of time left to continue doing so—until Enforcer let the thrill of domination and torture take over.

He'd known it the moment the girl quit moving and would no longer respond to cold water in her face. He had killed her...and he would pay. He even considered the possibility that Jefe would kill him—a life for a life. But to mutilate and humiliate him the way he had? Enforcer wasn't sure he could ever accept that and be loyal to his boss again.

Then again, what choice did he have? Where else was there for him to go? Though he knew of other brothels and slave compounds in the area where he might be able to get a job, if he went to one of them Jefe would find him sooner or later—more than likely sooner—and what the man would do to him then would make having his ear cut off seem like child's play.

Jefe had given Enforcer a couple of days off to let his wound begin to heal, but soon he would be required to return to his normal duties. He shifted his weight on his bunk in a futile effort to get comfortable and tried to ignore the screaming pain on the side of his head. He would eventually adjust to hearing out of one ear, but would he ever adjust to looking in the mirror and seeing that ear gone? He doubted it. And that left only one option: bide his time until he could get revenge against the man he now despised above anyone else on earth.

Chapter 22

Jonathan had spent the better part of Saturday morning tinkering and fussing with his VW, and at last it was sounding more like an actual car than a cantankerous lawn mower. He slammed the engine cover shut and stood up to survey his handiwork. The Bug would keep him going for several more months before it needed any more serious attention. He was pleased.

"Got it fixed?"

The question came from behind him, and Jonathan turned to see his dad standing just a few feet away, smiling, as the midday sun caused his red hair to look as if it were about to burst into flames.

Jonathan returned the smile and nodded. "Yep. Running like a charm now."

"Glad to hear it, son. You need a reliable car when you leave for school in the fall. Getting close, isn't it?"

Stiflingly so, Jonathan thought, surprised at the emotion that swept over him. Was he getting a case of leaving-the-nest jitters, or was it just because he was going to Bible college where he felt he didn't really belong? Of course, he had no idea where else he belonged, so Bible college was as good a place as any, and better than most.

"Very close," he said. "The summer's going to fly by. Starting next weekend I'll be working a lot more hours."

His father's gaze didn't waver or his smile fade, but Jonathan was certain he saw a flicker of uncertainty in the man's green eyes.

"You know your mother and I are very proud of you," Michael said. "Leah too."

Jonathan nodded. He didn't doubt that, though he often wondered why. He'd never really done anything exceptional. His greatest desire—playing professional baseball—was nothing but a pipe dream that would never come true. His grades in school were slightly above average but nothing to set the world on fire. He'd always kept his nose clean and stayed out of trouble, but he was a pastor's kid after all. It was expected of him. Where was the reason for any pride?

"I know," he answered, ignoring the questions that danced in his mind. "And I appreciate it. I won't let you down."

His father reached out and clapped him on the shoulder. "I know you won't, son. I have complete confidence in you."

Jonathan watched the man he so admired turn and walk back into the house, as a sense of inexplicable shame washed over him.

Michael's heart constricted as he stepped back inside, the realization that his only son was only weeks away from moving out of their home and beginning his life as an adult.

Oh, sure, he'd still be a student, living and studying in a Christian atmosphere, and for that Michael couldn't be more grateful. But the pending loss of the little boy he'd once taught to throw a baseball and ride a bike loomed large as he made his way to the kitchen for a cold drink.

"Hungry already?"

Rosanna's question interrupted his melancholy musings, and he looked up to find her gazing at him from her spot at the kitchen table.

He smiled. "Not really. Just thirsty."

She started to rise from her seat, but he motioned her to stay where she was. "I'll get it," he said, opening the refrigerator door. "Can I get you anything while I'm here?"

"I'm already having a glass of sun tea," she said. "I just made it this morning. Help yourself."

He did, and then joined her at the table.

"You were up early this morning," he observed, swirling his drink to help the ice cubes do their job with the still sun-tinged tea.

Rosanna smiled, her brown eyes warming his heart more than the sun had done when he'd been outside talking with Jonathan. "I woke up thinking about the meeting tomorrow," she said, sipping from her own glass as she continued to hold him with her gaze.

"Me too," he admitted. "Though I have a sense of peace about it, and excitement, too, it's the urgency that seems to override my thoughts and feelings about it."

She nodded. "Yes. It's as if God was holding the door open, just waiting for us to step inside and get this thing started. I know many people around the world are answering the call to help these people, but I honestly believe we've been called to do something on a personal level right here at our church."

Michael marveled yet again at the amazingly compassionate and compatible wife God had given him. How he prayed that his children would one day share such complete and joyous relationships with their own spouses.

"Jonathan's got his car fixed," he commented, and Rosanna nodded. "But I still have a hard time accepting that he's not going to be living here in a few weeks."

The tears that sprang to Rosanna's eyes made her appear more beautiful than ever, if that was possible. Michael took her hand and held it tightly in his own. He shouldn't be surprised to realize that his wife was taking their only son's imminent departure even harder than he was. He would have to make a point of keeping her feelings at the forefront as they made this first transition from a full household to a somewhat empty nest. And that meant drawing closer than ever to the heart of their Father.

The night had dragged out until Chanthra thought she and little Lawan would never get any sleep. But at last the final customer had exited the room and closed the door behind him. Lawan was asleep before the sound of the man's footsteps reached the bottom of the stairs.

Chanthra was tired but knew she needed help falling asleep this night. She was too stirred up, and she couldn't imagine why. She was relieved to see Lawan eating more regularly, but she was disturbed that the child continued to ask her to sing whenever they were alone. Chanthra knew she did not have an exceptionally good voice, but the little girl seemed to thrive on the few songs Chanthra remembered from her early childhood. She had even heard Lawan hum along on occasion, and it disturbed her more than she wanted to admit. Certainly the songs weren't unheard of, and others no doubt knew them. But they were Christian songs, songs of Chanthra's parents' faith. How could Lawan know them unless she too came from a Christian household?

The very thought nearly crushed the air from Chanthra's lungs. How was it possible that the loving God her parents worshiped would allow not one, but two, of His worshipers' children to be sold into slavery? Was this God unable to protect His own people, or did He simply not care enough to bother?

With trembling hands she reached for the familiar pipe that contained just enough of what she needed to get her through until morning, when a fresh supply would arrive to sustain her through another day.

Chapter 23

MARA HAD RESTED FOR MUCH OF THE DAY, DOZING A little in the sun after preparing breakfast for her owners and cleaning up after them. Her biggest challenge had been not to look directly at Enforcer, though it seemed the huge bandage on the right side of his head called to her each time she was anywhere near him.

If my tio did that to Enforcer for killing Jasmine, even if it was an accident, what will he do to me if he knows what happened at the motel last Sunday? And surely he does. She shivered at the thought, despite the warm sunshine overhead. Jasmine could never have held out and not told Enforcer the whole story. Her tio knew…and he would not allow her to go unpunished forever. It would do no good to tell him she hadn't known what Jasmine was going to do and that she'd intervened as soon as she'd realized what was happening. Would Jefe at least take that into consideration and lessen her suffering? She was certain he wouldn't mutilate her the way he'd done to Enforcer, for that would lessen her value in the eyes of the paying customers. It was the not knowing that haunted her when she was awake and plagued her dreams when she slept. She almost wished her tio would hurry up and get it over with, however bad it might be. But then, she reasoned, that was probably exactly why he didn't; part of her punishment was wondering and dreading what he would do.

"Let's go! The customers are waiting. Time to get ready for work!"

The command interrupted her thoughts, and her eyes snapped open to see Enforcer standing before her. So, he was returning to his duties. She wasn't surprised. Jefe wasn't one to allow slacking off for healing or any other physical need.

She pulled herself from the chair and headed for her room. She'd been told her "date" for the night had requested that she come dressed in red, from head to toe. An easy accommodation. She'd certainly had stranger requests.

Jonathan was having an unusually busy Saturday afternoon and evening. He'd been delivering pizzas as fast as he could get them loaded into his car and find the address on his map. One of his buddies had suggested he get a GPS, but he'd laughed at the idea. His boss wasn't about to pay for one, and he wasn't about to spend his hard-earned money on something so frivolous. Still, his tips were mounting up, and he appreciated it. He'd spent every dime he had on parts for his car.

He grinned as he cruised down yet another street with three more piping hot pizzas in the backseat, the delicious aroma reminding him that he it was getting close to his break time and he needed something to eat. The car was running like a proverbial top, and he couldn't be more pleased. *I might be broke,* he thought, *but my car isn't, and that's what counts!*

In less than twenty minutes the last of his three deliveries was made, and he decided to find a quiet spot to pull over and devour the small "everything but the kitchen sink" pizza he'd brought along for himself. He glanced around. Why did it always seem he ended up within shouting distance of that motel? He sighed. No sense trying to resist the pull. He'd just drive the extra two blocks and park out front while he ate.

The approaching night was warmer than usual, with little breeze and no hint of the usual evening fog moving in from the ocean. It was the first night that really felt like summer, and he was glad he'd brought his mini-cooler of cold drinks. He flipped it open and pulled out a bottle of sweetened green tea, something Leah had gotten him started on, and unscrewed the top. He was in the middle of taking a big swig when a van with darkened windows pulled up in front of him and stopped.

In a matter of seconds the driver's door opened and a mountain of a man with a bandage on the right side of his head got out and made what appeared to Jonathan to be a visual sweep of the place. His eyes landed on Jonathan, who nearly choked on his tea. What was it about that van and its driver that made him so uncomfortable? He wasn't sure, but he found himself second-guessing his decision to eat his dinner in that particular spot.

Without another moment's hesitation, he returned the lid to his bottle of tea and started the engine. He didn't glance back until he was at least a half-block away. Slowing as he approached a stop sign, he peered into his rearview mirror. In the dim glow of the street lights he saw several girls climbing out of the side door of the van and looking up toward the second floor of the motel. One of them was dressed all in red.

Jonathan was sleepy, but he'd had no trouble dragging himself from bed that morning, despite the fact that he'd had only a few hours of sleep. It had been nearly two in the morning when he'd finally finished his shift and made it home, but he'd fallen asleep the moment his head hit the pillow. When the alarm on his cell phone had buzzed him awake at seven, he remembered why he was actually interested in attending church that day. He felt only a slight stab of guilt over the fact that his enthusiasm had nothing to do with the worship or sermon, but rather with what would follow shortly after.

Sitting on the pew, he glanced at his watch. The time coincided with what he imagined was the pastor's final point, leading to a benediction and the dismissal of the congregation. Then he'd head straight to the classroom for the planned meeting about organizing an outreach to those trapped in human trafficking. Jonathan had managed to do a little online research over the past week since his run-in at the motel with the two girls. The scope of this tragedy was monumental, and he was stunned at the statistics. Somehow he'd always thought of it as something that took place on a small scale in some faraway, backward country. Now he knew better.

From the corner of his eye, he noticed Leah closing her Bible. That meant the pastor was done and would ask them to stand. He wondered if Leah was as anxious as he was to get out of here and on to the meeting. There was no doubt that their parents were excited about it; he knew they'd been praying for the last several days for a good turnout at the meeting. They'd all know shortly if their prayers had been answered.

He stood to his feet, with Leah on one side and his mother on the other. Eyes open, he stared down at his feet as the pastor spoke the words of blessing: "The Lord bless and keep you..." The words were as familiar to Jonathan as the soft organ music that played in the background. He cut his eyes to the side, just past where his mother stood, to the polished black loafers that were his dad's trademark. The perfect family, together in church, leaving in moments to attend a meeting about ministering to victims of modern-day slavery. How was it possible? How could his family's pleasant, predictable life be so in contrast with others living only miles from them in conditions he couldn't even imagine?

The terrified eyes of the half-dressed girl running from the second-story motel room seemed to float in his memory, and he shook his head to try to clear his vision. Instead he saw the face of the older girl, seeking him out for a final look before stepping back inside the room. Had it been a silent plea for help…or was she simply responding to a moment of curiosity? He would undoubtedly never know since he would probably never see either of them again. Yet he somehow realized he would never be able to forget them…or stop praying for them.

Chapter 24

The pictures lined the mantle, bright square and rectangular images of smiles and exaggerated poses for the camera. Diane wondered, as she did so often these days, why she left them there when they brought her such pain. But to put them away would be to give up hope, and she would never do that—not so long as there was a breath left in her body.

She picked up her favorite picture and brought it close to examine its familiarity once again. Jasmine. What a beautiful child! From the moment Diane first laid eyes on her nearly thirteen years earlier, even before the squirming bundle was cleaned up and weighed or measured, the grateful mother had thought she just gave birth to the most perfect child on earth. All the years of waiting while she and Franklin pursued their careers before finally deciding they were ready to have a baby suddenly seemed so ridiculous. What worth was any of it in light of the angelic creation that was now her very own daughter?

In all fairness, Franklin had been as smitten by his first and only child as Diane had. But now…now that she'd been gone for weeks with no word and the police failing to actively look for her, implying that the fragile girl in the pictures was just another runaway who had rebelled against her parents' strict rules... Franklin dared to tell her that she needed to back off, to accept the inevitable and stop torturing herself with false hope.

Tears sprang to her eyes as she pressed the picture against her chest. Torturing herself? And why shouldn't she? If she'd been a better mother, Jasmine would be home with them right now instead of... missing. If only Diane had continued to drive her precious daughter to and from school instead of allowing her to walk the streets with her friends.

She shook her head. Franklin was right. She was torturing herself, but she couldn't help it. She wanted her baby back, but with every passing day, she knew the chances of that ever happening grew dim.

But she had to try. She took a deep breath and gazed one last time at the smiling five-year-old on her first day of kindergarten—blonde braids, shining blue eyes, the whole world ahead of her...

Jasmine had trusted them. As much as she'd fought for her independence and her right to "hang out" with her friends, she no doubt believed that her parents would always be there to protect her, to rescue her if she got into trouble. Diane had believed it too, but now she knew better. When her only child disappeared and needed help, her parents hadn't even known where to look for her.

She replaced the picture back between the others and wiped away the tears. She had work to do. There were flyers to distribute and post. She'd already blanketed their own neighborhood and most of those nearby; it was time to move out a little. Today she planned to start walking the streets of Chula Vista, a relatively large San Diego suburb that would take a lot of time to cover. But then, she had plenty of time these days. Sometimes it seemed time was the only thing she had left.

Michael checked his watch again. Two minutes until the meeting was officially to start, and only seven people had shown up. Four of those seven were Michael and his family. How was that possible? The announcement had been in the bulletin this morning, and the pastor had even mentioned it from the pulpit. Didn't people realize how important this was?

He shook his head, chiding himself. Who was he kidding? Human trafficking was a hard sell. Visiting residents at the old folks' home was one thing, or even making sandwiches to distribute to the homeless in the park... but modern-day slavery? Who wanted to think about anything so ugly, let alone get involved in rescuing and ministering to those caught up in it?

Sighing, he leaned back in his chair and decided to wait five more minutes before getting started. He was relatively sure that Barbara, the lady in their church who was already actively involved in the ministry, would show up. She'd said she would anyway, so they really should wait for her.

He glanced around the room. He wished now he'd arranged a half-dozen chairs or so in a semicircle in the front of the room. After all, it was always preferable to have to add chairs for a larger-than-expected crowd than to look out at an almost vacant room with a handful of people sprinkled throughout and all the other seats empty. But it looked like that was what he was going to have to work with.

The five minutes had come and gone, and no one else had joined them, not even the one lady who knew enough about this sort of ministry to give them some start-up direction and momentum. Something must have come up or she would have been here by now. No sense waiting any longer.

He stood to his feet and turned to face the meager gathering. His wife and children sat together on the front row, the seat between Rosanna and Leah, which he had occupied just seconds earlier, now as vacant as the thirty-plus other chairs arranged in neat rows throughout the room. An elderly couple named John and Sue Compton, with gray hair and glasses, who had been at the church nearly since its founding and came to every meeting ever held on the property, smiled up at him expectantly from the third row, while an overweight thirtyish gentleman, whom Michael knew only as Randy, eyed him suspiciously from the back row. This was going to be interesting.

He cleared his throat. "Welcome," he said, avoiding the pointless "everyone" he would otherwise have tacked on at the end of his greeting. "Let's open in prayer, shall we?"

Two gray heads and one slightly balding one joined the Flannery family in ducking forward while Michael thanked God for the opportunity to meet together to discuss this great need, and then invited God's presence and direction before ending with a weak "amen." When he raised his eyes, Michael was both surprised and pleased to see that two younger ladies he knew were active in the women's group had slid in the back door and waited for his amen to take seats on the back row but at the opposite end from Randy.

Nine people. Hardly a mighty army to tackle such a formidable task, but after all, they did serve a mighty God, and Michael was convinced it was He who had called them together that day. Encouraged by the thought, he stood a bit straighter and opened the meeting with what little he knew about human trafficking. The elderly couple was soon dozing in their seats, while Randy sat with arms crossed over his chest, and the two young women appeared to be listening politely. His family showed the most interest, and he found himself wondering why they hadn't just called a family meeting at home instead of bothering with opening it to others.

He had scheduled the meeting for a full hour. Whatever was he going to say to these people to keep it going that long?

Never on Sunday.

Jefe nearly laughed aloud at the implications. How well he remembered the movie! He'd seen it countless times over the years and never tired of it. Newer movies disgusted him—no plot, no depth, no class. Just spectacular special effects to make up for the lack of everything that made movies worth watching. What was this world coming to anyway?

Chewing his steak and eggs and staring out the window of his favorite seaside eatery, he watched the noonday sun play on the dark Pacific waters as he remembered the many Sundays at The Reeds when he'd made unbelievable profits in a matter of hours. Those were the days! But that sort of thing was just too risky now. Better to keep the activity at safer venues.

The sea was relatively calm today, with only a handful of surfers dotting the expanse, looking like seals in their black wetsuits, perched on their boards as they waited for the next swell.

Ridiculous waste of time, he thought, stabbing another chunk of meat smothered in salsa. *You can't make a living floating around in the water all day. The bums should get a job and make something of themselves.*

His eye caught the lithe shape of a young girl in a bikini making her way down the packed sand near the water's edge. Young. Attractive. Innocent. Exactly the kind that brought the most money. He sighed. Too bad Enforcer and Destroyer weren't with him. He'd have them follow her and watch for a chance—

Nah. Too risky. Better to find them on an empty street or a back alley, taking a shortcut on the way home from school.

He nearly choked at the memory, as a vision of Jasmine floated in front of his eyes. What a beauty she'd been when Enforcer first grabbed her and brought her to him! Jefe had commended the man for his quick thinking when he spotted the girl waving good-bye to her friends and heading off by herself. He'd followed her for less than five minutes when she turned down an alley and practically invited the abduction. It was like finding a golden goose dropped right down into his lap, straight from heaven! And Jefe had always wanted one white-skinned blonde for his stable. Jasmine had been perfect. If only that overgrown idiot hadn't gotten carried away and killed her. A young girl like that could have brought in a small fortune over the next ten years. Now she was dead. What a waste!

Jefe dropped his fork onto his nearly empty plate with a clatter. The reminder of his lost revenue had stolen his appetite. If ever he sensed a twinge of guilt over what he'd done to Enforcer, he reminded himself of the great loss the man had dealt him and he realized that he had no reason to feel guilty. If anything, he had shown mercy in his restraint. He only hoped that each time Enforcer looked in the mirror at his lopsided head that he remembered he owed his life to his boss.

Chapter 25

"I DON'T BELIEVE THAT."

The statement came from the back of the room. Michael knew its origin but was surprised by the passion behind it.

Seven heads, including the two gray ones that bobbed back to life at the unexpected turn of events, turned to look at the man who had spoken those four words, interrupting what certainly hadn't been a lively discussion but had at least been an agreeable one. The topic was understandably tough, and Michael felt as if he'd been swimming upstream for a good twenty minutes by this time. The declaration of unbelief stopped him cold.

"What don't you believe?" he asked, forcing himself to maintain a pleasant tone and not allow his irritation to show through. After all, Randy had sat back there like a bump on a log since the meeting started, contributing nothing to the discussion, and then suddenly he spouts off as if he's some expert on modern-day slavery statistics. He had a lot of nerve.

The not-yet middle-aged man with the thinning brown hair lifted his chin. "I don't believe what you just said about this human trafficking stuff taking place right here in our own country. Thailand, maybe. I've seen TV specials about it. India, Africa...backwards countries. Not like ours. It doesn't happen here."

Michael clenched his jaw, biting back the words he wanted to spit out and asking God to give him wisdom. Before he could answer, Celia, one of the two women who had slipped in late, stood to her feet. "That's where you're wrong," she said.

If the room had been silent before, it was airless now—all oxygen sucked out of it as they waited to see who would speak next.

The attractive young woman stood her ground and stared down the man who had raised his head defiantly to glare at her. He dropped his gaze only slightly, even as Barbara, the woman familiar with ministry to human trafficking victims, stepped quietly through the back door and waited in the back of the classroom. Michael was relieved. Her timing and expertise could be crucial.

"How do you know I'm wrong?" he asked, shifting his attention back to Celia. "You some kind of pro on the topic or something?"

She took a deep breath. "Actually, I am," she said. "I was kidnapped by human traffickers when I was thirteen. It's only by the mercy of God that I escaped and I'm still alive today."

The oxygen returned to the room in a whoosh, as all eyes snapped to attention. Michael was as stunned as anyone, but he sensed the mood of the meeting had just shifted—in a very big way. Perhaps the afternoon wasn't going to be a wash after all.

Lawan lay in the semidarkness of early morning, grateful that her last customer had come and gone and she was alone on her filthy mattress, free to think about her life before she came here. No one would interrupt her imaginings, as she dreamed of being rescued—at least not until tomorrow evening. And in a few hours she'd get some breakfast to fill her always hungry stomach.

In the beginning, she had thought she could starve herself to death, but she just hadn't been strong enough. When the girl named Chanthra had sung to her—the same song that Lawan's mother used to sing to her at bedtime—her appetite had won out over her death wish, and she had eaten an entire bowl of noodles. It seemed she had been hungry ever since, but the boss man and his female assistant gave them only enough food to keep them alive. The gnawing in their stomachs never stopped. Lawan wondered if that was part of the reason Chanthra was always puffing on that pipe of hers. The older girl told her it was the only way to get through from one day to the next, but Lawan had refused the offer to share the pipe's contents. Somehow she knew the day she gave in to it was the day she gave up all hope of escape.

"*Maae,*" she whispered, softly so as not to disturb her roommate. It was obvious from Chanthra's deep, even breathing that she was asleep. "*Maae,*" Lawan repeated, closing her eyes and pulling up a picture of her mother's beautiful face. Wrinkled, yes—younger than she looked, Lawan knew. But beautiful, nonetheless.

Warm tears trickled from the girl's eyes as she remembered how her mother smelled when she held her in her lap. Oh, how she longed to snuggle against her *maae*'s shoulder once again, to be home with her parents and her little sister where she belonged!

The memory sliced through her heart like a hot, jagged streak of lightning. What was she thinking? Her little sister had been gone from the family for nearly two years now—since she was a toddler. Lawan's parents had explained that it was the only way they could ensure Mali's safety and give her a good future, as they had for Lawan's older sister, who had been adopted by a wealthy Chinese family before Lawan was born. The poverty-stricken peasants simply couldn't care for more than one child, and Lawan would be the one to stay with them. For Mali, a home and family far away, in a magical land called America where everyone had big houses and plenty of food, was the greatest gift they could give her. Lawan had recoiled in horror at the thought that her parents might have given her away instead of her sisters, but now she wondered if it would have been a kindness after all. At least she wouldn't have ended up in this horrible place.

The thought that her parents had now lost all their children tore at her heart. The one child who was supposed to stay with them and care for them in their old age had been stolen in an instant when she foolishly wandered too far from her village, and now she was trapped in this filthy room. Oh, how her poor *maae* must be crying herself to sleep these nights, wishing she had at least one of her daughters back! But now that Lawan, whose name meant beautiful, had been so horribly defiled, would she still want her? Would anyone ever want her again, except to use and humiliate her?

The thought was more than the child could bear, and she flopped over onto her stomach to bury her sobs in the mattress that had hosted her defilement with so many customers over the last few nights that Lawan had lost count.

Enforcer was back at work, determined to ignore the ongoing pain on the side of his head. Tonight he would pick up the girls as he had done so many times before, and he knew that none would ask about the bandage that covered his wound. They knew better. He might be mutilated, but he was still fearsome, and he wasn't about to take any taunting from the low-life females that worked for Jefe.

But it was Jefe himself who bore the brunt of Enforcer's growing hatred. Though he still respected and obeyed his boss outwardly, inside the man was seething. It would take time—lots of time—for him to plan his revenge. But he didn't mind. The important thing was that one day, when Jefe least expected it, he would pay for what he had done. Sure, Enforcer had made a mistake in killing the girl. But so what? It wasn't like he planned to do it. She had just pushed him too hard, refusing to cooperate the way he wanted her to. He hadn't really hit her hard enough to kill her—at least, it didn't seem that way. How was he supposed to know she was so weak? And besides, there were plenty of others out there to take her place. Jefe didn't have to act like she was the only one. Maybe next time around they'd find one even younger, with more years to turn a profit for them.

He crossed his feet as he lay on his bunk, staring at the ceiling and waiting until it was time to retrieve the girls from the motel. Jefe was entertaining one of his favorite girls tonight—his niece, of all people—which Enforcer found revolting.

What a pervert! With all the other slaves to pick from, why would he want to spend time with his own niece? Sick, that's what it is. Sick! He jerked his head in a nod to no one in particular, more determined than ever to wait for just the right moment to settle the score with the man who had hacked off his ear. And once that score was settled and Jefe was dead, the world would be a lot better place. What happened to the slaves after that would be up to him and Destroyer. And if Destroyer didn't see things Enforcer's way, then he could join Jefe in the flames of hell.

Chapter 26

IT WAS THE CLOSEST MARA HAD COME TO TEARS IN A VERY long time. She'd had a tough time stopping them up when Jasmine died, but now this—another humiliating night at the hands of her own uncle. It was almost more than she could bear.

The disgusting man had at last released her to return to her sleeping quarters, and she lay in silence on her bunk, blinking back the wetness in her eyes and listening to the soft snores of the others who shared her room. She knew they'd all had a rough night too, but at least it had been with strangers. True, her tio had been the first to steal her innocence and had taken advantage of his position as her owner many times over the years since, so this was far from a unique experience. But it had been a while since he'd called her to his room, and she'd hoped he'd finally lost interest in her. Apparently not.

Is it possible to hate anyone more than I hate Jefe? I don't see how. If I hated him any more than I do right now, my heart would explode. I would die on the spot. And then I'd be free!

She squeezed her eyes shut. If only it were that simple. But she could not let herself die before she had exacted revenge on the man who had promised to be her protector and benefactor but had instead betrayed her in the most horrible way. Oh, how she despised him!

His words echoed in her ears, causing her to shudder at the memory of his touch as he had grabbed her arms, pulled her close, and whispered in her ear, "Don't think I've forgotten your part in Jasmine's death. You're as responsible as Enforcer, you know. He may have killed her, but you set her up by not watching her more closely." He had pulled back then and looked down at her, his dark eyes like ice. "You will pay whenever and however I decide, even if it includes another visit to the box. Do you understand?"

Her nod was automatic; she had learned long ago that there was no point in resisting or arguing. Tio would do whatever he wished to her, and there was nothing she could do about it—at least not yet.

Then the ice in his eyes had melted, and the smile that spread across his pock-marked face had frightened her more than the hatred she'd seen there just seconds earlier. "Good," he'd said. "Now, let's enjoy the evening together, shall we? You may be getting older and you may have made some mistakes along the way, but we're still family—and you're still my favorite girl. That's why I've always taken care of you and given you special treatment. You know that, don't you?"

Again she nodded, though she had to fight the wave of nausea that swept over her. Family. They were family! And it made her shame so much worse.

Angrily wiping the tears from her cheeks, she gritted her teeth and determined to put the ugly memory from her mind. She had to be strong. She had to survive, at least for a while. And she had to take her revenge on her tio before he took his on her.

Monday morning. A new day, a new week, and a new neighborhood to cover with "missing child" flyers. Diane had managed to cover several blocks Sunday afternoon, but today she was determined to get an early start and make a dent in blanketing the large town of Chula Vista, so close to the Mexican border, with pictures of her precious Jasmine. She couldn't even allow herself to consider what so many, even the police, had suggested to her—that even if Jasmine had been kidnapped and not just run away, she could very well be deep in the heart of Mexico by now. If that was the case, Diane realized her chances of getting her daughter back alive were nearly nonexistent.

And so she clung to the hope that the people who took Jasmine had come to realize what a sweet and special child she was and were therefore treating her well. Diane couldn't bear the thought that the girl was being hurt or tortured or abused in any way, and the possibility that she might already be dead was not even an option. If she didn't believe she would one day get her daughter back safe and sound, she would have ended her life by now. There was simply no other reason to go on.

The morning fog had burned off early that day, and the Southern California summer sun already shone clear and warm. Diane didn't even notice. Her only focus was posting the flyers on every telephone or utility pole she came across, though she'd been warned that it was technically illegal to do so. Illegal? So what? What were they going to do, arrest her? Diane lived and breathed for only one reason: to find and rescue her daughter. If she couldn't do that, then it really didn't matter what they did to her. She just wished Franklin would stop mourning in private, as if she didn't know what he was doing, and find some active way to help her in her quest to locate their daughter. How he could continue getting up every morning and going to work as if nothing had changed was something she would never understand. The career that had once been so important to her now meant nothing. She continued to use up her vacation time and personal and sick leave days to canvas neighborhoods and post flyers of Jasmine's face with the hope that someone, somewhere, sometime would recognize her and know where she was. And if their daughter wasn't safely home when Diane ran out of paid days to take off, she would quit her job. Franklin made enough to support them both anyway. Let him go to work and pretend all was well; she would continue her campaign until it succeeded... or she died trying.

Graduation week. Jonathan was through with finals and basically just had to show up at school for a few hours today and tomorrow, and then he was through until Thursday's ceremony. As the dismissal bell rang and he walked across the familiar campus to the parking lot to retrieve his Beetle and head for work, he wondered again why he couldn't drum up at least a little enthusiasm about what was supposed to be a major milestone. No more high school! The passage from childhood to adulthood as he left for college. Dorm living. Campus life. Attractive young ladies. Limitless possibilities and opportunities for the future.

But all he could think about was yesterday's meeting at the church. It had been a bit humdrum at first, and he even felt a little sorry for his dad, standing up there in front of such a meager audience, trying to raise a little enthusiasm and discussion for the project. Then the guy in the back row announced his disbelief in what Jonathan's dad was saying. If that wasn't enough, the next thing they all knew they were listening to a woman named Celia tell of her experience of being kidnapped at the age of thirteen, right off the streets of San Francisco, and sold into slavery. That she lived to tell the story was truly a miracle, and that story had raised goose bumps on Jonathan's flesh.

Is that what those two girls he'd seen at the motel went through every day? Was that the sort of life they were forced to live? How was it possible that today, right here in America, in the twenty-first century, slavery could still exist—and the entire country hadn't risen up to abolish it?

Abolish. There was that word again. Jonathan wasn't sure yet what he would do to fight this horrible crime of human trafficking—something he now knew was the fastest growing illegal industry in the world—but the one thing he did know for certain: he was an abolitionist. Period. There was no compromising on the issue. No legalization, no establishing or overseeing of conditions, no unions to monitor pay or benefits. Just abolition. He would settle for nothing less. If it cost him his life—whatever that meant or however that played out—so be it. At least he was no longer without direction.

He tapped the VW's accelerator and then gunned it and headed out of the parking lot to begin his shift for the evening. Maybe delivering pizzas would help get his mind off the shocking truth of human trafficking—at least for a few hours.

Chapter 27

BUSINESS HAD BEEN SLOW AND THE TIPS LIGHT, BUT Jonathan didn't mind. He'd expected that on a Monday afternoon. But his old faithful Bug was running just right, and the early summer weather was perfect, with only a slight breeze as the sun edged downward toward the western skyline. He couldn't see the Pacific from the residential areas where he delivered a few pizzas on his route, but he could imagine the setting sun shining down on it before it all faded to dark.

Two more deliveries and he could head back to the restaurant to see if there were any new orders. If not, he'd busy himself in the kitchen or bussing tables. No tips in that, but it kept him busy and guaranteed his job until he left for school in a few weeks.

A relatively new black van with darkened windows, driving slowly in front of him, caught his attention. Why did it look familiar? Of course. He was fairly sure he'd seen it at the motel when he ran into those two girls. And he was absolutely certain he'd seen it on Saturday night, back in front of that same motel, unloading girls—one dressed in red.

A chill passed over him, and he slowed to keep his distance. If he recognized the van, the driver might recognize him as well. Somehow he sensed that wouldn't be a good idea.

The van pulled to the curb and stopped, though Jonathan could tell the engine was still running. A big man with a bandage over his right ear got out of the driver's door and walked to a telephone pole by the sidewalk. Jonathan slowed even more, knowing he should drive by but captivated with watching the man's actions. He seemed to be studying a flyer attached to the pole. Then, abruptly, he ripped the flyer from the pole, crumpled it into a ball, and carried it back to the van with him, just as Jonathan drove by. The driver lifted his head and locked eyes with Jonathan, whose heart skipped a beat as he tore his eyes from the man's angry glare and continued down the street. *Did he recognize me? Will he think I'm following him? I'd have to be pretty stupid to do that, but what if he...?*

He stopped at the four-way and then glanced in his rear-view mirror before making a right turn. The driver was already climbing back into his vehicle. Jonathan could only hope the man didn't decide to follow or confront him.

He forced himself to drive the speed limit so he wouldn't attract attention—from the man in the van or from the police. But as he continued to glance backward in the mirror, he felt his shoulders relax when he saw the van continue through the four-way stop without turning to follow him.

He'd dodged another bullet. But if he pursued his involvement with ministering to those trapped in human trafficking, how many more bullets would he successfully dodge before one of them found its target? It was obvious this was no child's game he was playing. The stakes were high. But what was the alternative? Run away and leave the job for others more courageous than he?

A part of him responded well to the thought, but the memory of two pairs of eyes—one pair hazel, one blue—would not allow him to do that. If only he hadn't been at that motel when the younger girl tried to escape—for he was certain that's what she had been trying to do—then he could have enjoyed his last carefree summer before college. But he had been there...and he had seen enough to know that human trafficking was real, and it had a face. At least two that he knew of. And those faces haunted him, day and night.

He couldn't ignore them. He couldn't deny them. And he couldn't leave the problem for someone else to solve. He had become an abolitionist, whether he liked it or not. If that required some bullet-dodging in the process, he would just have to learn how to move quickly—and pray more effectively.

"Candy?"

Leah smiled. The little girl who had been born into poverty in Thailand only three years earlier, spending the first eighteen months or so of her life with scarcely enough food to keep her alive and arriving in the States weighing little more than the average six-month-old, had quickly made up for lost time. The child had a voracious appetite and ate nearly anything that was set before her. But nothing made her eyes light up more than candy. It didn't matter what kind—peppermint, butterscotch, chocolate—she loved it all. And apparently, as she and Leah worked at building a tower with the child's plastic blocks, candy had suddenly popped into Anna's mind.

"You want candy?" Leah asked.

The little girl with the dark almond eyes and pixie-cut black hair laughed and clapped her hands. "Want candy!"

Leah, sitting cross-legged in front of their teetering block building, laughed and pulled the child into a loose hug. "All right," she said. "Your mom said you could have one piece, but only after you pick up your toys. Are you through playing blocks now? Do you want to put them away?"

Anna's eyes sparkled and she nodded. "Put toys away," she said, knocking the tower over with one swift smack and turning back to Leah. "Candy!"

Leah laughed again. "Candy it is—but toys first. Let's get them put away."

The excited child began to move the blocks from the floor where they were scattered into the toy box that lay open beside her bed. Leah watched her with delight. How blessed was she to get paid for spending time with such a delightful little girl! Leah had done a lot of babysitting over the last couple of years, but none of the children had been as much fun or as easy to get along with as Anna. Leah couldn't help but wonder if it had something to do with the child's past. Did she remember the days of deprivation and therefore appreciate her life more now? Or was she just born with a sunny disposition that so perfectly reflected her Thai name—Mali. Flower. Yes, that was exactly what Leah thought of each time she watched Anna playing or learning. She was a flower, opening up and beginning to bud. What a glorious bloom she would one day bring forth!

Thank You, Lord, Leah prayed silently, as she helped Anna retrieve her blocks and return them to the toy box. *Thank You for rescuing Anna from a difficult life that I can't even imagine and bringing her here to be with us.*

A tinge of regret tugged at her heart, as she thought of the family who gave up such a lovely child in order to give her a better life. The Johnsons had told Leah the story of Anna's adoption, including that she had a family who was unable to provide for her and had made the supreme sacrifice so she could have a chance to survive. How hard that must have been! Leah breathed a silent prayer for that bereaved family, so very far away on the other side of the world.

When his boss closed up at ten o'clock on the dot, with the kitchen already cleaned up and no reason to hang around due to lack of customers, Jonathan was relieved. He wasn't picking up much in the way of tips anyway, and he was tired. It had been a long day, and he was ready to go home and catch a few hours of much-needed sleep. Tomorrow would be a slow day at school, but he still had to get up fairly early to be there.

As he buzzed down the street with his windows open, enjoying the cool night air, he found himself humming a song and keeping tune with his thumbs on the steering wheel. Would he ever make enough money to afford a car with a radio that worked? He laughed. Did it matter? Probably not—at least not in most parts of the world, where getting enough to eat every day was way up the line on the priority list, with working radios not even a blip on the necessity radar screen.

He was nearly home and about to make a left turn onto his street when he noticed a white sheet of paper, attached to a utility pole, flapping lazily in the breeze. The memory of the van and the man ripping a sign off another pole earlier that day caused him to slow down. Was it possible there was a connection between the piece of paper he was looking at now and the one the man had torn down and crumpled into a ball that afternoon? Probably not. Then again, he'd never know if he didn't check.

He eased his faithful ride to the edge of the curb and shut off the engine, since he didn't trust his emergency brake. Climbing out of the car, he wondered why he hesitated. What was the big deal? What could possibly be on that piece of paper that would make him feel so apprehensive?

He shook away what was surely a baseless concern and strode purposely toward the pole. The night was fairly dark and the light limited where he stood, but even before he took the paper from the pole and held it close to his face, he knew why he'd resisted looking at it. Somehow he'd sensed what he would find there, and he was right. Though the girl was smiling and her eyes weren't frightened in the picture as they'd been when she stared up at him in the motel hallway, Jonathan would recognize her anywhere. It was the young blonde who had run from the motel room almost straight into his arms. The girl he had abandoned because he had no idea how to help her, and so he had chosen to believe the man who claimed to be her father.

Father. Of course he hadn't been her father! He was her customer, her "john," and she was being forced to perform whatever lewd acts he demanded of her. Why else would she have tried to escape? And now here she was, a happy version from her former life, smiling up at him and condemning him for leaving her there to a fate so horrible Jonathan couldn't even imagine it.

He crushed the paper to his chest and returned to his car. Climbing inside, he breathed deeply and waited until the wetness in his eyes had cleared enough for him to drive. He had failed the girl once. Now he had a chance to help her by calling her parents whose number was at the bottom of the flyer. But how would he ever drum up the courage to face them after what he'd done?

He turned the key, tapped the accelerator, and headed down the street toward home. That good night's sleep he'd been anticipating now looked as if it wouldn't materialize after all. Just as well. He had a lot to think about—and even more to pray about between now and the next morning. Something told him he was about to get a lot more practice at dodging bullets than he'd ever imagined.

Chapter 28

ENFORCER WAS MORE THAN MAD; HE WAS WORRIED. HIS anger at Jefe had kept him going since the worthless weasel of a man had cut off his ear. But now Enforcer realized he might be in trouble again. It was bad enough that he slipped up and killed the kid, but now her picture was plastered all over town. What if somebody recognized her and called the cops?

He paced back and forth in his small room, not even bothering to turn on the light. He'd already delivered the girls to a couple of different motels for the night, so he had time to think before he had to leave to pick them up again. But what was he going to do about the flyers? Even if he drove up and down every street in town removing them, the girl's family might put up more where he'd already taken them down. Sooner or later…

He stopped. Wait a minute! Who was going to see them and connect the girl to their operation? No one except the slime balls who used their services, that's who! And they weren't about to call the cops and tell them how they recognized the girl in the picture. Even if they did it anonymously, they'd be cutting their own throats by putting the business at risk. Enforcer knew there were other enterprises like theirs in the county, but he had to admit that Jefe had managed to make his business one of the most popular, as well as one of the most profitable. He only used attractive slaves, and he set no limits on what the customers could do to them so long as they didn't cause any permanent damage. Even temporary injuries, if they were visible, required extra compensation. As a result, the customers knew they would get quality service when they called Jefe.

The service will be even better when I get rid of the old man, Enforcer promised himself. *Destroyer and I can run things without Jefe's help—and I can run it alone, even without Destroyer, if I have to. So long as Jefe doesn't see the flyers, I'm home free. I'll just have to hope he doesn't catch sight of one of them, or I just might lose my other ear.*

He smiled into the darkness. *All the more reason to eliminate that no-good creep before he finds a reason to punish me again.*

Adung had wakened them early, hours before she normally came in to demand they bathe and get ready for the night's customers. The sun couldn't have been up for more than a couple of hours when the middle-aged woman who never smiled but served the boss man unquestioningly burst into their room.

"Get up," she demanded. "You must work this morning. One of the day girls is sick, and we have customers waiting."

Chanthra groaned silently. She hadn't even had time for a smoke to dull her consciousness. And now they had to work again, so soon after finishing a busy night! This wasn't the first time such a thing had been demanded of her, but it would be the first for little Lawan, who still lay unmoving on her mattress. The poor child had been worked nearly to death the night before, as word of her youth spread and her popularity grew. Chanthra worried that the girl might not survive long at all, and working double shifts would certainly not help.

But there was no escaping it. They must do as they were told or neither of them would survive the day. Chanthra pulled herself from bed, planning to nudge Lawan and get her moving. Adung beat her to it, though she didn't use a gentle nudge to wake the girl.

"Get up," she bellowed, kicking Lawan in the side and spurring a yelp of pain and fear. Wide-eyed, the child jumped up and stood cowering beside her mattress, shivering.

"Did you hear me?" Adung screamed. "I said get ready to work! We have customers waiting."

Lawan's eyes opened even wider, as she whimpered, "But it's not time yet. It's still early."

Her face red with rage, Adung slapped the child and knocked her to the floor, where she kicked her again. "Don't you ever talk back to me, you worthless piece of garbage! If you do, I swear to you that I will kill you! Do you understand?"

Curled into a ball on the floor, Lawan nodded. "Yes," she gasped. "I... understand."

Adung kicked her once more but with slightly less force this time, and then turned and walked toward the door. "Fifteen minutes" she called back over her shoulder. "Be cleaned up and ready. The customers are waiting, and they're growing restless. You don't want to make them mad now, do you?"

She slammed the door behind her, leaving the girls alone with the sound of Lawan's sobs. Though Chanthra wanted to gather the child in her arms and comfort her, she knew Adung had meant what she said. They had fifteen minutes and no more—and they'd better be ready.

With that in mind, she picked up the weeping child and carried her to the bathtub down the hall.

It was nearly two in the morning, and Franklin still hadn't fallen asleep. How was he supposed to function at work without sleep? How long could they go on this way?

Not caring if he woke Diane, he threw back the covers, slid his feet into his waiting slippers, and grabbed the robe at the foot of the bed before heading out the door and down the hallway to the kitchen. He'd never been one for warm milk, but a hot toddy couldn't hurt.

Or could it? Franklin had realized he was on his way to developing a serious drinking problem in his early twenties, but then he'd met and married Diane and had been able to stop the booze, cold turkey. Diane wasn't a drinker, not even socially, so they never had anything in the house to tempt him. But lately Franklin had been buying a little "alcoholic comfort" as he called it—sneaking it in and hiding it in the garage where he knew Diane would never look. It's not that she had forbade him to drink or even had any idea that he'd had a problem with it when he was younger, but he saw no reason to alarm or confuse her with all she was already experiencing.

As if I weren't going through a lot myself, he thought, retrieving his bottle and relaxing at the anticipation of what was to come. *After all, she was my daughter too, and I loved her just as much as Diane—*

He stopped at the realization that he was referring to Jasmine in the past tense. His hands trembled as he filled the cup, added a dab of sugar, and put it in the microwave for a quick warm-up. His father had taught him about hot toddies when he was a child, and had even let him sip them on occasion, helping the vulnerable boy develop a taste for them. How he would love to be able to sit across the table and share one with his father right now—to pour out his heart and tell him how much he missed his daughter and how he'd give anything to have her back.

He'd also tell him how he tried to blame Diane for letting Jasmine walk to school with her friends, but how he really blamed himself because, after all, he was Jasmine's father and it had been his responsibility to protect her. Now he'd failed. Jasmine was dead; he knew that beyond question. He'd held out hope for a while, but one night recently he'd felt the last shred of that hope slip away. She was gone, and there was nothing he could do to bring her back.

Diane would never give up, though. She'd keep walking the streets and posting those flyers and waiting for someone to call and tell them that Jasmine was alive and well. Franklin knew that would never happen. It infuriated him that Diane couldn't accept that. It was bad enough that his wife no longer cared about her job and left all the responsibility for maintaining the household and paying the bills to him, but at least if she could accept their loss, they could grieve as a couple.

As it was, they no longer had a connection to hold them together. All Franklin had now was the temporary warmth of his hidden bottle. He removed the warmed drink from the microwave and sipped it, sighing as he felt the relief flow down his throat and through his veins. Yes, he would drink a cup of this each night—only one cup, no more—and he would be able to sleep. If he could sleep, he could work, and if he could work, he just might survive.

"Franklin?"

He spun around at the sound of Diane's voice. She stood in the kitchen doorway, her short blonde hair disheveled, her makeup smeared, her eyes puffy. She'd been crying again. Franklin had heard her after they went to bed, but he'd pretended to be asleep.

"I heard you get up," she said. "Having trouble sleeping?"

He nodded, pulling the cup closer to his chest and wrapping both hands around it protectively.

"If that's tea you're drinking, I'd love some."

He swallowed. Their marriage had been so good once. They never lied to one another or did things behind each other's back. What had they come to? But then, their only child had disappeared. Dead. Jasmine was dead. He wanted to scream the words at Diane and make her believe it, but he just couldn't be that cruel.

"Sit down," he said. "I'll make you some tea."

She nodded, her smile tentative. "Thank you. That would be nice."

Trembling again, he turned his back to her and set his cup on the counter beside the sink, pushing it back a bit so it was partially hidden by the cookie jar. Then he filled a cup with water, put it in the microwave, and found a box of herbal tea in the cupboard.

Chapter 29

THE AROMA OF COFFEE LURED MICHAEL DOWN THE STAIRS and into the kitchen, where Rosanna stood at the sink, slicing fresh fruit. How many mornings over the last couple of decades had he stepped into this room and seen her standing in almost the exact same spot, preparing his breakfast so he could head off to work once again? More mornings than he could count. She almost never slept in and left him to fend for himself, even when she didn't feel well, and she was always up and moving before the kids had to get ready for school. What a treasure she was, even if most women might consider her old-fashioned.

He shook his head and smiled as he walked up behind her, as amazed as ever that this beautiful, intelligent woman who could have married someone rich or powerful, or become anything she wished, had chosen instead to devote her life to being his wife and the mother of his children. He felt her immediate response when he slid his arms around her waist and kissed her neck.

"Good morning," she said, leaning her head back against his chest. "I was just about to come up and wake you."

"I smelled the coffee," he murmured into her hair. "Couldn't resist."

She laid down her paring knife and apple and turned to face him, his arms still around her waist. "Hmm. So you could resist me, no problem, but not my coffee, is that it?"

He lifted his hands in mock surrender. "Guilty. I'm afraid you've got me pegged. It's all about your coffee." He smiled and kissed her forehead. "That's why I married you, you know."

"I do know," she laughed. "Now make yourself useful and set the table, will you? I'll have breakfast finished in two minutes or less."

He chuckled and turned to the cupboards to retrieve cups and plates. "All right," he said. "But remember, I'm timing you."

The table was set and he'd just settled into his chair next to Rosanna who, true to her word, had everything ready in less than two minutes, when Jonathan appeared in the doorway.

"You're up early," Michael observed. "Can't wait to get to your last day of school?"

The tall young man grinned as he joined his parents. "Sort of," he said, pouring a glass of orange juice. "I really don't have much to do today, but it is kind of nice to know it's the last day."

"Two more days until graduation," Rosanna commented, passing him a pitcher of milk for his cereal. "I still can't believe it."

Jonathan laughed. "Mom, that's because you still think I'm your little boy."

She set down the milk and fixed her eyes on him, though her lips twitched and gave her away. "You *are* my little boy," she declared, shaking a finger at him, "and don't you ever forget it!"

"Yes, ma'am," he answered, snapping a mock salute.

The friendly banter continued until Leah joined them, her thick red hair hanging past her shoulders in curly wet ringlets. "What's going on down here?" she asked, flopping down in an empty chair and snagging a piece of toast. "Did I miss anything?"

Rosanna raised her eyebrows. "Only grace," she said. "You are going to thank God before eating that, aren't you?"

Leah's cheeks flushed only slightly. "Of course I am," she said. "I always do. You know that."

Michael waited with the others as Leah bowed her head and offered a silent prayer before chomping into her bread. The conversation resumed then, and his heart warmed at the rare occasion to have his entire family at the table for breakfast. With Jonathan leaving for college soon, these occasions would become even rarer.

"So," Leah said after finishing her toast and reaching for another piece. "What did you all think of that meeting on Sunday? I thought it was boring—no offense, Dad—until that guy Randy stirred things up and then Celia jumped in. I've seen her around the church but don't really know her, do you?"

Before anyone could answer, Leah went on. "And I sure didn't know what was going on in her life before she came to the church. Wow! Here we are trying to start an outreach to people trapped in modern-day slavery, and we've got a lady right there in our own church who used to be one. That's amazing, don't you think? I mean, it's one thing to hear about these poor people on TV, but you sure don't expect to actually run into one of them, do you?"

Michael noticed Jonathan's face blanch, as he dropped his eyes and set his spoon down in his half-eaten cereal bowl. "I better get going," he mumbled, nearly jumping up from his chair to carry his bowl to the sink. "I'll see you all later."

Before anyone could ask why he was in such a hurry, Jonathan was out the door. Michael heard the Beetle's engine rev up and roar down the street. No way could the boy be that anxious about getting to school, even if it was his last day. Something else was definitely bothering him, and no doubt it had something to do with Leah's remarks.

Jonathan's stomach was so tied up he nearly overshot the entrance to the school parking lot. Flipping on his blinker at the same instant he turned into the driveway, he wasn't surprised by the horn blast from the car behind him.

"Sorry," he called into the mirror as he waved an apology. The gesture he received in return was less friendly. Snagging a parking place, he turned off the engine and sat for several minutes, staring out the front window but seeing nothing. He'd tossed and turned and prayed and worried for hours before finally falling asleep the night before, but for some reason he wasn't tired this morning. He was, however, a nervous wreck. How was he going to get through this day? By remembering what he'd decided in the wee hours of the morning before he finally drifted off, he reminded himself. And by knowing that he would follow through, no matter what.

The rap on his driver's side window jolted him back to the present. Snapping his head around toward the sound, he spotted Jason, one of his baseball buddies, leaning down and peering inside.

"What's up?" Jason called.

Jonathan took a deep breath and pasted on a smile before opening the door. "Not much," he answered. "What's up with you?"

Jason punched Jonathan's arm, causing him to flinch. "It's the last day of school, man. That's what up!"

Jonathan nodded. "Sure is," he agreed, forcing a cheerful tone into his voice. "Thought we'd never make it."

Jason laughed. "That's for sure. Especially me. At least you got good grades and college waiting for you. Me? I'm doing good to get that high school diploma on Thursday."

They headed across the parking lot toward the classrooms, joking as they walked. Just when Jonathan thought Jason would peel off in another direction and leave him alone so he could return to his thoughts, Jason said, "Hey, let's celebrate with a game this afternoon. We get out of class early, and I know we could get enough guys together to play. None of them are planning any serious partying until Thursday night, so why not spend our first free afternoon doing what we like best? You know you're dying to get that pitching arm fired up again, am I right?"

Jonathan nodded and smiled. Jason was right. There was nothing he'd like better than throwing a few this afternoon, but he already had plans. And he knew that if he changed them now, he'd never work up the nerve to do it later.

"Sorry," he said. "I'd like to. Seriously. But another time. Tomorrow maybe. Just not today. I... already have something planned, and it's really important."

Jason frowned. "Are you kidding me? You've got something to do that's more important than baseball?" He laughed. "Knowing how you feel about that, it must be life-and-death."

Jonathan felt his eyes widen. "You just might be right," he said, and then turned and walked away before Jason could say another word.

Michael and Barbara sat across the desk from one another in Michael's office. When he'd arrived for work that morning and found her waiting for him, he knew it was important—and he was certain it had something to do with the meeting on Sunday.

"I'm so sorry I was late to the meeting the other day," she said, skipping the formalities and diving right into the topic at hand. That didn't surprise Michael. From what he knew about this dedicated, middle-aged woman, she had a heart as big as all outdoors but a no-nonsense attitude that kept her inside the necessary safe boundaries of such a difficult ministry as working with victims of human trafficking. "I had every intention of being there on time," she continued, "but my daughter wasn't feeling well that day and I had to pick up my granddaughter from her Sunday school class and drop her off at home before I could come. It wasn't the sort of meeting where I'd want to bring a four-year-old."

Michael nodded. He couldn't argue with that. He sometimes wondered if he was making a mistake getting his own children involved in something that could prove dangerous, but they seemed determined to be a part of it.

"I understand completely," he said. "I just appreciate your coming at all. As it turned out, you really didn't miss much. I wasn't generating much response until Randy stirred the hornet's nest and got things going."

Barbara grinned, the compassion in her pale blue eyes speaking to Michael of why she was so successful in such a mercy ministry. "I must admit, when I walked in and heard Randy's question and spotted Celia sitting across the room, I wondered how it would play out."

Michael raised his eyebrows. "So you knew about Celia?"

"Sure did. In fact, I guess you could say she's one of 'my girls,' as well as one of our few success stories. I've worked with her for a while now, but I had no idea she was planning to come to the meeting. And I certainly didn't expect her to stand up and tell her story. But I had a chance to talk with her yesterday, and she explained that even though she hadn't planned to talk about her experiences, she just couldn't let Randy's challenge go unanswered." Barbara lifted the plastic foam cup of coffee Michael had poured for her when they first connected in the outside office and took a sip before going on. "Unfortunately, Randy's mistaken idea that this sort of thing only goes on in faraway lands is a common misconception. Thank God Celia had the courage to correct that. I think it changed the entire course of the meeting, don't you?"

"Absolutely," Michael agreed. "To be honest, I was going nowhere fast before Randy unwittingly turned the tide. By the time Celia was done, I think even our doubting Thomas was nearly in tears."

Barbara's smile was soft, if perhaps a bit sad. Though her short black curls showed only a hint of gray at the temples, she suddenly appeared ten years older. "Exactly. There's nothing more convincing than to hear such a personal and tragic story from a survivor. Sadly..." Her voice trailed off as she struggled visibly to maintain her composure. "Sadly, so many never survive to tell it."

Michael nodded, his own throat constricted at the thought.

"So," Barbara said after a brief pause, her full smile returning to once again light up her round face, "where do we go from here? How do I help? I'll do whatever I can." She leaned forward and lowered her voice as if sharing an important secret. "And Celia and her friend Monica have offered to do the same. Monica doesn't share any of Celia's past, as I'm sure you know since Monica's been here at the church for years, but she has a passion to help people affected by modern-day slavery. Both women identify themselves as abolitionists—as do I—so we want to know what we can do to get this ball rolling before the next meeting. But I just want to caution you against taking on too much or reinventing the wheel. There are a few excellent ministries to victims of human trafficking already established in the area. They love it when churches partner with them. I would suggest starting out that way and seeing where God leads."

Michael's heart felt light, as Barbara's suggestion was exactly what he'd been hoping to hear, at least for now. As difficult as it was to face such a horrendous crime as human trafficking head-on, he was certain that God was directing their efforts. Their group might be small, but it was dedicated and mighty because God was their strength. It would be exciting to see where He would take them in this venture, but he was relieved to think they could join others who were further along in this journey of rescue and recovery...and abolition.

Chapter 30

THE DISMISSAL BELL HAD RUNG, CATAPULTING JONATHAN and his classmates out of high school and into the new season of their lives. For some that meant goofing off for one last summer before heading off to further their education somewhere. Others went straight to work or joined the military, while some, like Jonathan, planned to work and save as much money as possible before starting the new college-student phase of their lives. He had several hours before he had to report to work to begin his delivery shift this Tuesday afternoon, and there was something important he needed to do.

His heart thumped against his chest as he pulled up in front of the familiar baseball diamond where his dad had spent so many hours teaching him how to throw a curve ball that would confuse the batters and a fast ball that would stun them. Right now he didn't feel like pitching either one. He just wanted to be there for a while and think.

The empty dugouts beckoned, and he scuffed his shoes as he shuffled toward the nearest one and took a seat on the lone cement bench. How many games had he sat through in this very spot, watching his teammates take their turn at bat while he waited for his chance to return to the pitcher's mound? Nothing had seemed more important then. He couldn't even have imagined anything bigger than the outcome of whatever particular rivalry was playing out on the field. Now it all seemed like a million miles and another lifetime ago.

"Forgive me, Lord," he whispered, surprised that he was talking to God when he'd thought prayer was the farthest thing from his mind. And yet his heart burned with the longing for connection to the only One who knew the answers Jonathan sought or the future he would experience.

"I've been so wrapped up in myself for so long, Lord. I had no idea—"

His voice cracked at the memory of the woman named Celia, only a few years older than him, sharing a story that sounded like something out of a horror film. But she wasn't just telling them about a movie; she was telling them about the life she had lived and what she had survived to be able to stand there that day and open their eyes to a reality more hideous and terrifying than any of them could have imagined. That Celia had experienced it was bad enough; to realize that the two girls Jonathan had seen at the motel were probably still experiencing it even now nearly brought him to his knees.

He blinked back tears, the grassy field in his vision nothing more than a green blur. "I want to help them," he whispered, once again surprised by his words. "I know Leah says you let me see those girls at the motel so I'd get involved in some sort of outreach or ministry to people like them, and I'm fine with that. But... I want to help them—those two girls. I feel so... responsible somehow. Like I should have helped them when I saw them, should have done something—at least tried."

A sob shook his shoulders, and he didn't even try to hold it back. The guilt was choking him, and he needed to be free of it. Could he work his way out of it by helping others escape that life? Would Bible college help? Would praying more or studying his Bible every day show him the way?

I am the way...

The words echoed in his aching heart. How many times had he heard them quoted over the years, even read them himself? "I am the way, the truth, and the life." Jesus had spoken those words to His disciples. But there was more. "No one comes to the Father except through Me."

No one. Only one way. Jonathan believed that...didn't he? His mind did, but...what about his heart? Would believing it in his heart finally stop the pain and longing that even now pounded against his ribcage?

If you confess with your mouth the Lord Jesus and believe in your heart that God has raised Him from the dead, you will be saved.

The familiar verse from Romans nearly knocked him from his seat. Jonathan had talked to God many times throughout his life, but suddenly he realized God was talking back, using the Scriptures Jonathan had learned over the years.

Was it really that simple? Was it just a matter of believing what the Bible said about Jesus and then confessing it to others? There was only one way to find out.

"I believe in my heart that Jesus is Lord and that You raised Him from the dead," he said aloud. "I believe that if I confess my sins like the Bible says, You'll forgive me and cleanse me. I want to be Your son, Lord—truly Your son! Your child, forever. I want to know without a doubt that You love me and I belong to You. Please, Father, show me. And then never, never let me go! I want to be with You forever."

A wave like warm honey oozed from the top of his head, down his shoulders, and even into his heart until he no longer doubted that God Himself had heard and accepted him. And though he still had no idea how he was going to do what he knew he must, he also knew he wouldn't have to do it alone.

He stood to his feet and walked from the dugout toward his car, passing the bleachers where so many times he'd heard the cheers of the crowds. This time the cheers seemed to come from heaven itself, and though tears continued to flood his eyes, he didn't stumble even once.

Jonathan sat in his car, parked in front of the neat, modest home in a middle-class neighborhood much like his own. He'd already made the phone call to the number he'd seen on the flyer. When he'd explained to them that he'd spotted the picture of their daughter and thought he might have seen her, the woman on the phone had burst into tears and handed the phone to her husband. The man had seemed wary and even suspicious, but had invited Jonathan to come to their home to talk. Jonathan was surprised when he turned onto the street nearly twenty miles from his own home that the place wasn't crawling with cops. But being suspected of a crime and mistakenly arrested were the least of his concerns. How would he tell the girl's parents how he'd happened to see their daughter and yet had done nothing to try to help her?

I will never leave you or forsake you.

The words came with great assurance to his heart, and with a deep breath he opened the car door and stepped into the street. This would be one of the most difficult things he had ever done, but he knew he would never rest until he did it.

He'd scarcely made it to the curb and stepped up onto the sidewalk before the front door opened and a man stepped outside. He looked about the same age as Jonathan's dad, with graying hair and a stare that immediately fixed itself on Jonathan and didn't waver. But it was the woman who tore at his heart. She stood beside her husband, her blonde hair short and looking as if it had just been done by a professional hairdresser minutes earlier. But her face looked haggard and scared, years older than the rest of her. Jonathan imagined that the look he saw there mirrored what the woman felt in her heart.

He drew within a few feet of the porch and stopped. "I'm Jonathan," he said. "I called you a little while ago."

Jonathan noticed how the woman's frightened blue eyes resembled an older version of Jasmine's when he'd seen her at the motel. His heart squeezed at the memory.

The man nodded. "I'm Franklin Littleton, and this is my wife, Diane." Jonathan could tell Mr. Littleton was fighting to maintain his composure, even as his wife clung to his arm as if she would faint at any moment. "You...you said you may have seen our..." His voice cracked but he recovered quickly. "Our daughter, Jasmine."

"Yes. I believe I did."

He nodded again. "Come in," he said. "We'd like to hear what you have to say."

Jonathan took a deep breath and followed them inside. How glad he was that he'd made the stop at the baseball field first. He couldn't imagine going through this on his own.

So, that was how Enforcer had decided to earn his way back into Jefe's good graces—by bringing in a new girl to replace Jasmine. Mara knew her tio really wanted a young one, closer to the age of the little girl who had died in the box, since those were the most requested by the customers and they had the most years of service ahead of them. She also knew he'd be happy with the new one, even though she was probably closer to fourteen or fifteen. She looked even younger, and she was gorgeous. Best of all, she was absolutely terrified, and that's what Jefe liked best.

The girl sat bound and gagged in a chair in Jefe's office, her wide green eyes wild with terror, as they flitted from Jefe and Enforcer to Mara, resting with Mara slightly longer as if she held out some hope that the only other female in the room might be an ally who could help her escape. If she only knew…

"So," Jefe mumbled over the lit cigarette that bounced between his lips as he spoke, "you found her at the beach."

Enforcer nodded. "Sí, Jefe. She was with another girl, walking in the sand by the water. I watched them for a while because they were headed away from the crowds. Sure enough, this one left her friend for a minute to head for the bathroom. No one could see the entrance to the women's side, so I just waited till she came out and grabbed her from behind. With my hand over her mouth, she didn't even have a chance to scream. By the time she figured out somebody had grabbed her, I'd stuffed her into the back of the van and locked the door." He grinned. "Piece of cake."

Jefe nodded. "And you're sure no one saw anything."

"Are you kidding? Her friend's probably still waiting for her outside the bathroom."

Jefe chuckled. "Maybe you should go back and get her too."

Enforcer looked surprised. "You really want me to, boss?"

"Of course not." Jefe frowned. "You think I'd take a chance like that?" He returned his attention to the terrified girl, who whimpered behind her gag as he reached out to stroke her face. "So, my pretty one, you've come to join our family." He grinned. "You'll like it here. We take care of our own." He leaned down until his face was only inches from hers. "But I expect complete loyalty in return. Do you know what that means?"

The girl shook her head, her whimpers silent for a moment.

"It means you will do anything and everything I tell you. And if you don't?" He kissed her forehead. "If you don't, you will find out what it means to betray me." He stood up and looked toward Enforcer. "Isn't that right, *amigo*?"

Enforcer's head jerked back at the question, and his eyes widened. Then he nodded and touched the bandage on the side of his head. "That's right, Jefe."

Jefe smiled and turned to Mara. "Even my own niece will confirm what I say, won't you, Mara?"

Mara nodded, her heart heavy as she watched the scene playing out before her. She knew now why her tio had included her in this conversation. He was going to make her responsible for the new girl's behavior. It would be up to her to make sure she obeyed without question and didn't try to escape, as Jasmine had done. It was obvious Jefe still blamed her for that, and even if he didn't punish her directly for that failure, he would exact a horrible price if she failed him again.

"Sí, Jefe," she said. "We must never disobey you or betray our family."

"Exactly," Jefe agreed, removing his cigarette and stubbing it out in the ashtray on his desk. Then he turned back to the girl who was now trembling visibly, as tears coursed down her cheeks.

"You are a pretty little thing," he said. "You'll be a great addition to our family and our business. And since I am the jefe, the boss of that family and business, it is my responsibility to train you properly." Without moving his eyes from the girl, he said, "Enforcer, take her up to my room and secure her there. I'll be up as soon as I've talked with my niece for a moment."

As Mara watched Enforcer throw the struggling girl over his shoulder and carry her from the room, her muffled cries reaching a frenzied peak, she braced herself for what was to come.

"You failed me with Jasmine."

No leading up to it; just a direct hit right between the eyes. No sense denying his words or trying to argue or reason with him. She hung her head, knowing her tio liked it when others willingly humbled themselves before him.

"Sí, Jefe," she whispered, her eyes downcast as she watched his silver-tipped cowboy boots so she could brace herself if he stepped toward her. "I did. And I am very sorry."

"You should be," he said, moving to stand directly in front of her. "It was your failure that resulted in the girl's death. You know that, don't you, Mara?"

She nodded.

He jerked her chin upward so she'd have to look at him. "I didn't hear you," he hissed, his dark eyes squinting at her.

She willed herself not to tremble, but she couldn't hold it back. "I'm sorry, Jefe," she said, praying her teeth wouldn't start chattering as well. "It was my fault she died, yes. And I will never do such a thing again."

Jefe paused, continuing to stare into her face. It was all she could do to force herself to return the gaze, but she knew he would punish her if she didn't. At last he dropped his hand from her chin and nodded.

"Good," he said. "You're my family. Flesh and blood. I've taken care of you since you were a little girl. I've treated you well and given you special favors. I should be able to count on you, to trust you, don't you think?"

"Sí, Jefe. Always."

His smile was cold. "Then I will go against my better judgment and give you another chance to prove yourself with that new girl. Don't let me down."

"I won't, Jefe."

He nodded again and then jerked his head toward the door. She was dismissed. He had other interests at the moment, but she couldn't let herself think about them. If she began to care for this new girl even the slightest bit, it would be the end for both of them. She would have to do exactly as her tio had commanded her and make sure her new protégé did nothing to cause them any more grief.

Chapter 31

ENFORCER SAT IN THE WARM AFTERNOON SUNSHINE IN THE courtyard, feeling almost smug in his newfound self-assurance. His plan was working. He was regaining Jefe's trust. And that would be essential when it was time to exact revenge.

He touched the side of his head as he had just an hour or so earlier when he stood in Jefe's office after delivering his new captive. How he despised the man who had deprived him of his right ear, but how he had delighted in watching his response to the gift Enforcer brought him—young, innocent, and completely unexpected. Enforcer could hardly believe his good luck. Jefe had sent him on a simple errand that took him past the beach, so he'd decided to stop for a few moments to enjoy the clean salt air and watch the waves as they rolled onto shore. What a bonus when he'd seen the two young girls in their skimpy bathing suits strutting past him, away from the crowds and watching eyes. He couldn't have set the scene better himself. And when the more attractive and younger of the two had veered off toward the isolated and deserted restroom, it was just too good an opportunity to pass up.

Now he listened to the crying and occasional screams that came from Jefe's private room, and he knew he had made some serious points with his boss. There was nothing the lecherous pervert liked better than breaking in a new girl, terrifying her into submission. Now if she'd just behave and help Jefe recover some of the income he'd lost due to Jasmine's early demise, Enforcer might just find himself in the perfect trusted position to carry out his plan.

Of course, he had to admit that he didn't really have anything specific in mind yet. Much of it would have to be improvised when the time was right. But he would watch and wait—and when that right time came, he wouldn't hesitate to do what was necessary to even the score between himself and Jefe, once and for all.

Jonathan's heart was an odd mixture of heavy and weightless. It had nearly finished him to sit in the Littletons' living room and tell them what he'd seen and how he was nearly one hundred percent sure the younger of the two girls was Jasmine. He cried when he told them how she'd tried to escape, only to be taken back inside the room by a man who claimed to be her father and another, slightly older girl claiming to be her sister. When he told them he had come to believe that both claims were false and the girls were actually being held against their will, forced into sexual slavery, he thought Diane Littleton would faint on the spot. But the parents had insisted on hearing every detail before calling the police so Jonathan could repeat his story to them. Though the two officers who'd come to the Littletons' house seemed skeptical that the girl he'd seen was really Jasmine, Jonathan was relatively sure that the girl's parents believed him. And for now, that was all he could do about any of it.

The police had taken his contact information and said they'd be in touch if they had more questions, and then he'd said good-bye to the Littletons and gone on to work. It all seemed surreal as he took a break from his deliveries, parked on a hill overlooking the ocean, and watched the sun go down as the sky changed colors. He tried to eat the calzone he'd brought from the restaurant before heading out on his deliveries, but he just couldn't make himself take a bite. He sipped his soda instead and rewrapped the sandwich for later.

"It broke my heart, Father," he said aloud, reliving his visit to the Littleton home even as he embraced his newly established intimacy with God.

It broke Mine too.

The echo stunned him as the truth of the words penetrated his mind. Why hadn't he realized that before? If it pained him to realize what Jasmine and others like her went through, how much more must it pain the heart of God? That people made in His very image could subject others made in that same image to such tortures was nearly unfathomable. And yet Jonathan now knew it was hideously true.

How were Jasmine's parents dealing with it? No doubt there was a spark of hope that she was at least still alive and somewhere in the area, but to realize what she must have been enduring since she first disappeared could easily crush them beyond recovery.

"Oh, Lord," Jonathan prayed, "please rescue Jasmine—and the other girl that was with her too. There must be so many like them, and so many families like the Littletons, grieving and hoping."

He gripped the steering wheel and lowered his head to lean against it. "Never let me forget them," he whispered. "Keep me praying for them and doing anything I can to help them—the girls and also their families. Please, Father..."

The young teenager named Jolene had never been so terrified or miserable in all her life. Why didn't someone come to rescue her? Surely her friend Heather had reported her missing long ago, since Jolene was sure it had been nearly twenty-four hours since she'd been kidnapped. Once her parents realized something had happened to her, they would have called the police immediately and wouldn't stop looking until they found her. By now they must be searching everywhere...though the horrible man named Jefe said they'd never find her.

She lay in the muted daylight of the stifling, airless room, bruised and bleeding, her hands cuffed to a bedpost. When the ugly brute with the bandage over his ear had deposited her here, she had no idea what to expect. And then the one who claimed to be the boss of their "business" and "family" came in and showed her exactly why she was there. The only thing that got her through the ordeal was the certainty that when he was finished using her, he would kill her and she would be free of him. But he hadn't killed her. Instead he had left her there, telling her to think about all he'd told her while he violated her—about what would be required of her in the future and what would happen if she fought it or tried to escape, not just to herself but to her family. And then, just before leaving her there alone, he told her that when she least expected it, he would be back to continue her indoctrination.

Tears slipped from her eyes, but she couldn't even cry out for he'd replaced the gag in her mouth before he left. And besides, who would hear her if she did call for help? Even the pretty girl with the big hazel eyes who'd stood in Jefe's office earlier had given her no indication that she would help her in any way. No doubt she was as frightened as Jolene—maybe more so for it was obvious she'd been here at this horrible place much longer.

Oh, Mama, she thought, *all I want is to be back home with you and Daddy! I always said you were too strict because you didn't want me to go places with my friends. Why didn't I listen to you? If I'd been at school today like I was supposed to, none of this would have happened. Oh, Mama, I want to come home. Please, please, find me! Come and get me, Daddy. Please! I don't want to die, but it's better than this. Help me, Daddy! Mama, please...*

But silence was her only answer, as tears continued to drip from her eyes, down her cheeks, and into her long, matted auburn hair.

Chapter 32

CHANTHRA DIDN'T FEEL WELL. IT WASN'T THE FIRST morning she'd wakened feeling sick to her stomach, but she knew from experience that she wasn't really sick. She was pregnant again, and her boss man wouldn't like it. This would be the fifth time in as many years, and Chanthra knew the routine. Once her condition was obvious, Adung would come with her bag of torture instruments, tie her down and gag her so she couldn't scream, and then "eliminate" the problem. Chanthra would be given extra drugs to get her through the procedure and a couple of days afterward, and then she would have to return to work—with a stern admonition not to allow it to happen again.

As if she could do anything about it. The men were given protection when they paid the fee for their time with the girls, but Chanthra could only encourage them to use it. If they opted not to, there was nothing else she could do.

She glanced over at little Lawan, still sleeping. Chanthra imagined that if the child weren't so thin and haunted-looking, she'd actually be quite lovely. After all, her name meant beautiful, and Chanthra imagined her parents had thought her so when she was born. The thought reminded her of her own mother's explanation when Chanthra had asked her how her name had been chosen.

"There was a full moon that night," her mother had replied, her eyes drifting back to a pleasant memory. "It lit the darkness of our little home, and I believed it was a sign from God that you would have a good and blessed life." Her dark eyes had grown sad again, and Chanthra knew she was trying not to cry. "Now I know that will only happen if your father and I practice selfless love, as the Savior did." She smiled, though the sadness remained, as she reached out to stroke Chanthra's cheek. "Always remember that, my daughter. Anything we do regarding your life is only for your good, to give you the blessed life that our Savior wants for you."

Chanthra pressed her own hand against her gaunt cheek then, remembering the warmth of her mother's touch and realizing how difficult that day must have been for her. No doubt she was already considering giving up her daughter so she would escape the abject poverty into which she had been born. If only she had known what lay ahead for her firstborn child, surely she would never have allowed the transaction to take place.

It's too late now, Chanthra reminded herself. *If my parents are even still alive, I will never see them again in this life. My only hope is in the next.* She squeezed her eyes tight against the hot tears that stung them. Was there any hope for her? Would God accept one so unclean and spoiled? She knew what her mother would say, for she remembered the stories of *phra yaeh suu* and how He forgave and accepted any who came to Him. Did that include her—even her? Oh, how she prayed it was so! If she just had that assurance before she died, she could endure the rest.

Wednesday night. Tomorrow would be Jonathan's graduation. But from the way Jonathan brushed it off as just another day, Leah thought she was probably more excited about it than he was. How could he be so casual about such a major event? She had only two more years until her own graduation, and she knew she'd be bouncing off the walls with anticipation when it was her turn.

She'd heard him come home a few minutes earlier. Maybe she could catch him before he fell asleep, and they could talk about it.

Sliding into her robe and slippers, she tiptoed from the room and down the hallway to her brother's door. It was closed, but he'd always said it was never closed to her. She knocked.

"Come in, sis."

"How'd you know it was me?" she asked, opening the door and stepping into the softly lit room, where he lay, still fully clothed, on top of his bed, his arms up and his hands under his head.

He grinned. "Sixteen years of living down the hallway from you?"

Leah returned his smile. Touché! Exactly why she knew him so well—and why she was so puzzled by his lack of enthusiasm over his pending graduation.

She plunked down at the foot of his bed. "What's up?" she asked. "Why aren't you excited about your graduation tomorrow?"

His eyebrows shot up. "Who says I'm not?"

Leah shook her head. "Sixteen years of living down the hallway from you, remember? I know you, bro. No way are you acting like I'd expect you to. Graduation's a big deal, you know."

He nodded. "I know. And I guess I am excited about it...in a way. But..."

"But what? Something's bugging you, isn't it?"

Jonathan sighed. "Yeah. It sure is. I haven't been able to get my mind off those two girls I told you about last week. You remember. The ones at the motel?"

Leah nodded. "Sure. I remember. And I knew that was bothering you, but I thought going to that start-up meeting at church the other day would help you put it in perspective." She paused before continuing. When she spoke again, her voice was low. "We can't save them all, you know."

"I know." His voice caught, and she waited, not wanting to embarrass him by mentioning the tears she saw him blink away. "But we have to try," he said.

"We are trying—all of us. That's why we had that meeting. Dad told me today that he talked to Barbara, the lady from church who's involved in that ministry, and she said there are groups we can join right here in our area that are already working to help these people."

"But... Celia. The one who told about her life in captivity and her escape..."

Leah knew her brother's tears had returned, so once again she waited.

"Those girls I saw? They're living that life right now, the one Celia escaped."

Leah laid her hand on her brother's knee. "You don't know that for sure."

"Yes I do. I know that Jasmine's been missing for weeks, and—"

"Jasmine?"

He blinked and sat up on the side of the bed next to her, hanging his head and staring at the floor as he talked, explaining to her about the big man in the van and the flyers around town. When he told her about visiting Jasmine's parents and talking to the police, her heart raced with fear.

"Jonathan, you'd better be careful! These people do *not* play nice! Have you told Mom and Dad about this?"

He shook his head. "Not yet. I didn't want to spoil the graduation ceremony tomorrow. I'll tell them as soon as it's over. I just hope the cops don't call or come here to see me before that."

Leah felt her eyes widen. "Do you think they will?"

He shrugged. "I don't know. I had to give them my contact information, and they said they'd be in touch. I'm sure they'll show up sooner or later."

"You should have gone to them first, instead of calling Jasmine's parents."

"I thought of that. But I wanted to be sure it was the same girl. The only way I could do that was to see more pictures of her. I knew her parents would have plenty."

"And did they show them to you?"

Jonathan nodded. "Yes. And it was her. No doubt about it. That's when we called the police."

"That must have been so hard for you—going to their house, I mean, and telling them what you'd seen."

"It was. But at the same time, it gave them hope that she was still alive." He shook his head and sighed, still staring at the floor. "I could never have done it alone."

Leah frowned. "What do you mean?"

Lifting his head, he leveled his soft brown eyes on hers and said, "There's more to the story. And I think you're going to like this part—a lot." He smiled then, and the sadness in his eyes seemed to melt away as he told her about his stop at the baseball field and his commitment of his life to Jesus.

"I have direction now," he said as he finished the story. "Maybe not all the details of what that direction includes, but at least I know I'm not heading there alone. There's a purpose for me going to Bible college, and I'm excited to find out what it is. Wherever it leads me, I know it will include serving the Lord."

It was Leah's eyes that now burned with unexpected tears, as she threw her arms around her brother's neck. "Oh, Jonathan, I'm so glad! This is the best news ever!"

Jonathan chuckled. "I thought so too. And first thing in the morning, I'm going to tell Mom and Dad. That should be the best graduation present any parents ever received, don't you think?"

Leah's concerns for her brother's safety were quickly forgotten, as joy over his having received Jesus as Savior washed over her. They were now truly brother and sister for eternity, and that was all that really mattered.

Diane Littleton lay in the dark, staring up at the invisible ceiling and wondering what her little girl was enduring at that very moment. It was the first time since Jasmine had disappeared that she had even allowed herself to consider the thought that her precious daughter might be better off dead.

The very idea pierced her heart like jagged metal, but if the young man Jonathan was right about what he'd recently seen at that motel, then her previously innocent daughter had been forced into a life of torture and degradation—one she might never escape alive. The sliver of hope Dianne had first felt when she realized that Jasmine had been seen alive less than two weeks earlier dimmed in the dark reality of what her life had undoubtedly become.

Still, as Franklin had reminded her just before he dozed off, there was now a good chance that their only child was still alive and living somewhere nearby. The police had expressed some doubt that a human trafficking ring would abduct her and keep her in the area, but at least Jonathan's report had spurred them to resume looking for the girl Dianne knew they thought had simply run away.

Jasmine would never run away, Diane fumed, angry that others didn't realize their family was different; it didn't fit into statistics or probabilities. They were a close family. They loved their daughter, and they just wanted her home. She had been happy here and would never have left on her own accord. Oh, how Diane hoped the police at last believed that! If so, then there was hope—hope that they would at least find Jasmine, simply because they would be actively looking for her. What condition their little girl would be in if they did find her was something they'd all have to deal with later.

Chapter 33

THE MORNING CLOUD COVERING HAD BURNED OFF EARLY, leaving a clear blue sky overhead and a mild ocean breeze holding the temperatures down to comfortable. Michael had never felt more excited and proud than he did at that moment, as he sat in the bleachers overlooking the high school football field, decorated with yellow and blue balloons and streamers to honor the school colors. Chairs were set up in neat rows, one after the other, extending across and backward to seat the entire 700-member graduating class.

And his son was in it. Jonathan, the firstborn of their two children. The son he'd longed for. The boy he'd taught to play baseball and who ended up being able to throw a meaner curve ball than Michael himself. But oh, how his heart had ached to watch that only son grow into the early stages of manhood without seeming to grasp his need for a personal relationship with Christ! Michael had prayed many, many times—alone and with Rosanna and in his men's Bible study group—that Jonathan would come to that place of understanding and make that commitment before leaving for Bible college. And God heard...and answered.

When Jonathan made the announcement at the breakfast table that morning, Rosanna had burst into tears, declaring that she'd never been happier while Jonathan teased her about having a funny way of showing it. Michael noticed that Leah hadn't been surprised by the news, so quite obviously the two siblings had already talked about it. He was glad. It was a blessing to know that his children were so close.

And now he was about to experience the joy of watching his only son walk the aisle to receive his high school diploma. Could it get any better? *Oh, Lord, thank You,* he prayed silently. *You have blessed me more than I could ever have imagined!*

Of course, Jonathan had said there was something else he wanted to discuss with them at their after-graduation dinner that night, but Michael wasn't concerned. Jonathan had officially been born into the family of God, so what else could possibly matter? They would deal with Jonathan's other concerns later. The students were beginning to file onto the field, their gowns flowing in the breeze and their tassels waiting to be moved to the opposite side before the caps went flying into the air. It was time to celebrate.

The van had just pulled up and parked in front of the familiar motel, dropping off Mara and two of the others for their evening's work, when Mara noticed a black stretch limo pull by.

High school graduation, she thought, watching the limo turn the corner and disappear from sight. *That must be what that's all about. Jefe said we'd have a lot of extra business starting tonight and running through the weekend—graduating seniors paying for our services themselves, and others having them paid for by older men, even their fathers. What kind of father gives his son such a gift?* She nearly snorted in contempt. *The kind of father like my tio, no doubt. Scumbags. Trash! The only kind who pay money to be with people like me. There are so many of those lowlife men out there. They pay for their own parties all year and then give their graduating sons a treat for themselves. I wonder what the graduates' mothers would think about that.*

"Get going," Enforcer growled, shoving her from behind. "Time is money, remember? The customers are waiting . . . and they're always right."

He laughed under his breath as he urged the girls up the stairs, following close behind. Though each of the three was going to a different room tonight, Mara knew they all wondered the same thing. What would the night bring? Would their customers be kind, weird . . . or even violent? Mara knew that a client might start out one way and end up another. She'd had men smile and call her "baby" one minute and then beat her the next. One man had even started out threatening to kill her, only to curl up on her lap and cry before the night was over. What was wrong with the male population of the world that they acted this way? She would never understand them—and she would never trust them. It was just that simple.

Taking a deep breath and shaking her head to rid herself of such thoughts, she stepped inside the door Enforcer opened for her and smiled seductively at the young man who waited for her. He was young enough to be one of those high school graduates she'd been thinking about, but he was also tall and muscular and could no doubt snap her neck without breaking a sweat if she upset him in any way. She would have to make it a point not to do so.

Rosanna lay nestled in the crook of Michael's arm, her head resting on his shoulder. How many nights over the past couple of decades had she fallen asleep in just such a position?

How many discussions had filled the night air as they considered the events of the previous day or the possibilities of the one to come?

Tonight was no different, except that the events of the day had been monumental, to say the least. At the top of the list was receiving the news that their son had finally made his walk with Christ personal and committed himself to following Him—wherever that might lead.

And then there was the graduation ceremony. What joy and pride had swelled their hearts as they watched their tall, handsome son receive his high school diploma, ready to begin the next season of his life at Bible college!

But it had been the news he'd shared with them during their celebration dinner at their favorite restaurant that had left them reeling throughout the remainder of the meal, as well as talking and praying long into the night.

"Did you notice Leah's face when Jonathan told us about visiting that girl's parents? She already knew."

Michael grunted. "Yeah, I noticed. It seems our children confide in one another before bringing us into the loop."

Rosanna sighed. "I suppose we should be glad they're so close."

Silence was Michael's only response.

"So what are we going to do?" she asked.

"About?"

"About what Jonathan told us. The police are involved now. Surely we should do something. We are his parents, after all."

"We've already done something," Michael said. "We've listened to Jonathan, advised him, and prayed for him. What else can we do?"

"But...what if there are repercussions? Jonathan has stepped into something that could prove dangerous."

"True." Michael paused. "Then again, what choice did he have? He was just doing his job of delivering pizzas when he saw those girls, and when he recognized one of them in the picture on the flyer, he had to let those poor parents know. Though I must admit, if he'd asked my advice first I would have told him to go to the police and let them tell the girl's parents what Jonathan had seen. But I understand why he did it the way he did. He just wanted to be sure."

"It took a lot of courage to go to their home," Rosanna said, trying to put herself in the shoes of the woman whose daughter was missing. What an emotional visit that must have been. True, they now had hope that their child was still alive, but they also had to face the possibility that she was suffering untold tortures in the meantime. Oh, how she prayed those parents would find their daughter safe and sound—and very, very soon! The realization of what they had been going through since their child's disappearance made her feel almost guilty for rejoicing at the good things that were going on in their own family.

"Jonathan has always been a courageous young man," Michael observed, pulling Rosanna's thoughts back to the present. "I just pray his courage doesn't get the better of wisdom in this situation. The more I learn from Barbara about her experience in ministering to those who have been trapped in human trafficking, the more I realize how evil and dangerous the people are who hold them as slaves. We need to walk very carefully, sweetheart—all of us—and pray for each other all the time."

Rosanna nodded. She had been thinking the very same thing.

Chapter 34

MARA HAD FALLEN INTO BED, EXHAUSTED AND RELIEVED that the evening was at last over. The young man who had been her "date" for the last several hours had at least been kind to her, and she was grateful. But now she wanted nothing more than to sleep.

She had just drifted off when she was jolted back to reality by loud voices. Whose? She shook her head and tried to focus. Tio, of course. And someone else...

Ah, yes, the new girl. Jolene, was it? Mara hadn't heard the girl speak more than a couple of words since arriving at the compound, but she had heard her muffled cries and screams coming from Jefe's room, so she quickly recognized the whimpering going on now in her own room.

The overhead light flipped on, and Mara blinked at the rude intrusion. The two other girls in the room looked equally perplexed, as all tried to focus on the reason for all the commotion.

At the open door stood the young girl, clad only in the now tattered and filthy bathing suit she had been wearing when she was abducted. Her slim body was covered with bruises and scratches, and she trembled under the verbal onslaught of her new owner.

"You failed me," he bellowed, adding a string of curse words that Mara had heard thrown in her direction many times. "The only reason I don't kill you right now is that you owe me—and you're going to pay. I took you in and personally trained you, and I expect to get my money's worth!" He reached out and grabbed her chin, jerking her head upward until she was forced to look at him. "Do you hear me, you worthless piece of garbage? I asked you to do one more simple little thing for me, and you refused. What kind of person refuses to show gratitude to someone who has given her everything?" He leaned toward her, squinting his eyes as he hissed in her face. "Scum like you, that's who. And don't think you're going to get away with it. I spent the last couple of nights training you, and starting tomorrow, you're going to start earning your keep around here. No more free ride, you got it?"

He waited, and when she didn't answer, he squeezed the sides of her chin until her lips were pushed together and she looked like a dying fish, gasping its last. Finally she nodded, her eyes wide as tears poured from them down onto Jefe's hand.

"Good," he said, letting her go. He did a quick sweep of the room before focusing on Mara. "Find her somewhere to sleep," he said. "I want her rested when she starts work tomorrow. Understand?"

Mara nodded. "Sí, Jefe." She recognized her tio's behavior and why he was acting the way he was with the new girl. It was something they'd all experienced in one way or another when they first came here—even the two young boys who also served as Jefe's slaves. He would personally "train" them in the business, and then let them know they had failed to meet his expectations, giving them one last chance to redeem themselves by serving others and making money for Jefe. It wouldn't have mattered what this girl had done or not done to please him; he would have exploded at some point and accused her of failing him, only to deposit her here with the others and order her to start working to pay off her "debt." Of course, Mara knew the debt would never be paid in full.

Jefe stepped toward Mara, glaring. "Don't think I've forgotten what happened with Jasmine. If you don't do your job with this one, I don't care whether you're my own flesh and blood or not. I'll hurt you like you've never been hurt before. Got that?"

Mara swallowed. She thought she'd surely been hurt every way there was to be hurt, many times over, and she couldn't even imagine what could be worse. But she wasn't about to find out. Whatever it took to keep Jolene in line, she would do—at least until she could find a way to finally rid them all of the scum who claimed to be her "flesh and blood." Only the anticipation of his death at her hands enabled her to keep her voice from trembling as she answered.

"Sí, Jefe. I got it. She'll be ready. I promise."

Lawan was worried. Something was wrong with Chanthra. She was smoking her pipe more often, and even getting sick when she tried to eat. What would Lawan do if something happened to Chanthra? Who would help her and take care of her? Even if Chanthra couldn't help her escape, at least she did her best to try to make things as easy as possible for her. Lawan couldn't imagine surviving in this awful place without her.

Sitting up on her mattress, she watched the older girl sleep. It was midmorning by then, and Chanthra was usually awake before this. Lawan had heard her earlier, though, vomiting into a small bucket beside her mattress. Was it from all that stuff she smoked? Why did she use it? Couldn't she just stop?

She had asked about it, and Chanthra had told her it was her "magic carpet ride" away from this place, but Lawan knew it was only a temporary escape and certainly not a healthy one. Even now, she watched Chanthra's uneven breathing and the rolling of her eyes beneath the closed lids. Was she dreaming of her home and her parents, as Lawan did? Oh, if only there was the slightest hope that she could one day return there, then it would make sense not to take the "magic carpet ride" with Chanthra's pipe. But with each passing day, Lawan grew more and more certain that neither of them would live long enough to return to their homes or their families, so what was the point? Why not drift away from the horror, as Chanthra appeared to do when she lifted the pipe to her mouth?

The temptation grew daily, as the pipe sat on the floor, next to the stinking bucket full of vomit beside Chanthra's mattress, beckoning Lawan as she shifted her gaze from her friend to the pipe and back again. Was that all she had to look forward to—to end up like the older girl who now wrestled with demons in her sleep?

Tears pricked Lawan's eyes. She was trying desperately to remember all her mother had taught her about *phra yaeh suu,* about how He loved her and had died for her and would never leave or forsake her. She knew in her heart that it was true, for she had received His love and forgiveness, and yet...

Help me, she prayed silently. *Don't let me give up and try to escape with Chanthra's pipe. Please,* phra yaeh suu. *I am so small and weak...*

Friday morning dawned clear and bright, with no morning fog or clouds to burn off before the sun could warm the air. Jonathan knew he should be sleeping in. After all, it was his first "official" day of freedom from high school. Graduation was behind him, and he didn't have to work until late that evening. So what was he doing up so early?

He chuckled to himself as he climbed into his blue Beetle and started the engine. *I'm up because I have way too much on my mind to stay in bed. I'm going to head for the beach and enjoy an early morning walk on the sand, and then maybe I can raise enough interest in a baseball game before I have to go to work.*

Jonathan hummed and kept time with his thumbs on the steering wheel as he zipped along familiar streets to his favorite spot on the coast. It was the only place that wasn't usually crawling with tourists, even at this hour. And there was nothing he liked better than walking on the packed, wet sand next to what was left of the breaking waves as they teased his bare toes before ebbing once again. If he got tired of walking, he'd climb the old wooden steps to the pier and find a place to sit in the sun and watch the handful of diehard fishermen who were sure to be there.

He wasn't disappointed. He parked in a nearly empty parking lot near the sand, just a block or so from the pier, and left his shoes in the car. His cut-offs and tank top were all he needed in the warm, salty air, even with the whisper of a breeze that blew in off the ocean.

Seagulls swooped and called to him as he made his way down the beach, but he hardly noticed them. And for once he was able to block out the burden of Jasmine and all the others trapped in such a horrific lifestyle. Jesus had become real to him—personal—and he no longer struggled with accepting what he'd once thought of as his parents' faith. It was his now, and nothing could take that from him. It was a joy he'd never experienced in all his years of sitting in church and Sunday school, or talking with his family about God. His heart had become new, and he recognized he would never be the same.

Wherever You take me, God, he thought, *it will be the right place. I know that now. And I know You have a good plan for my life. All I want to do is fulfill it. The rest just doesn't matter anymore.*

The cool water lapped at his toes, but he kept walking, feeling lighter than he'd ever imagined possible. For now, he just wanted to enjoy his newfound relationship with God; together they would face the rest later.

Chapter 35

I'M ONLY FOURTEEN," JOLENE WHIMPERED, AS MARA brushed the girl's long auburn curls in an effort to make her as enticing as possible for her first night's work. Mara had received her assignment directly from Jefe: capitalize on Jolene's youth but dress her as skimpily as possible. The two of them would serve a well-to-do customer together, a man known for paying well when he got what he wanted. Unfortunately he was also known for a sadistic streak, though he'd never seriously injured anyone . . . yet.

Mara sighed impatiently. "Hold still," she ordered, pulling back the sides of Jolene's hair and tying them together with a pink ribbon. She was certain Jefe would approve of the little girl look, combined with a very tight, short green dress that complemented Jolene's eyes and shimmered when she moved. The stiletto heels completed the look, though Mara imagined she'd have to help the girl balance when she walked. "And to tell you the truth, I don't care how old you are. Only fourteen? I thought you were about twelve. Either way, you're a lot older than I was when I started in this business."

The girl's head snapped around, her eyes huge as she registered her shock. "You were younger than me? Seriously?"

"Seriously." Mara yanked Jolene's hair until her charge turned back around and sat still. "Now let me get done here. We have to go. Jefe does *not* like to be kept waiting."

Jolene didn't move again as she asked, "But...how old were you?"

Mara shrugged. "Five or six. I'm not sure. It doesn't matter. It was a long time ago, and I had nothing to say about it. I still don't...and neither do you. So stop fighting it, and maybe you won't get smacked around so often."

Jolene's shoulders shook, and Mara knew the girl was crying again. Great! Not only did Jefe not like to be kept waiting, but he did not want his girls showing up with red eyes either.

"Listen," she said, smacking the girl lightly on the back of the head. "Those tears have got to stop. You're only making it worse for yourself—and for me. If Jefe can tell you've been crying again, we're both going to catch it. Understand?" When Jolene didn't answer but continued to sob quietly, Mara hit the back of her head again, a little harder this time. "I said, do you understand?"

Jolene hesitated only slightly before nodding. "Yes," she whispered. "I understand. And I'm trying not to cry, but..."

"But nothing," Mara scolded, coming around front to face the girl. "Look at me."

Jolene raised her head. Her eyes were still wet, and tears trickled down her made-up face, but at least the damage was fixable.

"I'm only going to say this once," Mara said. "I'm trying to save your life—and mine. So you'd better cooperate and stop crying right now. You're going to do exactly what you're told tonight, and every night after that. And get it through your head that no one cares how old you are. We have girls here younger than you, and two boys too. So knock off the pity party and get to work, just like the rest of us. Got it?"

Jolene swallowed, and her shoulders shook one last time as she took a deep breath and nodded. "Yes. I got it."

"Good." Mara grabbed a tissue and dabbed at the girl's face in an effort to wipe away the tears without damaging her makeup. "Now, let's get going. The longer we keep Jefe and our client waiting, the worse it will be for both of us."

Michael would have preferred to wait and have the second meeting for the ministry to human trafficking victims on Sunday afternoon again, but it seemed everyone except his family would be out of town or in some other way occupied and unable to attend. As it was, everyone was able to come Friday evening except Jonathan, who was working, and so the same handful of people who had met together for the first time on Sunday now gathered at the church to pursue their plans.

Michael was both pleased and relieved that Barbara had agreed to co-lead the group with him. He was even more relieved to see her occupying a front-row seat when he and Rosanna and Leah entered the room. The Comptons were huddled together in the same seats they'd settled into the first week, but at least Randy had moved up from the back row to sit right behind Barbara. Celia and Monica were also there.

No new faces, Michael thought. *I'd hoped some others would join us, but at least none of the originals have baled, so that's encouraging. We're all here—except for Jonathan. I really hate for him to have to miss, but I know he needs the money and can't afford to take off of work... especially on a Friday night. I'll just have to fill him in tomorrow.*

He took a deep breath and stepped to the front of the room, as Rosanna and Leah sat down in the front row next to

Barbara. Michael knew that Barbara planned to present her suggestion to join with one of the three existing human trafficking outreaches in the area, outlining each one and letting the group choose. It sounded like a good plan to him. No sense reinventing the wheel.

He smiled and welcomed the group, and then bowed his head in prayer. It was time to get started.

Jonathan could feel his muscles tense and his stomach churn, though he willed them to stop. After all, a pizza delivery at a motel was hardly an unusual event. And it wasn't like anyone would suspect him of being there for any reason other than to deliver pizza, especially now that his boss had insisted they put the plastic "Slice of Italy Pizza" sign on top of the car whenever they were working. But why did he have to come to this motel? The memories were just too strong.

"Help me, Lord," he whispered as he turned down the block leading to the motel where he'd encountered Jasmine fleeing toward him, her face contorted with fear. Would he ever be able to forget that haunting image, knowing he'd done nothing to help her? Where was she now? Was she all right? Would the police be able to find her and return her to her parents? When Jonathan had told the police about the incident, they'd said it wasn't unusual for trafficking rings to frequent certain locations, including motels. Jonathan imagined they were checking into this one, talking with the owner and managers, and patrolling the area more often.

He pulled into the parking lot, near the office, and shut off the engine. There sure weren't any patrol cars in sight now. Somehow he'd thought there would be.

Exiting his car, he reached into the back and retrieved the order—two pizzas, one with everything and one cheese only—and scanned the room numbers until he located the right one. Upstairs, not far from the spot where he'd seen the two girls and the man who had claimed to be their father. Willing his heart to return to its normal rate, he approached the stairs and began to climb. Muffled sounds of indistinguishable TV shows drifted from various rooms, but otherwise, it was a relatively quiet Friday evening—except for the music coming from one of the rooms farther down the hall. It wasn't extremely loud, but the pulsating beat was sensual and repetitive. Jonathan determined to ignore it as he reached his destination and knocked on the door.

The family that greeted him—father, mother, and two adolescent boys—paid him quickly and gave him a substantial tip, as the boys tore into the cheese only pizza before the parents could close the door to join them. Jonathan smiled to himself as he turned away and headed back down the stairwell. It didn't seem that long ago that he was that age, getting excited about pizza and dreaming of a career in the major leagues. A lot had changed since then, most of it in the past couple of weeks.

Back in his car, he steered toward the street, determined to block out the thoughts that danced through his mind. Out on the street he slowed to a stop and stared up at the second story of the motel, wondering what he'd do if once again he spotted those two girls—or any girls, for that matter—racing from a motel room. Would he have the courage to help them next time? Even if he did, would it be the wise thing to do?

Father, he prayed. *When I'm supposed to do anything, please show me.* He sighed, tapped the accelerator, and drove away.

Chapter 36

ENFORCER STEERED THE VAN ONTO THE STREET IN FRONT of the motel just as a familiar looking VW Beetle turned off the street and drove off into the night. Why had the car seemed familiar? Was it just because there weren't many of them left, or . . . ?

He slammed on the brake. Of course! It was the pizza delivery car that had been parked out in front of the motel one night recently, with some young guy sitting inside, and then he'd seen it again when he snatched that flyer off the pole. Jasmine had finally admitted she had tried to get help from some pizza delivery man. Could this be the one? Jefe had warned him too many times not to ignore coincidences that just didn't make sense. And this was one of them.

He glanced up at the second story of the motel. All was quiet. Mara and the new girl weren't going anywhere, so they could just wait a little longer for him to pick them up.

As fast as he was able in the large vehicle, he hung a U-turn and drove through the stop sign and down the street in the direction he'd seen the VW disappear. He just hoped he could catch up with it.

Yes! There it was. He'd recognize those little red VW taillights anywhere. The guy was less than a block ahead of him. Enforcer was going to find out where the guy was headed, and even if he couldn't confront him tonight, he'd catch up with him sooner or later. All he had to do was get close enough to read the sign he'd seen on top of the car—

He was closing in on the smaller vehicle when his phone beeped. Cursing, he flipped it open and pressed it to his left ear—the only ear he had left, he reminded himself. "Yeah?"

"Yeah, what?" came the response.

Enforcer took a deep breath before answering. "Yeah, Jefe," he said.

"That's better. Where are you?"

He considered telling his boss why he was heading away from the motel rather than toward it, but thought better of it. "I'm... just a few blocks away from the pickup."

"Good. Get over there, quick. The motel manager called and said things are getting kinda rowdy up there. You know he doesn't like to attract attention with too much noise—and neither do I, especially now that the cops are nosing around more often. Looks like we're going to have to consider changing locations again soon. Meanwhile, get up there. Now."

Enforcer squinted his eyes, straining to read the sign on the car ahead of him. "Slice of Italy Pizza." Good. Now he knew where the kid worked. That was enough for now, though he would have preferred to settle the situation tonight.

He watched the taillights grow smaller as the distance between his van and the VW increased. He sighed, biting back the words he wanted to say. "I'm on it, Jefe."

"See that you are. I don't want any trouble, understand?"

"I understand." Enforcer flipped the phone shut and cursed again before slowing down and turning back toward the motel. Whatever Jefe wanted, Jefe got. Enforcer clenched his jaw. First chance that came along, all that would change. For now, he would do what he was told. He didn't want to risk losing another ear—or worse.

The early morning bouts of nausea were becoming more violent, but Chanthra had dealt with them before. She knew what she had to do, though she dreaded it. She had no choice; she must tell the boss man that she was pregnant again—and he wouldn't be happy. Several days of lost business and income would be the result for him, as well as a painful procedure for Chanthra and the loss of yet another life, as new and tiny as it was. Chanthra told herself it was ultimately for the best, for even if she were allowed to give birth to the baby, what sort of life would it have? As soon as he or she was old enough, the child would be used for the perverted pleasure of Chanthra's owner. No, it was a kindness to end its life now, though Chanthra dreaded the pain she would endure as the abortion was done without any anesthetic.

She glanced at her pipe. Last time she'd been given an extra portion and allowed to smoke before Adung began the operation; Chanthra prayed she'd be afforded the same privilege again. As bad as she knew it would be, it would undoubtedly be worse without her pipe.

A moan caught her attention, and she turned toward the sound. Lawan still slept, exhausted from a long night's work. The young girl was very popular with the customers and often entertained more men in one evening than Chanthra had ever done. She wondered how long her little companion would survive such abuse. Would it be a blessing if she too passed on from this life quickly, even as the baby inside Chanthra would do within hours of the boss finding out of its existence?

Lawan twitched and cried out, though it was obvious she still slept. Chanthra's heart yearned to go to her and comfort her, but what could she do? What comfort could she offer the child? There was none in this place. Only the comfort of the pipe... nothing more.

Chanthra pulled her attention from Lawan and picked up her pipe, thinking to blur her reality as much as possible before doing what she knew she must, but a wave of nausea swept over her again, and she heaved what little was left of last night's dinner into the filthy pail beside her mattress.

Mara tried in vain to sleep on one of the two double beds in the room, even as Jolene's sobs and whimpers continued in the bed next to her. The middle-aged man who had been their date for the evening had shown an immediate preference for the new, younger girl and had scarcely paid any attention to Mara at all.

Fine with me, she'd told herself, glad to be away from the man as she steeled her heart against the compassion she felt for Jolene. It would only get them both in trouble. She knew that and turned her head away so she couldn't see, even in the nearly dark room, what was going on just a few feet from her.

"Please don't hurt me again."

The begging and pleading was the toughest part for Mara to ignore, worse even than when the man had grown angry with Jolene and thrown her to the floor, causing a loud crash and bringing forth a cry of pain and fear from the wounded girl. It was after that when Jolene had begun to beg for mercy, but Mara knew it was pointless. She'd long ago given up expecting mercy from those who saw no reason to give it. Jolene would soon learn the same lesson, but meanwhile it was painful to listen to her.

Thoughts of Jasmine vied with Jolene's whimpers for Mara's attention. Mara squeezed her eyes shut tight, as if she could block out Jasmine's face or Jolene's pain. It hadn't been but a few nights earlier when Mara and Jasmine had huddled together in an identical room in this very motel and Mara had told her companion about The Reeds, warning her never to go there under any circumstances. A pointless warning, she realized, as the girl hadn't lived long enough to get near the place. Was Jasmine the lucky one after all? Listening to Jolene's pitiful sounds behind her, Mara couldn't help but think that was so.

No way out, she told herself silently. *No way... unless Jefe is dead—*

The knock on the door interrupted her thoughts, as well as the whimpering from the other side of the room. The man cursed and yelled, "Who is it? We're busy in here."

The familiar voice was low. "It's me, Enforcer. Let me in."

More cursing accompanied the man as he slid into his clothes and padded to the door, opening it just a crack but leaving the chain lock attached.

"What are you doing here?" the man demanded, his voice lowered only slightly. "I paid for six hours. I've still got nearly half of that left."

"Open the door," Enforcer insisted. "I'm not going to talk out here where everyone can hear me. Besides, you're not supposed to use the chain locks. I'm supposed to have access at any time."

"Whatever." Grumbling, the man opened the door and then shut it as soon as Enforcer had stepped inside. "Make it quick," he said, glancing toward the bed where Jolene lay, quiet now. "I'm in the middle of something."

Mara watched in the dim light as Enforcer's eyes swept the room. He snorted. "Yeah, so I see." He redirected his attention to the shorter, smaller man in front of him. "Listen, what you do up here is your business. You paid, and you can do whatever you want with the girls—except cause any serious damage. It doesn't look like that's the case, so go ahead and finish what you paid for. But keep the noise down, will you? Jefe got a complaint from the manager, and he doesn't like that."

"Hey, can I help it if the young one cries all the time?" the man demanded. "You oughta teach your girls to keep quiet."

Enforcer's gaze moved in the direction of Jolene, and he nodded. "She's new," he explained. "We're still training her. Next time bring duct tape or something." He pointed at Jolene. "For now, you shut up, you hear me? If we get any more complaints, they're coming out of your hide. Got it?"

Then he turned toward Mara. "That goes for you too. Keep her quiet, or this time you won't get off as easy as you did with the other one."

Mara swallowed. The threat of punishment for what Jefe and Enforcer saw as her failure with Jasmine had just been compounded by the possibility of her failing with Jolene as well. She'd better not take anymore chances. If she got sent out on a date with Jolene again, Mara would bring the duct tape herself.

Chapter 37

Rosanna was up early, even though it was Saturday and she didn't need to be. It had been quite a while since she'd made a big breakfast for her entire family, and she'd wakened thinking about how few chances she'd have to do so once Jonathan left for college. And so she'd bounded out of bed and hurried downstairs to start chopping veggies for omelets and melons and pineapple for a fruit salad.

As she stood at the sink preparing the food and watching through the window as the sun burned through the thin marine layer, she smiled. It was going to be another gorgeous San Diego day, and she was going to be sure it started off right. A nice time of visiting and eating around the table was the best imaginable way to kick it off. If that sun did its job and completely dispensed with the fog by the time the food was ready, she might even set the table outside on the patio. They hadn't had breakfast out there in ages!

She heard the shower go on upstairs as she retrieved the eggs from the refrigerator. Right on time! She could count on Michael to wake up within twenty or thirty minutes after she got up. He said he just couldn't sleep without her there and always knew when the bed was empty. Apparently that was true, as she hadn't been downstairs long and already he was awake.

Cracking the eggs into a bowl, she smiled at the memory of how pleased Michael had been at the meeting the night before. Though they hadn't had any newcomers to add to their numbers, neither had they had any dropouts. And the mood had changed dramatically since the opening of their first gathering the week before. She and Michael agreed that everyone there had seemed enthusiastic about joining with one of the existing groups already working with trafficking victims, providing housing and exit counseling and even job training so those so deeply wounded could find healing and a new place and purpose for their lives. Even Randy's previously negative and skeptical attitude had changed, and he seemed anxious to get started, as did they all.

Rosanna retrieved the whisk from a nearby drawer and began to beat the eggs. Like Michael, she was sorry Jonathan hadn't been able to attend the meeting, but they understood that he'd had to work. She glanced back out the window. There was his car, the "Slice of Italy Pizza" sign still perched on top. He was supposed to take it off when he wasn't working, but he'd probably been tired when he got home and just forgot. But for now, what could it hurt if it stayed on a little longer? After all, the car was safely home in their own driveway.

She smiled. It was going to be a great day. Now to make sure the rest of the family was awake so they could all eat together.

Saturday had passed in a haze, with Chanthra floating in and out of consciousness, grabbing for her pipe each time the pain became too intense, which was most of the time. The memories of the actual procedure were too horrific, even in her drug-induced fog, to allow herself to relive. Adung had been rougher even than in the past, seemingly angry that Chanthra had gotten into such a predicament again. But how could she have prevented it? It wasn't as if she had a choice in the matter. The actions that led up to her pregnancy were forced upon her, night after endless night, though it did no good to attempt to offer such an excuse. If the boss man and his assistant, Adung, said it was your fault, then it was, and there was nothing to be said or done about it except as they decided.

In addition to blocking out the memory of the painful procedure, Chanthra also refused to allow herself to think of the life that had been ended in the process. She knew Adung threw out the remains with the day's trash, and all Chanthra could do was pray that the baby who never saw the light of day now lived with the Light of the world.

My maae used to call You that, she thought, wondering if her disjointed musings counted as a prayer. *The Light of the world. She said she heard that from somebody once... can't remember who. Light. Oh, how I wish for Your Light in this dark place!*

She heard herself moan and was surprised that she had made a sound. She was usually quite disciplined in keeping her thoughts and feelings to herself. Now she felt a light touch on her arm, and she turned her head. A vision of Lawan's face swam and swirled into view. The girl's mouth was moving. Was she speaking to her? She strained to concentrate.

"I'm here," the young girl whispered, her voice soothing. "I've been here, praying for you, all day. Even tonight, when... when I'm working, I'll still be praying."

Comfort, warm and oozing, seemed to slide down Chanthra's body, beginning at the top of her head and working its way down to her toes, erasing even the agony that had ripped at her insides for hours. Dear Lawan! The girl had become like a sister to Chanthra, and her presence meant more than she would ever have imagined. Thank goodness the child was still too young to experience what Chanthra had been through today, though if she lived long enough, her time would surely come. The thought forced hot tears from Chanthra's eyes, and she knew at that moment that she'd gladly give up her own life if poor little Lawan could somehow escape.

Light of the world. Was it possible that *phra yaeh suu* still cared for her and was somehow shining into this dark place through Lawan, who now prayed for Chanthra? She imagined it was just the effects of her pipe that allowed her to consider such a thing, but oh, how she wished it could be true!

Jefe stubbed out another smoldering cigarette butt in the ashtray beside his bed and pulled himself to a sitting position. He knew he should probably quit smoking. The coughing that woke him up in the mornings was getting worse, but the only thing he wanted when he opened his eyes was a drink of tequila and a smoke. Why should he deny himself? He worked hard, didn't he? He had a lot of responsibility and stress, and he needed something to ease all that. Too many people depended on him to keep them fed and clothed and a roof over their heads, including his own niece. Did they appreciate all he did for them? He doubted it.

He threw his legs over the side of the bed and sighed. Though he'd had the company of one of the two male slaves in the compound last night, he'd sent him back to his room after only a few hours. The boy was bruised and battered, but not enough that he wouldn't be able to return to work that evening. Jefe had enjoyed the entertainment for a while, but he got bored quickly and always made it a point to sleep alone, with his door locked. He had never trusted anyone, and he saw no reason to change that policy now.

He picked up his cell phone and dialed the kitchen number. Destroyer answered.

"Who's cooking this morning?" Jefe asked.

"Mara and Jolene," came the answer. "You said Mara should train the new girl in everything, so we figured that meant cooking too."

Jefe smiled. Maybe today wouldn't be such a bad day after all. His coughing had eased up, and he was starting to feel a few hunger pangs.

"Tell Mara to bring me some coffee," he said. "And some steak and eggs. And tell her to be quick about it. I'm hungry."

"Sure, boss. Anything else?"

Jefe chuckled. "Yeah. Tell her to bring the new girl with her. I want her to feed me . . . personally."

After a brief pause Destroyer said, "You want them both? What about breakfast? Who's going to finish cooking?"

Jefe scowled. This was the perfect example of the insolence and ingratitude he dealt with daily. When would they learn?

"You do it," he said.

"Me?"

"You. And do it right, or you just might end up with a lopsided head like Enforcer."

Picturing the furious look that no doubt covered Destroyer's face at that moment, Jefe laughed aloud and clicked the phone shut. They might not appreciate all he did for them, but they would definitely obey him.

Chapter 38

LEAH HAD BEEN PLEASANTLY SURPRISED BY THE SPREAD that had awaited her when she descended the stairs that morning. Her mother hadn't gone all out with a family breakfast like that in a long while, and eating it outside in the morning sunshine had been an added bonus.

She smiled as she rang the bell at the Johnsons' front door. Though her mother hadn't said as much, obviously the breakfast event had been spurred by the realization that they wouldn't have many more occasions like that before Jonathan left. That unspoken knowledge, which they all shared but didn't address, had made their time together that much sweeter, as they discussed everything from the weather to human trafficking to the ridiculous looking pizza sign Jonathan was required to sport on top of his dilapidated Beetle.

The door opened, bringing Leah back to the present. Nyesha Johnson greeted her, the milk chocolate color of her skin glowing in the sun, which was now almost directly overhead.

"Come on in, Leah," she said. "Anna will be thrilled to see you, as always. I didn't tell her you were coming because I knew she'd never eat her breakfast or take her midmorning nap. She should be waking up any minute now."

Leah stepped inside, the coolness of the entryway contrasting with the warmth of Nyesha's welcome. "I was pretty excited about coming myself," she admitted. "I love spending time with Anna."

Leah followed Nyesha into the kitchen, where Leah once again marveled at the stunning color scheme of the room. It was as if God Himself had splashed the walls with bright autumn leaves and sprinkled the air with heavenly gold dust. Nyesha had told her when they first met that she loved bright, bold colors, and it showed in the way she dressed, as well as the way she decorated her home. Leah had teased that perhaps that was why they had such a beautiful "rainbow family"—one white, one black, one Asian—and Nyesha had admitted she just might be right.

At Nyesha's invitation, Leah plunked down on the bench in the breakfast nook, wondering for what she imagined was the thousandth time if it was fair or right for her to accept payment for something she so enjoyed doing. She'd told both Nyesha and Kyle that she'd babysit Anna for free, but they wouldn't hear of it. And so she had decided that she must have the most perfect job in the entire world.

Nyesha placed two glasses of lemonade on the table and sat down across from her. "So," she said, "tell me about Jonathan's graduation. How was it?"

As Leah related the details, Nyesha listened intently, bursting into laughter when she heard about the junior varsity football team showing up in girls' cheerleader outfits to lead a humorous salute to the graduates at the end of the ceremony. Leah loved that Nyesha could laugh at the teenagers' antics; some of the adults had been offended by what they considered a lack of decorum and respect for a serious occasion. Thankfully Leah's parents hadn't been among those offended by the incident.

"What else is new in your life?" Nyesha asked. "We never get much chance to talk with Anna around, but I'd love to know what you're doing these days."

Leah was touched that this mature woman cared enough to inquire about the personal life of a teenager, but then that's just the way Nyesha was. Leah took another sip of her tart but refreshing drink and launched into an explanation of the new human trafficking outreach that she and her family were helping to start at the church. The entire time she spoke, Nyesha's dark eyes glistened with tears.

"This is so close to my heart," Nyesha said. "Kyle and I even considered coming to the meeting and getting involved ourselves, but I... I just couldn't bring myself to do it." She paused, closing her eyes for just a moment before continuing. "I've told you some of the story about how we got Anna, but not many of the details. There was a reason for that, your age being one of them, but also because I want to protect Anna and keep her story as private as possible. However, since you're getting involved in this ministry with your family, I think it's OK for you to know."

Leah frowned. It was obvious that Nyesha was quite serious about what she was going to tell her, and she was flattered that the woman considered her mature enough to hear it.

"Anna's Thai name is Mali, which means Flower. I think I've already told you that much, haven't I?"

Leah nodded.

"Anna is the youngest of three girls from a very poor family. We never met them, but we learned all this from the agency that set up the adoption. The family was adamant that they know details about Anna's adoption to be sure everything was legal and in order." She dropped her eyes before looking up and continuing. The tears that had pooled in her eyes earlier now dripped down her cheeks. Leah handed her a napkin to wipe them away, and Nyesha took it without missing a beat.

"It seems the family was near starvation and was afraid their firstborn daughter, who was five or six at the time, would die. When someone came to them, claiming to be from an adoption agency, and offered to pay them a nominal amount to place the child with a well-to-do family, the poor parents agreed. They were supposed to receive updates on the girl's progress, but they never heard another word. They had another child before Anna, but when they realized they simply couldn't afford to feed both of them, they decided it would be easier to find a legitimate home for the younger girl. This time they went through a reputable agency, and I understand they receive periodic updates on Anna's—Mali's—situation. Sadly, I recently learned from the agency that their remaining daughter has disappeared. They fear she's been kidnapped and possibly sold into prostitution."

Leah gasped. Anna's sister? A prostitute? "How...how old is she?"

"About seven or eight, I believe."

Seven or eight? The thought nearly sucked the breath from Leah's lungs. Her mind moved quickly from the disappearance of the one sister to the apparently shady adoption of the oldest girl. Was it possible she too had been sucked into the ugly human trafficking scene? Suddenly the reminder that modern-day slavery was about more than nameless, faceless victims swept over her, as she fought a wave of nausea.

Nyesha reached across the table and laid her hand on Leah's. "I'm sorry. Maybe I shouldn't have told you all this after all."

Leah shook her head. "No. I'm glad you did. Really. I need to know it if I'm going to get involved in this ministry. And I guess, deep down, I did know it, but..."

"I know. It's when it becomes personal that the ugliness of it all nearly overwhelms us. I'm afraid that's why I didn't come to the meetings at the church. I'm afraid I'd never let Anna out of my sight again, even for a moment."

Leah nodded. The realization that one or both of little Anna's sisters might be trapped in such a hideous life nearly made her crazy. Something had to be done to stop this evil thing that apparently permeated every corner of the world. But she was only one person, a teenager who hadn't even finished high school. How could she possibly be any help?

"Mommy?"

The tiny voice from the sleepy little girl who stood in the doorway, rubbing her eyes and holding her favorite stuffed teddy bear under her arm, changed quickly as the child's dark eyes opened wide in recognition. "Leah?"

Leah pushed her previous thoughts from her mind and held out her arms to the three-year-old who had escaped what her sisters may not have. The child squealed in obvious delight and scampered into Leah's embrace, still clutching her teddy bear with one hand.

"You came! You came!" Anna cried, bouncing on Leah's lap.

The teenager laughed, her heart light once again. "I sure did," she said. "And I'm so glad you woke up. I'm going to stay with you for a while this afternoon while your mommy and daddy take care of some errands and shopping. What do you think of that?"

Anna's eyes lit up, and her dimples deepened as she dropped her bear and clapped her hands together. "Yay, God!" she cried.

Nyesha and Leah laughed. Yay, God, indeed! It was going to be a fun afternoon, and Leah breathed a silent prayer of thanks.

Enforcer was not a happy camper. Jefe had sent him on so many errands and demanded they be done in such a short span of time that he hadn't even had time to stop for lunch. And if there was one thing Enforcer especially hated it was missing a meal.

Driving the van back toward the compound from his last stop, the windows down to enjoy the warm afternoon sunshine, he wondered if he had time to at least stop at a drive-through somewhere and grab a quick sandwich. If he didn't, it would be hours before he had a chance to eat again. As soon as he got back to the compound, Jefe would have him delivering the merchandise to various spots—the usual motel as well as a couple others—and he was forbidden to stop anywhere with them in the car.

He glanced at his watch and cursed. He was late already, and Jefe would be furious if he didn't get back immediately. It didn't matter that the reason he was running behind was because Jefe had given him too much to do and not enough time to do it. Logic didn't work with Jefe; the man saw all explanations as attempted excuses, and dealt with them accordingly. Enforcer decided it was better to be safe than sorry. He'd just have to get back as quickly as possible and let his stomach growl until he delivered the last girl this evening. Then he could go eat at his leisure.

He had no sooner made that decision than he turned the corner and got hit with the tantalizing aroma of freshly baked pizza. His favorite food! He'd know that smell anywhere. He glanced to the right and then the left, and sure enough, a little hole-in-the-wall Italian place greeted him enticingly.

Enforcer's mouth watered. "Slice of Italy Pizza" the sign read, and Enforcer could almost taste the pizza. Those little obscure places that had been around forever, as this one appeared to have been, always had the best food.

Wait a minute. Slice of Italy Pizza? Wasn't that what that plastic sign said on top of that old VW Bug he'd seen hanging around the motel lately? Yeah, he was sure of it. This was the place the kid worked. He nearly laughed out loud. So, tonight he'd kill two birds with one stone. The minute he got through delivering the girls for their evening's work, he'd head right back to Slice of Italy Pizza for a long-overdue dinner...and a confrontation with the guy who'd been turning up in the same place way too often lately. The kid had better be able to convince him that he'd just had a lot of deliveries in the area, or Enforcer would have to find a way to make him tell the truth.

Sunday morning in the Golden Triangle dawned muggy and still. No breeze lifted the filthy curtains or blew through the bars of the room's only window. But Chanthra didn't even notice. She knew only that she was on fire, burning slowly and painfully, with no end in sight. A small girl sat beside her, periodically mopping her head with a wet rag. Who was she, and why was she crying? Even more puzzling, why was she praying and singing about *phra yaeh suu*? The only time the child left Chanthra's side was when the older woman came into the room. Quickly the girl scurried to the mattress a few feet away, but her eyes remained on Chanthra while the woman laid her hand on Chanthra's forehead and clucked in obvious disapproval.

Chanthra knew she should know the woman's name—the child's too—but the fire was too great. She couldn't concentrate, couldn't think, couldn't do anything but moan and beg for water. The pain inside her was almost greater than the pain of the fire—almost, but not quite. Where was her pipe? That would help, she was sure of it. But when she ordered her hand to reach for it, nothing happened. Why didn't someone help her? Did this mean she was dying? Was she already feeling the flames of hell? Her mother had told her she would go to heaven when she died because she had accepted *phra yaeh suu* as her Savior. But had He accepted her? Oh, how she prayed He had, for she had no other hope.

The woman was gone now, and the child was back. Chanthra sighed. The pain in her body did not ebb with the girl's presence, but the ache in her heart did. For that, she was grateful.

Chapter 39

IT WAS TURNING OUT TO BE ONE OF THE NICEST SATURDAYS Jonathan could remember in a very long time. Sharing breakfast outside on the patio with his parents and sister had started it off with a bang, and then he'd had a call from a couple of his buddies looking for someone to join them for a few quick innings. He'd accepted in a heartbeat.

"Burn one in, Flannery!"

"Show us what you got, Big Red!"

Jonathan ignored the catcalls and the Big Red nickname he'd been stuck with since he'd first gotten involved in sports—which was at a fairly young age. Even now, with his focus on Bible college and the new ministry to victims of human trafficking, his love of baseball still set his heart to pumping with excitement. He supposed he'd always enjoy the feel of a ball in his right hand and the sounds of the crowd chatter ringing in his ears. But no longer was the game his greatest passion. Turning his life over to Christ, once and for all, had changed everything.

He reared back and let one fly, the round missile slicing through the air so fast he could have sworn he heard it whistle.

"Strike three!"

He'd done it again, struck out three batters in the bottom of the ninth, resulting in numerous pats on the back and "atta boys." But now it was time to go home and grab a quick shower before heading for work.

Less than an hour later, after scarcely stopping long enough to say hello and good-bye to his parents as he zipped in and out, he left the house, freshly scrubbed and ready to deliver pizzas. With the "Slice of Italy Pizza" sign firmly attached to the top of his car, he putted down the street, whistling and tapping his fingers on the steering wheel, reminding himself yet again that one day he just might be able to put a radio in his ride.

He was still whistling as he opened the back door and stepped into the steamy kitchen where the smell of tomatoes and garlic had become a permanent fixture. Jonathan's boss, Sal, intercepted him before he could check the delivery list.

"The cops were here," he said, his meaty face redder than usual as he squinted in what appeared to be a mixture of curiosity and suspicion. "They want to talk to you—ASAP." Sal raised an eyebrow. "Any idea what that's about?"

Jonathan smiled as reassuringly as he could. "Not a problem," he said. "I made a report about something I saw a few days ago, and they said they'd be in touch. Probably have a few more questions for me or something."

Sal studied him a moment before answering. "OK, kid. If you say so. You're a good worker, and I got no reason not to believe you." He reached in his pants pocket and pulled out a card. "This guy said for you to stop by the station and ask for him. I told him you'd probably come by on your break later this evening, and he said that'd be fine."

Jonathan nodded and glanced at the card before slipping it into his wallet. He'd get some deliveries made and then stop by the station on his break, as Sal suggested. No doubt it was just routine, but he'd feel a lot better once he knew that for sure.

Jonathan had no sooner raced through the house and headed off to work than the doorbell rang. Michael and Rosanna, sitting in the family room discussing various subjects, not the least of which was the new outreach to trafficking victims, stopped midsentence and eyed one another in surprise.

"You expecting anyone?" Rosanna asked.

Michael shook his head. "Apparently you're not either."

"Not that I can think of. Leah's at the Johnsons' place babysitting, and Jonathan's gone to work. Besides, both of them have keys."

Michael smiled. "Well, I guess there's only one way to find out who it is, right?"

He stood to his feet and headed for the entryway, with Rosanna following close behind. When Michael opened the door, Rosanna was pleased to see Barbara from church, standing there with a pink box and a smile.

"Forgive me for not calling first," she said, "but I was on my way home from a women's luncheon with this leftover pie . . ." She indicated the box in her hands. "They insisted I take it, though I couldn't imagine what I'd do with an entire pie. But I was driving past your house and thought why not take a chance and see if they're home? Maybe they'd be willing to help me out with all this dessert!"

Michael laughed and opened the door wider. "You came to the right place," he said as she stepped inside and leaned over the box to return Rosanna's hug. Michael took the pie from her and carried it to the kitchen, while the ladies followed. Rosanna often had to fight resentment when her time with Michael was interrupted, but Barbara was a delightful woman—and besides, she'd brought pie. How could she not be pleased at such a turn of events?

In moments they were gathered around the little maple table in the corner of the kitchen, sipping iced tea and savoring peach pie. Rosanna couldn't help but think that Jonathan and Leah would love to have been there to join them.

"I must confess," Barbara said between bites, "that this was a great excuse to stop by and talk to you both about last night's meeting. I thought it went very well, didn't you?"

"It sure did," Michael agreed. "All the tension from the first one was gone, and thanks to you, I feel like we have some direction now."

Rosanna nodded. "I agree completely. That first meeting was a bit rocky, at least at first—until Celia stood up and shared her story. And now that you've given us some options of local ministries already established in this outreach, I think we're on the right track."

"I'm so glad you both agree," Barbara said. "And I'm thrilled that your kids want to get involved too. This is a major fight we're entering into, and it's not without danger. We're up against some heavy hitters, some really rough people with a lot of money that won't go down easily. We've got to decide now that we're in it for the long haul, and we need to pull together with others in the same battle. But remember, we have a Captain who's leading us, and we're going to win. We have to believe that." She leaned over her plate, her pale blue eyes shining. "It's the only hope for the millions of people enslaved around the world. Abolition! We can settle for nothing less."

Rosanna watched her husband's face as he nodded. She knew that determined look, and she agreed with him completely.

Finally! Enforcer had dropped off the last girl and didn't have to be back to pick any of them up for several hours. Nothing was going to stop him now. He was headed for Little

Slice of Italy to satisfy his growling stomach—and to see if he could spot that weasel of a kid who drove the VW and hung out near the motel.

Traffic was light as he took the back roads toward the restaurant, and the only thing that could stop him now would be a last-minute call from Jefe, wanting him to run another errand or bring him something to eat. He considered turning off his phone, but the price he'd pay if Jefe called and Enforcer didn't answer was just too high. He'd leave it on and take his chances.

In less than ten minutes he was standing at the counter in the cramped building, where the handful of tables and benches were all full. He waited behind a family who couldn't seem to decide if they wanted their pizza with or without mushrooms. It was all he could do not to push them all aside and demand some service before he passed out from hunger.

At last it was his turn. A small sausage and mushroom pizza and a cold soda sounded better than a filet mignon at the moment, and he gladly slapped his money down on the counter to pay for it. Another ten minutes and he was back in his van, digging in while he watched the parking lot for the familiar car.

He didn't have to wait long. He was halfway through his meal when the old blue Bug came rolling in. Enforcer watched closely as the tall kid unfolded himself from the driver's seat and headed into the pizzeria. In moments he was back, but this time without a pile of pizzas in his hands. The kid jumped back in his car, and Enforcer realized he was leaving. Was he off work already? Enforcer jammed what was left of his meal back into the box and started the engine. No way was he letting the kid get away without finding out why he spent so much time at the motel.

Rolling out of the driveway just seconds after the VW left, Enforcer followed at a safe distance, knowing that if he recognized the kid, the kid might recognize him as well. But he was trained at following people without being spotted, and he hung back just far enough not to be seen. He began to think the kid was heading home, which would be great. Enforcer could imagine nothing better than knowing where this bozo lived and being able to use that information any time he wanted. And then, in an instant, it all changed.

The police station? The kid is going to the police station?

Sure enough, the Volkswagen pulled into the parking lot next to the station, and the tall kid got out and headed for the front door. Quite obviously Enforcer wasn't going to be able to confront him now, but at least he'd confirmed his suspicions that the pizza delivery guy was trouble with a capital *T*. And he also knew where the kid worked and what his car looked like. It was just a matter of time until the two of them met face to face. And Enforcer would make sure that time came very soon.

Chapter 40

It was going to be a long night. Jonathan still had several pizzas to deliver over the next few hours before he could even think about going home. But it wasn't going to be easy to concentrate. All he could think about was the meeting he'd had with the detective at the police station.

They found a body. He shivered, despite the warm night air. A young girl—twelve or thirteen, they said. Thin. Frail. Battered. Possibly beaten to death. Oh, God! Is it her? Is it Jasmine?

Though his lunch break had come and gone, Jonathan hadn't even considered eating anything after leaving the station. How could he think about food when Jasmine's body might be lying on a cold slab at the morgue, waiting for the Littletons to come in and identify her...or not? After all, it could be another girl...couldn't it?

The possibility brought him little comfort. If it wasn't Jasmine, it was still somebody's daughter, someone's little girl whose life and dreams had been brought to a brutal end. How could he feel better about that? And besides, if it wasn't

Jasmine, that brought them no closer to knowing where she was.

He drove the dark streets, doing his job, collecting tips, and wondering if she was in one of the motel rooms he passed—either the motel where he'd seen her before or another one of the dozens that dotted the nearby neighborhoods. How widespread was this human trafficking thing? How many prostitution rings existed, right there in their own town and community? How many teenagers had disappeared over the years, only to be classified as runaways by the police when, in reality, they had been kidnapped and forced into slavery?

"Oh, Father," he whispered, "the reality of all this is darker than the night I'm driving through. You're the only source of Light, Lord, the only One who can help them. Use me, Father, any way You wish. Guide me into the purpose You have for me so my life won't be wasted. Show me what You want me to do with the years You've given me on this earth, Lord, and I'll do it—whatever it is. Thank You, Father."

His heart still heavy but hopeful, he turned down yet another street to deliver one more pizza to one more house full of hungry people. Did they realize the degradation and pain that others were going through, even as they awaited their pizza and enjoyed an evening together with family and friends? Probably not, Jonathan decided. After all, until just a couple of short weeks ago, he hadn't given it a thought either.

Enforcer's stomach was full at last, and his thoughts were hopeful as he headed toward the first pickup point to start bringing the workers back to the compound. The way he figured it, he now had an ace in the hole. If he didn't get a chance to deal with Jefe soon, he might be able to earn some brownie points by dealing with the pizza delivery kid. It seemed very possible that he might be on to them; the VW was turning up far too often to be a coincidence, and now he was making stops at the police station. But first he'd have to prove it—even if it meant getting the kid alone and beating the truth out of him.

He smiled at the thought. Beating up kids and women got old; they were too scared to put up a fight. But a tall, muscular young guy like the one nosing around the motel? He'd be more of a challenge for sure—and quite possibly a lot more fun.

Steering the van onto the familiar road that led to the motel, Enforcer was only slightly disappointed when he didn't see the beat-up Beetle sitting out front. Tonight probably wasn't the best time to corner the kid anyway. And besides, now that he knew where he worked, he could pretty much pick him off any time he wanted.

Enforcer parked the van and grinned. He might be minus an ear, but he'd even that score soon enough. Meanwhile, life wasn't really all that bad. His job provided him with enough thrills and other perks to make the rest of it worthwhile. He cracked his knuckles as he mounted the stairs. Tonight he was going to take advantage of one of those perks. All he had to do was decide which one looked the most inviting as he drove them home.

Mara had never intended to let herself get so close to the new girl, but here she was, lying on the bed with Jolene's head cradled on her shoulder. The elderly man who had been their companion for the evening snoozed peacefully in the bed next to them.

She sighed and shook her head. Men! She'd never understand them, and she'd certainly never trust them, but at least this one had been kind. Strange, yes... but kind, nonetheless. He'd paid quite a bit of money just to have the two girls sit and talk with him for several hours, and then he'd told them they could go to sleep. Pleasantly surprised and yet wary, Mara and Jolene had curled up together on one bed while their "new best friend," as he called himself, stretched out on the other and quickly began snoring. Jolene hadn't taken much longer to fall asleep herself, but Mara had lain there, alert and wondering if it was all just a ploy. Would the old man wait until they were asleep and then pounce? Or had they simply gotten away with an easy assignment tonight, a rare occasion that came along all too seldom but was always greatly appreciated?

Mara had finally decided on the latter, and now she lay beside the girl Jefe had charged her to watch, listening to her quiet, steady breathing. Why not let her rest while she could? No doubt tomorrow's appointments wouldn't be nearly as easy.

Jolene stirred, moaning as she twisted her head. Mara took advantage of the girl's movement to slide her arm from beneath Jolene's head. Mara's fingers had been starting to tingle, and she was glad for the chance to wiggle some life back into them.

"What's happening?" Jolene mumbled, and Mara turned her face toward the girl, marveling at how young she looked with her long auburn hair splayed across the pillow. Had she really been that age once? Yes, she reminded herself, and not that long ago. It only seemed longer because of the things she'd had to do in the interim.

"What do you mean?" she asked.

Jolene frowned. "Where are we? Why am I sleeping here with you?"

"Because that's what we were told to do."

Memory dawned in Jolene's expression, and she nodded. "I remember now." She pushed herself up on one elbow and peered over Mara toward the other bed. "He's sleeping too."

"Yes. Hasn't moved since he laid down."

Jolene fell back onto the pillow, obviously relieved. "Good. I hope he doesn't wake up before they come back for us."

"I don't think he will."

"Why did he do that?" Jolene asked, gazing up at the ceiling. "I mean, he didn't even touch us. Why would he pay all that money and then not... do anything?"

Mara shrugged. "I don't know. It happens once in a while. Not very often, though. You just have to enjoy it while you can."

Jolene nodded. "I want to go home," she said, her voice quiet but firm. "Why can't I just go home?" She turned her face toward Mara, her green eyes intense. "Why can't I just walk out that door and go home? I know they said they'd find us and kill us, and our families too. But do you think they really would? I mean, they don't even know where I live. They just found me at the beach. I could live anywhere for all they know."

Mara's heart raced as the girl pushed herself to a sitting position. "Seriously, Mara," she whispered. "Why do we have to stay here? The old man is asleep, and we should still have some time before they come to get us. Let's go. Let's get out of here while we can. Who's going to stop us?"

Before Jolene could get to her feet, Mara grabbed the girl's thin arm and yanked her back down. "I am. I'm going to stop you." She used her weight and strength to pull Jolene back onto the bed, and then straddled her and pinned her down, clamping a hand over her mouth before the girl could get past her initial shock and start yelling or screaming. Jolene's wide, terrified eyes pleaded for release, but Mara couldn't allow herself to be swayed by emotion. Jefe had made that all too clear already.

She leaned down and spoke directly into Jolene's face, her whisper more of a hiss as she tried to keep from waking the old man. "Don't you understand? It's not just your life at stake here. Even if you got away—and you probably wouldn't because we never know when Enforcer or Destroyer are right outside watching—they'd find me for sure. And I'm the one who'd pay. Don't you get it? Maybe you have somewhere to run, but I don't. That's why Jefe put me in charge of making sure you don't try anything. If you escape, he'll punish me worse than he ever has before." She took a deep breath, trying to calm the terror that churned in her stomach. "You have no idea yet how bad it can be, but I do—and there's no way I'm going to find out how much worse it can still get. So you're staying right here, understand? You try to run—now, or any other time—and I'll kill you myself."

Jolene's eyes grew even wider, and Mara shook her for emphasis. "I said, do you understand?"

Jolene nodded, as tears pooled in her eyes and began to spill over and drip down into her ears and hair.

"Good," Mara said. "Don't ever forget that, and we'll get along just fine."

Before she could decide whether or not to remove her hand and climb off the girl or wait another moment to be sure Jolene got the message, she heard a key in the lock. Without moving she turned her head back toward the door just as Enforcer made his entrance.

His eyes met hers, and he took in the scene in front of him before his ugly, meaty face broke into a grin. "I don't know what's going on here," he said, "but I like it." He glanced over at the customer, fully clothed and still snoring, on the other bed, and snorted before turning his attention back to the girls. "So, you got a worthless one tonight, did you? Well, don't worry, ladies. I was just thinking that I haven't taken advantage of some of the perks that go with my job lately, but now I know exactly how I'm going to make up for that."

Mara cringed as the huge man with the bandage still covering the spot where his ear once was moved closer to them, the look in his eyes promising an end to what had until now been a peaceful evening. She felt Jolene tense beneath her, and with good reason, Mara thought. Enforcer had forced himself on her only a few times through the years, but she had never forgotten the brutality of his attacks. It seemed now that she and Jolene were about to endure such an experience together.

Maybe she should have considered Jolene's invitation to join her and try to escape. No. Experience had taught her that her best chance of survival was not to fight the inevitable, and certainly not to attempt an escape. Those who did ended up regretting their decision, as Jefe made an example of them to the others. Whatever Enforcer had in mind for them now could never be as bad as what her tio would do to them if they tried to run.

Chapter 41

Sunday passed in a blur of pain and heat. Chanthra knew enough in her most lucid moments to realize there was medicine that could help her, but she also knew the boss man would never waste his money on one of his girls. There were many ways to get new girls to replace those who were lost. And Chanthra knew she was nearing the end of her useful years anyway. The owner might be glad to be rid of her.

What happened to my baby? she wondered. *Is it with* phra yaeh suu*? And my other babies, the ones they killed before? Are they there too? Oh, I pray so!* An ache clutched her heart at the thought. If only there was a chance that she might join them when she finally left this place. But a girl like her, one whose life had been given over to such filth and evil? Chanthra could not imagine that a pure and holy God would welcome her to a place so perfect as heaven.

Heaven. She smiled in spite of her pain. So many years ago, and yet she could still remember her *maae* telling her of such a place and how those who belong to *phra yaeh suu* would go there when they died. Chanthra could certainly believe that about her beautiful mother—her father, too, who had also worshiped *phra yaeh suu*. And once, when she was still young and innocent, Chanthra had accepted *phra yaeh suu* as well. But that was before she was spoiled, ruined beyond repair. Surely He could not accept or love her now.

A cool cloth on her forehead. Chanthra opened her eyes to see the face she was certain must belong to an angel. Yet why would an angel come to tend to her? No, it could not be an angel after all. It must be Lawan—sweet, faithful little Lawan. How dearly she loved the child! But oh, how she wished the girl could grow wings and fly away, far from this horrible place and back to the peace and safety of her home, wherever that might be.

The child was singing again. Always the girl sang softly to her of *phra yaeh suu*. How could it be that the songs she sang were all known to Chanthra, songs her own mother had sung to her so long ago?

The pain swept over her again, pulling her away from the sweetness of the girl's voice. Oh, how she longed to lose herself in the words of those songs! *Are You there,* phra yaeh suu*? Can You hear me? Oh, help me, please—even me,* phra yaeh suu*!*

The Johnsons had invited the Flannerys over after church, and the seven of them now sat outside on the patio behind the Johnsons' home, the warm afternoon sunshine muted by the shade of the two spreading jacaranda trees that bordered the otherwise open eating area. The bright red bougainvilleas splashed the rest of the yard with brilliant color, while the sweet fragrance of honeysuckle competed with the mouth-watering aroma of grilling burgers. Jonathan scarcely noticed any of it. His cell phone, set on vibrate, was clipped to his belt, waiting, and that call was the only thing he'd been able to focus on for the past couple of hours.

"Hungwy!" Anna pounded her fork on the table, drawing a smattering of giggles from the adults, though her father, who sat immediately to her right, was quick to correct her behavior.

"Is that the way we act at the table, Anna?" Kyle asked, his kind gray eyes holding his daughter's attention.

The little girl dropped her gaze, as her cheeks flamed in embarrassment. Her straight, dark hair, gleaming in a shaft of sunlight, scarcely moved as she shook her head. "I sowwy," she mumbled.

Kyle planted a kiss on the top of her down-turned head. "Good girl," he said. "Now why don't you show us all how big girls ask for their lunch?"

Slowly the child raised her head and moved her eyes from one face to the next. When she seemed comfortable with the level of compassion she saw mirrored in each expression, she grinned and said, "I'm hungwy—pwease!" Even Jonathan joined in the spontaneous laughter, and then bowed his head as Kyle led them in a brief prayer of thanksgiving for their food.

"Amen!" Anna's voice rang out above the others, leading to another round of laughter as they began to pass the platters of burgers and chips and salad, the small talk erupting in spurts around the table. Jonathan did his best to be a part of the group, but he couldn't help but try to will the phone to buzz.

He'd talked to the police early that morning, and they'd said they should have a positive ID on the body before the day was out. They'd promised to call him as soon as they did. But would they? On a Sunday? Jonathan imagined bodies could be identified on any day of the week.

His father sat beside him, the only one who knew why Jonathan was restless and reserved throughout the meal. Occasionally the older man laid his hand on Jonathan's shoulder or knee, giving a reassuring pat, which Jonathan appreciated. The two men had agreed not to mention the situation until and unless they knew for certain it was

Jasmine—and then only after they'd left the Johnsons' place to go home.

Jonathan was about to force down another bite of hamburger when the vibrating phone stopped him. Excusing himself, he set the burger on his plate and stood up to walk away from the table, catching his father's eyes in the process. Jonathan nodded and took several steps toward the other end of the yard.

The news brought mixed emotions. When he returned to the table, everyone else was caught up in a conversation about how much they liked the new choir director at church—everyone except Jonathan's father. Michael Flannery's green eyes followed his son every step of the way until Jonathan drew up beside him.

"It wasn't Jasmine," he whispered as he sat down next to him.

Michael nodded and picked up his burger. Jonathan did the same, though he could think of nothing else but what the detective had told him—which wasn't much, he realized. The man didn't tell him who the girl was except that she was a drowning victim, someone they'd been looking for since a boat capsized a few days earlier. Even that, the detective said, he was telling him only because it would soon be on the news. He hadn't even given the girl's identity, though Jonathan imagined that would be fodder for the evening broadcasts as well.

So Jasmine wasn't dead after all. Or was she? Just because this particular body wasn't Jasmine Littleton didn't mean the girl was still alive. And even if she were, where was she? Would the police find her before it was too late? Would that girl's poor parents ever see their daughter again? If they didn't, would it be his fault for not trying to help her when he saw her at the motel that night?

Jonathan sighed and dropped his burger back onto his plate. There was no point trying to eat it. He'd never get it past the lump in his throat. He knew the Lord had forgiven him—not just for the way he handled the situation at the motel but for everything—but right now that didn't seem to help the regret he felt in his heart over not trying to do something for those two girls. And he couldn't help but wonder if Jasmine's parents blamed him as well, though they'd been far too kind to mention it.

"Would you really do it?" the girl asked. "Would you kill me if I tried to get away?"

Mara looked up from the beat-up lounge chair where she sat, trying to absorb some of the late afternoon's dying rays before she had to clean up and get ready to go back to work. Jolene stood directly in front of her, the girl's thin frame blocking most of the sunlight, leaving only a slight halo effect of light around her. What was wrong with this girl? Didn't she understand English? Didn't she get it? What did Mara have to do to get through to her that she would do whatever she had to if it meant keeping Jefe from treating her any worse than he already did? She'd been weak before—with the big-eyed child that had shown up one day and died after being locked up in the hole, and with Jasmine when she hadn't watched her closely enough and stopped her before she tried to escape. Mara wasn't about to make the same mistake again. She would not grow attached to Jolene, and she would certainly not underestimate the girl's desire to escape. Quite obviously it was still an issue.

"Yes, I would," she answered, forcing as much cool determination into her voice as possible. "In a heartbeat." She squinted up at the girl's blank expression. "If you do anything stupid, it's either you or me, sweetheart. One of us will have to pay. And I guarantee you, it won't be me."

Jolene stood, unmoving, for a moment, and then nodded wordlessly and walked away. Mara could only hope she had finally gotten through to her.

Chapter 42

By the time the Flannerys left the Jacksons' place to go home, Jonathan was so obsessed with wondering about Jasmine's whereabouts and welfare that he told his parents and Leah that he'd see them at home later. He'd driven his own car over anyway, so why not find a nice secluded spot to spend some alone time with God and see if he could resolve the churning in his gut and the restlessness in his heart.

Windows down and fingers thumping the steering wheel in an unnamed melody, Jonathan found himself instinctively heading back toward the beach. He needed the steady thrumming of the whooshing waves and receding tide to still his thoughts and focus them where he knew they needed to be.

Be still… and know that I am God.

The familiar Bible verse from Psalms, words he'd heard countless times as a child but never personalized until now, whispered to his heart, calling him to come away from the noise and the voices and the activity, and just wait and listen. Gladly, he responded, looking forward to basking in the sweetness of God's presence, of drawing on the strength that he now understood could be found nowhere else.

"I need Your wisdom, Lord," he whispered as he squeezed into one of the few empty parking spaces available. He wasn't surprised at the crowd, even though the day would soon draw to a close. Sunday afternoon was a popular time at the beach, and people were reluctant to see it end, so they tended to stay as long as possible. But Jonathan was determined to find a quiet place, even if he had to walk a ways to do so.

The still warm breeze brushed his skin with the scent of salt as he stepped from his car, leaving his shoes and socks behind and rolling up his pant legs to just below his knees. He locked the car doors and dropped the keys into his pocket, then set off in the direction he imagined he would most likely find a secluded spot.

He hadn't gone far when he noticed a family by the water's edge. The father and son, who looked to be seven or eight, raced back and forth into the waves, splashing one another and laughing with delight, while the mother and pre-school age daughter stayed back where the water just lapped their feet. The mother coaxed her daughter in further, but the child refused to budge.

Jonathan smiled. That could have been his own family just a few years ago. He remembered the many times they'd come to this very beach, playing and laughing together, sharing peanut butter sandwiches on a blanket and building sandcastles until the sun set and they reluctantly packed everything up to head home.

I wonder if Jasmine's family had days like that.

The sudden thought sliced through his heart, nearly causing him to stumble at the sharpness of the pain. Of course they'd had days like that. He pictured Franklin and Diane Littleton as he'd seen them at their home that day. They were older than some parents, though still trim and fit.

Franklin had explained to Jonathan that Jasmine was their only child, born to them when they were in their mid-thirties and already deeply entrenched in their careers. With Jasmine's arrival, Franklin and Diane's lives had changed, taking on a deeper meaning and bringing them more joy than they'd ever imagined possible. Jasmine was everything to them—and now she was gone.

The man had nearly choked on the words as they spoke, and Jonathan had found himself wishing the man wouldn't be so personal. He didn't want to know how close they had been as a family and how devastated they were now that their daughter was gone. It was easier not knowing that, and yet, once Jonathan saw the flyers, he'd realized he had no choice but to come and tell the girl's parents what he'd seen. Somewhere in the back of his mind he'd held out a shred of hope that when he got to Jasmine's home and saw more pictures of her that he'd realize the girl at the motel had been someone else. But that hadn't been the case. He now knew for certain that the girl who'd tried to escape from the man at the motel was indeed Jasmine Littleton—and that he hadn't even tried to help her.

There was nothing I could do, he told himself for what seemed the thousandth time. He knew it was true, but that didn't take away the overwhelming feeling of guilt that seemed to ride on his shoulders twenty-four-seven. Even when everything else was going well, he sensed that load on his back, taunting him. Would he ever be free of it?

At last! He spotted the slightly grassy knoll off to his left, just far enough back among the dunes that no one else had claimed it but close enough to watch the sun sparkle on the waves as they rolled in and out on their endless journey. Jonathan settled in quickly, sitting with his legs bent upward in front of him, his arms resting on top of his knees, and his toes digging into the warm, grainy sand. It was one of the few times he actually missed having enough hair to feel the ocean breeze blow through it, but it was pleasant to feel it on his face.

Will I ever be free of this?

He hadn't planned to spit out the question so informally or without preamble, but he decided that God already knew that, so maybe it was best to get it out in the open.

I know I'm at peace with You now, Jonathan spoke silently. *And thank You so much for that, Father. But no matter how much or how often I tell myself that there was no way I could have known what was going on or helped in any way, I just can't seem to accept it. Maybe if I'd called 911 right away or something...*

His thoughts trailed off. He'd gone over them so many times before, like the water rushing in and receding, only to return again and again. Jasmine's face—and the other girl's—always there, teasing his memory, haunting his peace. What had happened to them? Where were they? And how had they ended up in such an awful life? Would they ever escape?

Too many questions, with seemingly no answers. Jonathan bowed his head and leaned it against his arms, which still rested on his knees. "I can't fix this, Lord," he whispered. "I can't go back and redo it. I can't find those girls and rescue them. I can't make it right for them or make the pain go away for me." He took a deep breath. "But You can, Father. So I'm giving it to You. The whole situation. All of it. I give up. Use me if You want to...or not. Whatever You want, Lord. Like Jesus said, Your will, not mine."

The waves crashed, as the setting sun and wind caressed his skin. He had no idea how it would all work out, but somehow he knew it would.

Jefe shook his head, annoyed at the scene playing out in front of him. Why would the new girl go to Mara with her questions and concerns, instead of coming to him? Hadn't she figured out yet that he was the one who cared for them all, who kept the entire business running smoothly so they could enjoy its benefits? He nearly growled as he watched the girl standing in front of Mara, who sat in the lounge chair looking up at Jolene. What were they discussing? Short and sweet, apparently, for after a brief exchange, the younger girl walked away. But Jefe didn't like the way Mara studied her. The last thing he wanted was for the girls to start caring for one another. When that happened, he lost control. And that was one thing Jefe was not willing to give up.

Stepping from the shadows into Mara's line of view, he suppressed the satisfaction he felt at her obvious surprise. She hadn't realized he was there, and he knew she was wondering if he'd overheard her conversation with Jolene. He hadn't, but it served his purpose to let her think he might have.

"So," he said, standing over her and smiling down, "have you had a nice day so far, *mijita*?"

Eyes wide, Mara nodded. "Sí, Jefe," she answered, the slight tremor in her voice betraying her otherwise peaceful demeanor.

"I'm glad to hear that," he said. "I like my girls to be happy—you especially. You know that, don't you, Mara?"

The girl nodded, her long brown hair moving only slightly in response.

Jefe let his eyes travel up and down the girl's body, a body he knew almost better than his own. He had trained her well, cared for her as he'd promised her parents he would do. Did she appreciate all he had done for her? He doubted it.

"How is the new girl working out?" he asked. "I hear she's becoming popular with the customers."

"Sí, Jefe," Mara repeated. "She is doing well. No trouble."

Jefe paused, allowing his gaze to hold hers until he knew she was adequately uncomfortable, though she obviously did her best to hide it. "Good," he said at last. "See that it remains so. Remember, I'm holding you personally responsible for her actions."

Mara blanched, and Jefe nearly laughed in satisfaction. Exactly the reaction he'd hoped for. Keep them on edge, nervous, eyeing one another rather than banding together against him. That was the secret to running a successful business. And he was just the guy who could do it best. His plans for tonight would reinforce that edge and keep them all on their toes. One way or another, he'd get the respect he deserved.

And besides, he loved surprises.

Tonight, Enforcer thought as he wolfed down a sandwich he'd bought when he was in town earlier. He knew he wouldn't have much time to eat later, as it seemed Jefe had special plans for the night.

Enforcer washed down a bite of salami and bread with a lukewarm soda. *Jefe wants to conduct one of his periodic inspections of the slaves and their dates, with me taking him from room to room to check out the action. He hasn't done that in a long time. I wonder why he wants to do it now.*

He shrugged. What did it matter? He got paid, whatever Jefe wanted to do, so what difference did it make? Besides, having the slime ball alone with him in the van all evening opened up all sorts of possibilities. Should he tell Destroyer what he had in mind? It would make it a lot easier if the two of them were in on this together, and he couldn't imagine that Destroyer wouldn't want in the minute he realized that getting rid of Jefe would mean they could run the business themselves—and finally get paid what they were worth. Enforcer was sick of working for peanuts and being treated like dirt.

He touched the bandage on the side of his head. Tonight just might be the perfect time to finally get revenge for what Jefe had done to him. All Enforcer had to do was watch for the perfect moment.

Chapter 43

LAWAN WONDERED IF SHE'D EVER BE ABLE TO STOP CRYING. She sat by Chanthra's side every moment she wasn't with a customer, cooling the older girl's forehead with water from a small bowl, singing to calm her, and praying desperately for her to find peace with *phra yaeh suu*.

"You knew Him once," Lawan whispered into Chanthra's ear when it seemed the girl was awake and lucid. "I know you did. Your *maae* told you about Him, didn't she?"

Chanthra nodded, moaning slightly but not opening her eyes.

"Did she...tell you anything else? About *phra yaeh suu* being the...Light of the world?"

This time Chanthra responded. She turned her head, eyes wide, and fixed her gaze on the younger girl. It was the clearest Lawan had seen Chanthra's eyes since before Adung had taken her baby from her.

"Light of the world," she whispered. "Light of the world! Yes. *Maae* told me that—many times."

Lawan nodded, her suspicions growing. Should she mention them? Would it upset Chanthra, make her worse?

Or would it comfort her and give her hope? She closed her eyes and breathed a silent prayer for wisdom.

"How did you...know that?" Chanthra whispered.

Lawan opened her eyes and frowned. "Know what?"

"About...about my *maae* telling me that *phra yaeh suu* is the Light of the world."

Is this Your answer? Lawan prayed. Should I tell her?

Peace flowed over her, settling her indecision. "*Kop koon,*" she whispered, thanking God for His answer.

"I think perhaps I know this about your *maae* because... because my *maae* told me the same thing."

Chanthra's eyes grew wide, and a smile touched her cracked lips. She nodded. "Yes. I understand. This is a good thing, isn't it? It makes us...sisters."

Lawan gasped. It was obvious she needed to press ahead. "I...I think maybe we truly are—sisters." She swallowed and took a deep breath before laying a hand on Chanthra's arm. "I think we have the same *maae*...the same parents."

She waited, watching as the words made their impact. At last Chanthra spoke. "It cannot be so," she whispered. "How would it be possible that a loving God would allow two from the same family to end up here, in this horrible place?" She shook her head. "No. No! It cannot be. It cannot. Surely God would not do such a cruel thing."

Lawan was confused, and growing more frightened by the moment. Hadn't God led her to share her suspicions with Chanthra? Why was she reacting this way? Wasn't it a beautiful thing that they should find each other, even under such dreadful circumstances?

She quickly dipped the cloth in water and did her best to calm Chanthra by applying the wet cloth to her forehead. "Shhh," she crooned, stroking her hair with one hand and holding the cloth in place with the other. "It's all right. We'll talk about it later. You rest now. Rest so you can get better. Please, Chanthra! I need you to get better."

At last Chanthra drifted off into a restless sleep, as Lawan stayed by her side, singing and praying as her tears dripped down onto the girl she was nearly certain was the older sister she'd heard about but never met—until now. She still wrestled with how that could be possible, since this was certainly not the life her parents believed Chanthra was living. But quite obviously things had not gone as they'd planned.

Mara and Jolene had been paired up again, but Mara imagined that was intentional. Jefe was going to make sure that Mara watched Jolene every moment of the evening. And Mara was going to make sure Jolene didn't try anything. This night was going to go smoothly if someone had to die in the process.

Mara frowned, as she stepped out of the van, with Jolene following close behind. The familiar motel loomed in front of them, but Mara was disturbed by the thought that had just passed through her mind. *If someone had to die in the process.* Why would she think such a thing? She shook her head, dismissing the snakelike sensation that crept up her spine. This was no time to get weird. She had work to do... and a girl to watch.

The sun had gone down, and a few stars twinkled overhead as she climbed the stairs ahead of Jolene and Destroyer. Apparently Jefe had other work for Enforcer tonight, as he was the one who usually drove them to their meeting spots. It made no difference to Mara, since she didn't care for either of Jefe's henchmen. She simply tolerated them, like she did everything else in her life.

Reaching the top of the stairs, she looked back at Destroyer for a cue about which direction to take. He nudged his head to the right, and she turned accordingly. She had no idea who or what was waiting for them when they reached the room, but she'd find out soon enough.

The sense of peace that had come from yielding an impossible situation to God followed Jonathan as he left the beach behind and headed toward home. He'd grabbed a quick burger near the pier since he hadn't been able to eat at the Johnsons', so now he had no reason to stop along the way. He seldom got an evening off to spend with his family anyway, so why not take advantage of it?

Except that his car seemed to have other ideas. How else could he explain the fact that he was now turning onto the street where he'd seen Jasmine and the other girl the night he delivered a pizza to the motel—the very motel that awaited him as he slowed to a stop? His heart lurched at the sight of the familiar van parked in the lot near the stairwell. Following the stairs to the second floor, he spotted a large hulk of a man following two young women to the right of the stairs. Was it possible? Could it be?

He tried to focus, leaning toward the open window and squinting his eyes for a better look. Both women looked very young, particularly the second one. In truth, she appeared to be no more than a girl, a preadolescent dressed nearly as skimpily as Jasmine had been the night she ran from the room and nearly collided with him in the corridor. The girl's hair was long like Jasmine's though he couldn't clearly see the color, and she was about the right size and shape, but...he just wasn't close enough to be sure.

He stared at the girl in front. Surely she was the older girl who had claimed to be Jasmine's sister, but again, he wasn't near enough to be positive. And the man walking behind them? He was big and burly, like the man he'd seen driving the van before, but he walked differently. And yet...he was nearly certain it was the same van.

He had to get closer; that's all there was to it. There was no way he was going to drive away without knowing. His heart raced and his palms felt clammy as he opened the door and stepped out into the warm night air. Sounds of nearby traffic and voices coming from a couple of the motel rooms drifted on the breeze, but he blocked them out. He knew he had to push past the fear and find out what was going on with those girls—whether they were the two he'd seen before or not. But how was he going to get past their monstrous bodyguard?

Reaching the stairway just as the girls and their escort stopped in front of one of the upstairs rooms, Jonathan clutched the railing with one hand. *Help me, Lord,* he prayed silently. *Give me wisdom, Father, and courage—and protect me, please!*

With no clear direction, he took the first step onto the stairs. He'd left two helpless girls behind once; he was determined not to do it again.

Chapter 44

ROSANNA WAS RESTLESS. SHE'D CLEANED UP THE KITCHEN after their light supper, which was actually more of a snack than a meal, since they were all still full from the barbecue they'd had at the Johnsons' place. Leah had gone up to her room, and Michael sat in the family room, reading. She'd tried to join him but just couldn't keep her mind on her book.

Instead she paced, back and forth from the kitchen to the entryway, wondering why she was suddenly so concerned about Jonathan. He was eighteen, after all, a high school graduate on his way to college in the fall. She knew she had to let go of him, be less protective, and yet...

She shook her head. *Stop it,* she scolded herself. *Jonathan is a big boy. If he had car trouble or something, he has a cell phone and can call for help. Stop creating trouble where there is none.*

But her heart refused to be quieted. After a long and futile wrestling match with her niggling doubts, she decided to trust what she'd learned over the years: that perhaps God was calling her to prayer. Experience told her it was a call worth heeding.

"Michael?"

She stood in the doorway to the family room, watching her husband as he raised his head from his book and looked back at her. As his eyes focused, a frown formed between his eyes. Quite obviously he read her concern before she even spoke it.

"What is it?" he asked, setting his book on the coffee table and rising to his feet. "Is something wrong?"

"I...don't know," she admitted, moving toward him, grateful for his outstretched arms. She moved into them and sighed as he pulled her close. "I'm just...concerned for Jonathan for some reason," she said. "I know it's not terribly late, but...I would just feel better if he were home safe and sound."

Michael kissed the top of her head. "Then we'll pray for that to happen," he said, pulling her gently toward the couch where he'd been sitting. "God knows exactly where he is and what's going on with him right now. Let's pray together for his protection."

Rosanna nodded, taking comfort in the warmth of her husband's hands holding hers as they bent their heads together and welcomed their Father's presence.

Jonathan was halfway up the stairs when he heard the footsteps coming toward him from the landing above. He froze, uncertain whether to continue upward or retreat. *Show me, Lord,* he begged.

Immediately he returned to the ground floor and ducked behind the stairwell, scarcely breathing as he waited. He knew God had directed him when he saw the big man who had escorted the girls walk away from the stairs toward the van and climb inside. He exhaled, relieved that at least he wouldn't have to deal with the gorilla who served as their bodyguard. All he had to worry about now was whoever was in the room with the girls.

When the van had departed from the lot and driven out of sight, he crept from his hiding place and once again began to climb the stairs. This time he made it to the top uninterrupted. Turning right, he walked as quietly as possible toward the room where he was sure the girls had gone. What did he do now? Knock? Call out to them? Pretend he was looking for his own room and was confused?

Pizzas. If he pretended he had pizzas down in the car and was just checking for the right room to deliver them, it would give him an excuse for knocking. And if the girls in the room really were the ones he'd seen before, it might help them remember where they'd seen him before. Would they welcome the sight of him, realize he'd come to help them? Or would they turn on him or reject him, or . . . ?

There was only one way to find out. He raised his hand and knocked.

Butterflies flitted around Enforcer's insides, making it difficult for him to concentrate on driving, particularly since he was driving Jefe's Jaguar instead of the familiar van. He dreamed of owning the Jaguar himself one day—after he had eliminated Jefe—but right now he was only the flunky driver, one who would be severely chastised and even punished if he so much as put the tiniest of scratches in the sleek black car.

He supposed he was nervous for various reasons, having driven the Jaguar only one other time being one of them. The main reason, though, was that he couldn't help but believe that tonight might be his chance to implement his plan against Jefe. The problem was that he had no plan—not really. He knew only that he wanted Jefe dead, gone, out of his life once and for all. Then he, Enforcer, would take over the business. No longer would he have to take orders from the spineless creep that sat next to him as they drove toward their first stop. No longer would he have to worry about angering Jefe and suffering his wrath. And no longer would he have to be satisfied with peanuts when he could have everything.

Yes, with all his heart he hoped that the opportunity would present itself tonight. Various scenarios had played themselves out in Enforcer's mind over the last several days, particularly since Jefe had told him of his plans for this night. They would stop in unannounced at the various locations where Jefe's slaves entertained their clients, confirming that all was going as it should and reaffirming Jefe's dominance and authority over the entire operation. It was an intimidation factor he employed just often enough to make it effective. And it presented opportunities that Enforcer might not otherwise have to be alone with Jefe at locations where anything could happen—and blame could easily be cast on others while Enforcer literally got away with murder.

He smiled as they pulled up in front of the motel and parked at the far end of the lot where the Jaguar was less likely to be scratched or dinged. This was only their first stop, and butterflies or not, Enforcer planned to make the most of any opportunity that presented itself.

Chapter 45

Mara nearly jumped, and Jolene's eyes grew wide at the sound of the knock on the door. Had Destroyer come back already? Had there been a mistake and they'd been brought to the wrong room? Mara certainly hoped not because once again, she and Jolene had been requested by the kindly old man who had done nothing to them the last time but cuddle and talk with them and then go to sleep. When the girls had entered the room and spotted him waiting for them, his grin warm and welcoming, they'd sighed with relief. It had appeared they were in for an easy night.

Now she wasn't so sure. If Enforcer was back, that wasn't a good sign. And if it was him, why didn't he just use the key? She tore her eyes from Jolene's and looked straight at the old man who sat on the edge of the bed between them, looking as surprised and confused as they felt.

"Are you…expecting anyone?" he asked.

Mara shook her head. "No. Are you?"

"No one," he said. "You're my only friends."

Mara's heart constricted, but she dismissed the feeling. No time for sentimentality. "Do you want me to answer it?"

The old man hesitated until the knock came again. His rheumy eyes widened behind his thick glasses. "Maybe you should," he ventured.

Mara rose from the bed, leaving the old man and Jolene huddled together. "Who is it?" she called through the door.

The only answer was another knock. She peered through the peep hole but couldn't see anything but a dark shirt. It was enough to tell her that Destroyer hadn't returned and that whoever stood at the door was tall, but nothing more.

"Identify yourself if you want me to open the door," she said, hoping her voice sounded more authoritative than she felt.

After a brief hesitation, she heard a male voice answer, "I'm the pizza delivery guy. I...have a pizza downstairs in my car, and I'm just trying to find the right room."

A buzzing began in Mara's ears and she felt lightheaded, as she remembered the guy from a couple of weeks earlier, the one she was pretty sure she'd seen parked out front on another occasion. The guy with the kind face whose gorgeous brown eyes she'd been trying to forget. Was it possible this was the same person?

She shook her head. No. It didn't matter if it was the same guy or not. They hadn't ordered a pizza, and he had no business at their door. "It wasn't us," she called to him. "We didn't order anything, and we can't help you."

"Please," he said. "Can't you just open the door for a minute? Maybe you can help me figure out which room I'm looking for."

The realization struck her that nothing stood between her and the stranger outside except the simple lock on the door, not even the extra security latch. Curiosity tugged at Mara as her hand snaked around the doorknob. What was she thinking? There was absolutely no reason for her to open that door!

She glanced at the pair on the bed. The old man still sat, wide-eyed and unmoving, while Jolene shook her head nervously and mouthed the word "no." *Strange,* Mara thought. *Just yesterday she would have been begging me to open the door so she could try to get away. Maybe she just feels safe with the old man.*

"Please," came the voice again. "Please, open up, just for a minute. Please?"

Kind brown eyes swam in her vision, even as she turned the knob and tugged the door inward. Every bit of her training from Jefe screamed at her not to do this, but she just couldn't seem to stop herself.

Chanthra drifted back into consciousness on Monday morning, wondering why it was so hot and why her *maae* wasn't sitting beside her. Her *maae* was always there for her, singing to her and praying for her, cooling her forehead with a damp cloth and spooning liquids between her parched lips.

"*Maae?*" Her voice was little more than a croak in the early morning gray, but the response was immediate.

"I'm here," came the answer.

Chanthra looked up. The face was familiar, but…not her *maae*. She squinted, trying to focus. "Who…are you?" she whispered.

Tears pooled in the girl's dark eyes, as she bent her head nearer, her tousled hair falling forward. "I am Lawan," she answered. "Your…sister."

Chanthra closed her eyes. Lawan? Sister? The name was familiar, but Chanthra had no sister. She had been an only child when her parents gave her up for adoption to a man who promised her a good home and plenty of food and nice clothes. Instead she had ended up here…

She remembered then. The brothel. Lawan was her roommate, a young girl who had recently been kidnapped and brought here to this horrible place. But why did the girl call herself her sister?

Chanthra opened her eyes. "Lawan," she said.

The girl nodded, bringing the damp cloth to Chanthra's forehead.

"Why...why did you say you were my sister?"

Lawan dropped her eyes, then raised them again. "Because I think I am," she whispered, leaning even closer. "You know the songs my mother sang to me. And she told me of my older sister, Chanthra, who was adopted by a wealthy family before I was born." Tears spilled over onto her cheeks then. "You are about the right age, but...but now I fear that my parents were wrong. You weren't adopted after all, were you?"

Chanthra's eyes burned, and her head throbbed. Without asking more, she knew the girl spoke the truth. She was indeed her sister. But how could it be that the *phra yaeh suu* would allow such a thing to happen—to bring yet another girl from the same family to such a place? Chanthra sensed that her own time in this earthly hell was nearly over, but was it just beginning for her own flesh and blood?

The instant the door opened, Jonathan knew he'd been right. This was the older girl he'd seen a couple weeks earlier at this very motel. Was Jasmine here with her?

Not waiting for an invitation, he pushed the door open and stepped inside, his eyes going straight to the old man and the girl on the bed. It wasn't Jasmine. His heart sank. He was so sure he'd find her here and return her to her parents.

"I..." He frowned and turned back to the older girl. "Do you remember me?" he asked.

She nodded. "But why are you here? What do you want?"

Emotions swirled in his heart, and he struggled to formulate the words. What did he want? To find Jasmine. To help her—and all the others like her—to escape. He looked at the old man, surprised at his age. "Who are you?"

The old man stood to his feet, shaking a bit as he did so. "I didn't mean any harm," he said. "I...just wanted some company. These girls are real nice to me. Real nice. They talk to me and listen and..."

His voice trailed off, as Jonathan stepped toward him. "I think you should leave," he said, surprising himself at the firmness of his command.

The old man didn't hesitate. Grabbing a light jacket from the room's only chair, he shuffled toward the door, edging past Jonathan as quickly as his old bones would allow. Turning back in the doorway, he nodded at Mara and then Jolene. "Thank you, girls. It was nice to make your acquaintance." Then he turned and disappeared from sight.

Jonathan stood between the girls, the door to the room still open. What would happen now? Would they run? Would they come with him if he asked? And where was Jasmine? Was it possible she was in another such room, right here in this same motel?

He had to know. Turning toward Mara, he said, "I'm here to help you...if you want it. But...I really need to know where Jasmine is. Her parents are looking for her, and—"

Mara's brown eyes opened wide, and then immediately flooded with tears. "Jasmine? Her parents are looking for her?"

Jonathan nodded. "Her mom put up flyers all over town. That's how I found out her name. I recognized her picture and went to her house and met her parents. They're trying so hard to find her, and when I saw you two walking toward this room, I thought sure I'd find Jasmine and—"

He stopped as Mara's face crumpled and she nearly fell to the ground. Grabbing her arms, he supported her as she sobbed. "Jasmine's dead," she cried, her tears wetting the front of Jonathan's shirt. "They killed her. She's dead—and it's all my fault!"

Holding Mara close, Jonathan looked over the top of Mara's head at the younger girl, still seated on the bed. If what the older girl said was true about Jasmine, he couldn't imagine how he'd ever tell the poor family. But for now he realized he had a bigger problem. He had to find a way to convince these two girls to come with him to the police station so he could get them some help. Why did he know that was not going to be an easy thing to do?

Chapter 46

Jefe and Enforcer made their way across the parking lot, waiting in the shadows until an old man had made his way down the stairs and driven away. Then they headed up the stairs toward the room where Destroyer had reported Mara and Jolene would be with their date for the night.

Jefe walked just ahead of Enforcer, maintaining his required spot in the pecking order at all times. Enforcer knew he was not Jefe's equal, simply his employee who did what Jefe told him—if he knew what was good for him. But Enforcer sensed it wouldn't be long until he found a way to level the playing field—once and for all.

Several feet from their destination, Jefe stopped, nearly causing Enforcer to plow into him from behind. Before Enforcer could apologize, Jefe turned and fired a warning glare, and then whispered, "The door's open."

Enforcer's hair rose on the back of his neck. Something was wrong.

Pulling his revolver from his pocket, he nudged ahead of his boss and approached the room. When he burst inside, gun at the ready, he was stunned to see a tall, familiar-looking kid, holding Mara while she cried, and Jolene sitting on the bed. What was going on here? He wasn't the one who had brought the girls here, so he couldn't be sure that the kid wasn't the one who'd hired them for the night, but somehow he doubted it. And if he wasn't, what happened to their date?

"What's going on here?" Jefe demanded, stepping up next to Enforcer. "And why is the door open?"

The looks on the three young faces in front of them ranged from shock to abject terror. It was obvious they were up to something and this was no normal evening "date."

Jefe turned to Mara. "You," he said, his voice slithering up Enforcer's spine. "Mara. My own flesh and blood. My own brother's daughter, whom I took into my own home and raised as my own. Will I ever be able to trust you? Will you ever learn? What do I have to do so you will finally stop betraying me?"

Mara shrank back into the tall kid's arms, as if he could protect her. Enforcer knew otherwise, since the gun in his hand gave him the only edge he needed. But was this the time to use it on a measly pizza delivery kid, or could he take advantage of this opportunity and finally get even with the man who had so humiliated him?

He pointed the gun at Jonathan. "I can settle this right now," he said, kicking the door shut behind him. "There's a silencer on this thing, and you'll be dead before anyone knows there's a problem."

The kid's eyes widened, but he pulled Mara closer, as Jolene whimpered on the bed.

Jefe laughed. "He's right, you know. We'll get rid of you and then get the whole story about what was going on here out of these girls—one inch of skin at a time."

"Or not."

Enforcer's words wiped the smile from Jefe's face, as he lifted his eyes to the bigger man's face. "What did you say?" he demanded.

"I said, 'or not.' Oh, I'll kill the kid—absolutely. But not until I've gotten rid of you, you slimy piece of trash. After what you've done to me, I should make you suffer first, but right now, I just want you dead. Then I'll take care of the nosy pizza delivery kid, and I'll have these girls—and all the others—to myself. I'm sick of living off your scraps and asking how high when you say jump." Enforcer felt his momentum growing as he saw the realization on Jefe's face turn to fear. "You're done, old man," he growled, pressing the gun against his boss's stomach.

Before he could fire, Jonathan slammed him from the side, knocking the gun from his hand and sending it spinning across the floor. "Get it," he cried as he wrestled the stunned Enforcer to the ground and straddled his chest. "Get the gun!" he shouted in Mara's direction.

Mara moved just in time, scrambling for the weapon ahead of Jefe and holding it out in front of her, pointing it at her tio. Her voice shook nearly as bad as her hands as she ordered, "Don't move, Tio. I mean it. Don't! There's nothing I'd rather do than pull this trigger."

"But, *mija,*" Jefe soothed, "I'm your tio. Your very own tio! How could you even think of such a thing after all I've done for you?"

From his prone position Enforcer saw Mara's face redden as she lifted the gun toward Jefe. "After all you've done for me?" The girl nearly laughed. "You mean, after all you've done *to* me!"

"Kill him," Enforcer growled. "Pull the trigger and kill him. You'll be doing us all a favor."

"No," Jonathan ordered, still struggling against Enforcer, who was determined to push the kid off him but hesitated each time Mara pointed the gun in his direction. "Don't do it. Just don't let him move. And call 911, please!"

"Jolene," Mara ordered, "get up and call, quick, or I swear I'll kill Jefe right now—Enforcer too!"

Though her hands still shook, Enforcer saw the determination in her eyes. Apparently Jolene did too, because she scurried to the phone on the desk and dialed, her hands trembling the entire time.

This was not the way Enforcer had envisioned things turning out this night—brought down by a pizza delivery kid and two females. But as long as Mara had that gun pointing at them, he really didn't see any other way to get out of this mess alive.

Lawan sensed that it wouldn't be long. She'd finally accepted that no one was going to bring any medicine to help Chanthra, though Lawan had begged for it, even promising to do anything they asked in exchange. But Adung and the boss man had just laughed, saying she'd have to do anything they asked anyway, and that Chanthra wasn't worth the money it would take to save her life.

And so Lawan continued her lonely vigil beside the girl she had come to believe was her older sister. If only there were some way to keep her alive!

"Oh, *phra yaeh suu,* You can do anything! You can heal her. You can save my sister."

Chanthra moaned and stirred, opening her eyes as Lawan watched. Was this God's answer? Was He going to heal her?

"I want to go," Chanthra whispered. "I want to go to heaven and be with *phra yaeh suu.* Do you think He will… accept me?"

Tears pricked Lawan's eyes. "Yes. Of course, He will. But… I don't want you to go. What will I do without you?"

"*Phra yaeh suu* will take care of you. You told me that Mali has gone safely to America, yes? And if *phra yaeh suu* brought you here to me, perhaps He will bring you to Mali as well. *Maae* always said He could do anything."

Lawan nodded. She remembered her *maae* saying that very thing, many times.

"Pray with me," Chanthra whispered, her voice growing weaker. "I am so tired, and I want to go now. Please, pray with me for forgiveness. I want to be clean when I die, to go into God's presence with no sins to hold me back."

The tears that had burned Lawan's eyes now flowed freely down her cheeks. She knew now that God's answer was to take Chanthra from her pain. Lawan would miss her, but she was glad for her. And was it possible that her older sister was right, that someday *phra yaeh suu* might reunite her with little Mali in America?

Lawan couldn't imagine how that could be so, and yet their *maae* had said that nothing was impossible with God. Whatever was His purpose for her life, He would do it—and Lawan wanted nothing else.

She closed her eyes to pray with her sister . . . and to release her into the hands of *phra yaeh suu*.

Barbara had come over as soon as Rosanna called. It was nearly midnight on Sunday, but the entire Flannery family was gathered together in the family room, rehashing the evening's events.

"What do you think will happen now?" Jonathan asked, directing his question at anyone who might have an answer, but particularly to Barbara who had the most experience in this sort of thing. "To everyone concerned, but especially Mara and Jolene."

"Jolene and any of the captives at the compound who are minors will go to child protective services until families are located and individual circumstances are sorted out," Barbara explained. "Mara and the others who are obviously from Mexico may be handled through the Mexican consulate, though it's more likely they'll benefit from the US law that affords them medical, psychological, and even financial help because they were victims of crime here in this country. It also offers the possibility of a fast track to citizenship. But I can assure you that however it's handled, we'll do everything possible to see that they don't return to abusive situations. We also have ministries on that side of the border who will take them in if they have nowhere else to go."

Jonathan nodded. Now that the man known as Jefe and both of his thugs were arrested and the compound shut down, he felt as if the very world itself had been lifted off his shoulders. His only regret was that it hadn't happened in time to save Jasmine. The thought that even now some official was sitting in the Littletons' home, delivering the tragic news, tore at his heart. But he knew he had done what he could, and he no longer blamed himself for not helping Jasmine when he first saw her. He was just grateful that God had allowed him to be used to break up this horrible human trafficking ring, and he was more determined than ever to devote his life to seeing modern-day slavery stopped once and for all.

Jonathan glanced up from where he sat and saw Leah watching him. Her smile was tentative. Did she know what he was thinking? She probably did. She always seemed to be one step ahead of him, especially when it came to spiritual matters.

He returned her smile. In just a few more weeks he'd be heading off to Bible college. Maybe he'd finally catch up with his little sister then. After all, they were on the same team now, and they had the same Captain.

The End

SPECIAL DELIVERY

Kathi Macias

PROLOGUE

IT WAS GOOD TO BE BACK IN SAN DIEGO, THOUGH Mara made it a point to avoid going anywhere near the area where she'd once lived as a modern-day slave. The memories were too ugly, and she did everything possible to block them out. When the topic came up—which it did all too often these days—she immediately changed the subject or walked away. It was an evil best left for others to combat.

The early summer sun shone warm on her dark hair, cut short now in a modern style that complemented her dainty features and accentuated her large hazel eyes. Her good looks and trim figure often drew whistles and comments, but she ignored them all. Having a man in her life didn't even rate at the bottom of her priority list.

Mara closed her eyes and let the mild breeze toss her hair and caress her skin. There was nothing she liked better than coming to the beach and finding a deserted spot to sit and listen to the waves rush in and break on the packed, wet sand. It was nearly impossible to find such a private place on the weekends, but this was midmorning on Monday, and the place wouldn't start filling up until closer to lunchtime. By then she'd be at work.

She smiled at the thought of her new job. She was a waitress now, making enough in wages and tips to rent a room and meet her basic needs. Though she'd taken advantage of UI benefits, specifically designed to help people from other countries who had been victims of crime while in the United States, it had still taken her nearly two years to get all the necessary paperwork cleared so she could not only come to the States legally, but to do so as a U.S. citizen. But she'd been persistent, determined to leave her homeland of Mexico, with all its violence and corruption and poverty, behind. Even with all that had happened to her here in Southern California during her youth, she knew that America held more promise for her than the country of her birth. And besides, what did she have to hold her there? It was her parents who had sold her into slavery, and her own uncle, her tio, who had stolen her innocence, held her captive, and served as her pimp until at last he was captured and sent to prison. So far as she was concerned, her family was dead to her. She had no desire ever to see any of them again.

Mara opened her eyes and watched a tanned, bathing-suit clad couple stroll along the sand in front of her, the waves lapping at their bare feet. Arms wrapped around one another's waist, they seemed oblivious to anything or anyone else, talking and laughing together as if they were the only human beings on earth. The thought skittered through Mara's mind that she might have a relationship like that one day, but just as quickly she excised it from her realm of possibility. At barely twenty years old, she'd already had enough of the male population to last her for several lifetimes.

Affirming that thought with a quick nod of her head, she picked up the towel she'd been sitting on and stood to her feet. She didn't have a car yet, but it was only a ten-minute walk to the seafood café where she was now employed.

Gainfully and respectably employed, she reminded herself. *Tio used to tell me I'd never be anything but a prostitute, and that he'd kill me before he'd let me leave. But look at me now—free as a bird while he rots in prison. Maybe there really is a God after all…*

Book club questions for this novel and all of Kathi Macias's New Hope fiction titles—plus resources to learn about and fight human exploitation—are available online at New Hope Digital, www.NewHopeDigital.com.

New Hope® Publishers is a division of WMU®, an international organization that challenges Christian believers to understand and be radically involved in God's mission. For more information about WMU, go to www.wmu.com. More information about New Hope books may be found at www.newhopedigital.com. New Hope books may be purchased at your local bookstore.

Use the QR reader on your smartphone to visit us online at **www.newhopedigital.com**

If you've been blessed by this book, we would like to hear your story. The publisher and author welcome your comments and suggestions at: newhopereader@wmu.org.

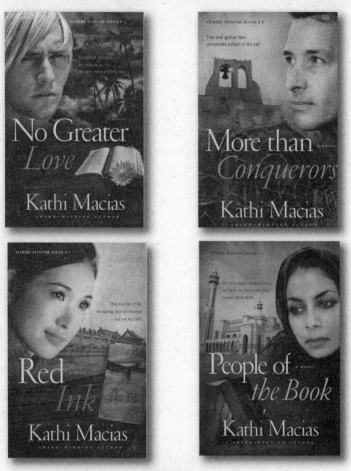